Sexy Street Tales Volume 2

Flexin & Sexin

Stories by

ERICK S. GRAY

ASHLEY & JAQUAVIS

TREASURE E. BLUE

DASHAWN TAYLOR

J. TREMBLE

NICHELLE WALKER

FLEXIN

Life Changing Books in conjunction with Power Play Media
Published by Life Changing Books
P.O. Box 423 Brandywine, MD 20613

Library of Congress Cataloging-in-Publication Data;

www.lifechangingbooks.net

ISBN - (10)1-934230812   (13) 978-1934230817
Copyright ® 2010

Photographer-Karim Muhammad
Project Coordinator-Nakea S. Murray

Gift —
($15.00)
9113
HJ

1139510 4 X

A NOTE FROM THE CREATOR

In the Summer of 2007 Flexin & Sexin Volume 1 was released and received well by fans of Urban Fiction and Erotica. In creating this series I wanted to give Street Fiction writers the opportunity to show fans their sexy side and for Erotic & Contemporary authors a chance to showcase their more edgy, street side. Life Changing Books was instrumental in the success of this series and I have to thank Azarel for believing in me and allowing my brain children who come to me in my dreams to see the light of day. K'wan, Anna J, Erick S. Gray and other talented authors gave readers a super sized dose of sexy street tales that made them crave the next installment. In Flexin & Sexin Volume 2 we've brought back the highly anticipated follow-up to Hit 'Em Up By Erick S. Gray, a sexy cautionary tale by the King Of Erotica J. Tremble, a fast paced thrill ride by New York Times Best Selling authors Ashley & JaQuavis, a scandalous love triangle penned by Treasure E. Blue, a chilling and seductive story by Dashawn Taylor and things are wrapped up with a fun and flirtatious piece by Nichelle Walker. Readers sit back, enjoy the delicious drama, thrills and chills...and of course the steamy scenes!

Happy Reading!

Nakea S. Murray

HIT` EM UP 2
ERICK S. GRAY

QUEENS, N.Y.

The traffic on the Triboro Bridge was like a parking lot. Cars and trucks moved at a snail's pace, with horns blowing and the summer heat making it almost unbearable to sit in traffic. It was late evening and a three-car accident caused two lanes to be blocked. The day seemed normal and rush hour was almost at an end with night trading off for the sun.

A four-door rusted old Chevy crept leisurely across the bridge, bumper to bumper with other slow moving cars. Two men, both of Jamaican decent sat in the Chevy. They looked impatient and intimidating. The driver was clad in a soiled wife-beater and dark shades. He was fat, with skin like night and a small scar lined his right cheek. The passenger was lean, with long Rasta dreadlocks down to his shoulders and had the same dark complexion like the driver. He wore an old black T-shirt, with a fading picture of Bob

Marley on his chest. He had bad teeth with bad breath to match. He smoked some kush rolled up in a long spliff and had a devious appearance about him.

"Bamba-claat traffic gettin' mi upset, yuh hear," the driver cursed.

His friend took another long pull from the burning kush and passed it to the driver.

"Mi gwan ask Afrika fa extra, mi done need ta put up wit' this hur…" the passenger stated.

The driver took a pull from the kush and his eyes looked wild. He stared across at the neighboring car and fixated his eyes on a young female driver behind the wheel of a BMW X5. She had her eyes forward and paid no attention to the two Rasta men in the Chevy.

"Hey pretty gal…yuh hear mi callin' ya pretty gal?" the driver called out with the spliff dangling from his mouth.

The young female driver glanced his way and expressed some disdain toward the disruptive catcall. She then decided to roll up her windows and turn on the air conditioner.

"Bamba-claat bitch, disrespectful, ya hear bredren. She gwan roll up da blood-claat window on mi. She don know who she dealin' wit', mi open dis door and smack fire out her ass," he exclaimed to his friend.

His friend laughed. He took a pull from the kush and replied. "All dem Yankee women disrespectful bredren, mi don pay her no mind."

The Rasta driver continued to glare at the female driver then began mocking her, making her a little nervous. Keeping her eyes forward, she contined to focus on the traffic, and never looked at the two men. She eased her X5 forward a little, not wanting to be alongside the old Chevy. The men in the car gave off an eerie feeling causing the woman to sighed and turn up the radio.

The Chevy was brimming with thick weed smoke with little summer air circulating through the car. The summer heat gripped their skins like it was flesh itself, and sweat began trickling down both of their brows. The driver coughed and began looking more impatient by the minute. He passed the kush to his partner and looked around for the X5. At that point, he noticed that she had switched over to another lane.

For some reason, it made him upset. He was daring to jump out, snatch the young girl out her ride, and throw her in the trunk of the Chevy. But the thick traffic and many eyes around made him think otherwise. Besides, the trunk was already occupied.

As the Chevy crawled inch by inch toward the tollbooths, Miranda was bound, gagged, and hidden in the filthy truck. She was butt-naked, and squirmed desperately to free herself in the under-sized space. Her wrists and ankles were tied tightly with duct tape, and her mouth sealed with it as well. Tears of panic and pain trickled from her burning red eyes, and her fingertips were bleeding and bruised.

Before she was forced into the trunk, her kidnappers, Fuji and Kaman both took their sweet time with her. They raped, beat and sodimized Miranda in a dark basement and left her body as well as her pussy sore and bleeding like she'd just given birth to quadruplets. Fuji and Kaman wanted their turn with Miranda before they delivered the package to Afrika's men.

As Miranda struggled in the trunk, she managed to peel the duct-tape from her mouth, but her limbs were still bound. She screamed out, "Help me, please…help me!" But the loud reggae music coming from inside the car drowned her out to the adjacent traffic on the bridge. She cried as she kicked and struggled for her freedom.

Fuji took another pull from the kush and stared at the city skyline from a distance.

"Mi sick of New Yak. Mi need a serious vacation bredren," Fuji commented.

"I feel ya mon…mi gwan tell Afrika we need ti plane tickets back ti Jamaica soon," Kaman laughed.

They were a quarter mile from the tollbooths. Fuji and Kaman had been working for the notorious Afrika for a month. When it came to seducing, deceiving and luring young females into the web of the dangerous and lucrative sex trade, they weren't as good or subtle as Tommy and Bay, Afrika's former workers.

Tommy had been dead for six months now, while Bay was in

a grave coma for weeks suffering from a gunshot wound to the back of his head. The entrance wound of the bullet was in his left occipital region and it passed into the periphery of the right temporal lobe, where it had lodged.

Several weeks after the shooting incident, Bay was transferred to a rehabilitation center. The doctors called Bay a miracle or a blessing. Bay was becoming relatively in good health with only slight general EEG changes. The doctors were saying that Bay was lucky to be alive because none of his important brain structures were injured, and secondly, the kinetic energy of the silvertip hollow-point bullet was rather low.

When Bay became conscious, doctors told him that he probably would have slight sensory disturbance in his fingers of the left hand and left-sided homonymous hemianopia. His recovery would be long and the projectile would be still lodged in the right temporal lobe.

Bay was happy to still be alive, but he couldn't forget. They'd killed his friend Tommy, and that bitch Carmen had set him up, but his biggest fear was Afrika. Bay knew too much about the operation and he knew for fear of being exposed, Afrika would probably send a hit squad to shut him up.

Bay knew he had to think up a plan fast because he was living on borrowed time. Bay wanted to, one, get revenge on Carmen and two, find and kill Africa before they killed him. It was inevitable that more deaths would follow.

Fuji and Kaman were far from being Bay and Tommy. Where Bay and Tommy used skills and lies to entrap their victims, the two Jamaican men used brute force and intimidation to capture women for Afrika's business. They didn't have time for games and lies, and the only thing that mattered to them was the five grand they received for every woman brought to Afrika's underground organization.

Miranda was a stripper in a Queens club, and unfortunately for her, Fuji and Kaman had their eyes set on her the minute they walked into the strip club. Miranda was on stage topless, clad in her G-string, and twirling herself around the long pole. She was the type of girl Afrika wanted for a Nubian prince in Africa.

Miranda was five-nine, with flawless brown skin, a thick and curvy figure, and a Caribbean background. She was from Trinidad and danced to pay her way through medical school. Her father was a sergeant for the NYPD.

Fuji and Kaman watched Miranda all night. They even flirted with her and gave her numerous tips while plotting for the right moment to strike. The men stayed 'till closing, which was four a.m. When the two men were asked to leave by the bouncer, they waited patiently outside in their parked Chevy for Miranda to exit the club. They wanted to kidnap her quickly and smoothly. The fewer eyes around the better.

Therefore, they sat parked and waited close by the club. Miranda exited the club by herelf fifteen minutes after closing. She walked to her truck with a confident stride, with her heels clacking against the concrete and her tight round ass in a pair of stylish Seven jeans. The block was dark, and the area vacant of people and activity. Her truck was parked a block from the club.

Fuji started the car while Kaman smoked on a large spliff. Both men's eyes were fixated on their victim, and a .380 lying on Kaman's lap. The Chevy came to a slow creep behind Miranda walking to her truck. Fuji blew smoke from his mouth with his scheming eyes never leaving the target.

When Miranda turned and noticed the car creeping, she put a little pep in her walk. Seconds later, she became nervous and slowly reached into her purse, searching for the small blade she always carried.

"Cuse me, beautiful," Fuji called out with a disturbing smile.

"I'm good," Miranda replied, not missing a step to her ride. She wasn't interested in anything he had to say or even try to sell.

"Pretty gal, why ya ignoring mi? Mi jus wan ta talk to ya," Fuji continued.

Miranda remembered him from the club and a shot of nervousness spread throughout her body. Her truck was only steps away. Miranda moved hastily with her keys in hand, blade in the other. Fuji navigated the Chevy closer.

"Why ya dissin' me, beautiful?" Fuji asked.

"Look, just fuck off!" Miranda shouted.

When she got near her truck, thinking she was safe and out

of harm's way, out of nowhere, Kaman ran up from behind and struck her with the gun before she could scream. She didn't even see him get out of the car. He pushed her in the trunk and the two sped off.

With every woman the duo kidnaped, before the delivery to Afrika's people, Fuji and Kaman always have their way with them sexually. With Miranda it was no different. They raped, abused and sodimized her for hours and when they were done with her, they bound her with rope and duct-tape, and tossed her beaten body in the trunk of the Chevy, like she was trash.

Miranda continued to struggle. She had ripped the duct-tape from around her mouth, so that gave her an advantage to scream for help somewhat, but the music and bass from the speakers drowned out her frantic calls. Miranda was burning up in the trunk as she struggled to free her wrists. She gnawed at the tape, feeling it cut into her mouth. She was desperate and the pain was nothing compared to her being held captive in a sex trade world.

She knew the car had to be in traffic because they've been stopped for a while. Miranda took a deep breath and tried not to continue to panic. She knew now was her chance to escape. She thought about her father being in the NYPD for fifteen years and began remembering the tips he'd given her if she was ever in any danger.

Miranda continued to gnaw through the thick tape. She felt it loosen around her wrists. She knew there was still hope. She felt the Chevy move more and she was racing with time. Her mouth began to bleed and her wrists started to feel numb. The unbearable heat in the closed trunk made Miranda want to pass out. She fought the agonizing heat and pain and tore at the tape with her teeth. Minutes later, she freed her wrist. Her feet came next, and with both her hands available, undoing her feet came easy.

However, the hardest part was getting out of the trunk. She searched for some kind of lever in the dark with her hands, but felt nothing. She took another deep breath and started to remember more tips from her father. The first thing Miranda started doing was trying to gain access to the brake lights from inside. She knew by gaining access, she would be able to pull out wires and have the lights fail, capturing the attention of the police.

Miranda ran her hands across the panel and then she pried it open with her hands. Once she had access to the wires, she ripped them all out, causing the brake lights to the Chevy to go out immediately. Next, Miranda searched in the dark with her hands for some kind of tool she could use to pry the trunk open. As her hand came across a tire iron, she felt her escape coming near.

She worked diligently to pry the trunk open by the sides. She shoved the tire-iron against the latch and tried to force it open. It took her a while, but she felt the latch weakening.

Fuji thought he heard some kind of thump come from the back.

"Bredren, yuh hear dat?" he asked.

"Mi don hear a dam thang, Fuji," Kaman replied. He was becoming upset and impatient with the thick traffic and scorching summer heat.

Fuji heard another thump come from the trunk of the car.

"Bredren… mi ain't hearing thangs, dem noise come from ti trunk."

Kaman began to listen attentively. Fuji turned down the radio and looked to the back.

"Fuji, de bitch stay put and tied tightly, she not runnin' nowhere," Kaman assured his friend.

"Kaman, mi tells ya sumthin' ain't right…mi fear she untied and scheming," Fuji proclaimed.

Kaman chuckled. "Bredren, mi knocked da bitch unconscious. She sleep 'till we in Jersey."

Abruptly, the trunk flew open and Miranda jumped out screaming.

"Mi told ya I hear sumthin'!" Fuji shouted.

Fuji quickly put the car in parked and he ran out the car with Kaman, gun in hand. He was furious as Miranda ran through the evening traffic butt-naked and screamed out frantically.

"Help me! Somebody help me!" she screamed.

Onlookers in their cars were shocked and in awe. Miranda slammed her bloody fists against car windows and windshields, yearning for someone's help. She looked like a mad woman escaping from the mental hospital. Her hair was in disarray, her naked body was bloody and bruised and her eyes wide with terror.

Fuji and Kaman chased her a few cars down, but the cat was already out the bag. Fuji gripped his .380 tightly and all he could do was glare at Miranda making her daring escape from them. He had the look of wickedness about him and if he had a clear sight, he would have shot Miranda in her back.

"Fuji, we need ti leave…she gon', bredren," Kaman said.

"Bamba-claat…that's mi money escaping!" Fuji yelled.

"Bredren, police be soon on da way," Kaman informed him.

Fuji looked around madly. He noticed that all eyes were soon on him and Kaman. Some men and women locked themselves in their cars, panicking. They rolled up their windows, trying to shelter themselves from any danger. Some people quickly exited their cars and ran for the nearest help, fearing the two Jamaican men were terrorists.

Fuji and Kaman rushed back to their Chevy, but with the heavy traffic on the bridge, fleeing by car was impossible. Police sirens began piercing the air and a group of officers hurried to the trouble spot by foot. They screamed codes into their handheld police radios with their guns out and ready to confront the two men.

Fuji knew that their only escape was to jump from the bridge, but he couldn't swim. Fuji stared at his partner in crime and exclaimed, "Bredren, we fucked up!"

Kaman reached into the backseat of the car and retrieved a fully loaded Glock 17. Kaman screamed, "Mi see no American prison!"

After his statement, he quickly fired at the first close officer. Blam. Blam. Blam. Blam. Blam

Two shots hit one officer in the vest and he went flying back. Fuji immediately followed action and let off a barrage of gunfire at the oncoming law enforcements. Panic soon overwhelmed the people on the bridge. Passengers and drivers swiftly ducked down in their cars, while others tried to escape the threat.

"Stay in your cars. Stay in your cars!" officers shouted, as they shot back.

More gunfire burst from the Jamaican's guns, as they shot at police without any remorse or care for the bystanders trapped in their cars or running from the scene. Police took cover behind cars, and it was too dangerous to return gunfire. Civilians were running by them screaming and blocking their line of fire.

"Get back in your cars! Get down! Get down!" cops shouted.

Fuji and Kaman didn't care about hitting innocent people. They still were shooting to kill. One lady exited her car out of fear and caught a hot slug in her back. She dropped dead in front of the police.

Bak. Bak. Bak. Bak. Bak. Bak.

Fuji shot rapidly. He ducked behind the Chevy and was ready to reload his extra clip. Cops tried to return fire, but it was risky because there were too many innocent people around. A normal traffic filled day on the Triboro Bridge had become completely chaotic.

Twenty-five cars down, Miranda sat in the arms of a caring woman, who covered her naked body with a blanket she carried in the trunk. Miranda sat crying and shivering in the elderly ladie's arms, while her husband gazed ahead at the madness taking place just a few cars ahead.

"Henry, get your stupid butt down before you get shot," the lady pleaded with her husband.

"Oh, my God, Leah, they are really shooting it out up there," he said in shock.

"Don't worry; honey…help is on the way. Just hold on, and we'll get you to a hospital," Leah assured Miranda.

Miranda tears flowed continually. She shook uncontrollably like there was a cold winter wind draped around her. Her body felt limp. She couldn't speak, but only cried and clutched onto the woman like her life depended on it.

"What did they do to you, poor chile," the lady cried out, still trying to comfort Miranda.

Miranda looked to be in a zombie condition, with her eyes wide and her body feeling cold on one of the hottest days of the month. The rape and abuse would forever haunt and disturb her.

Fuji reloaded his .380 and continued to shoot at police. Two dozen officers were now on the scene and ESU was approaching the danger fast.

"Mi give da bloot-claat police sumthin ti' fear….mi gun down batte boy cops!" Kaman shouted.

He went to the backseat, and lying on the floor was an Uzi machine gun. The men came ready for a confrontation. Kaman held the deadly weapon in his hands without hesitation or concern for any innocent life in front of him; he began spraying the bridge with a heavy barrage of bullets.

Bullets riddled many cars and hit dozens of people. Men and women took cover wherever they thought was safe. A few officers got in the way of the lethal weapon and were mowed down like grass.

"Officers down! Officers down!" cops squealed into their radios.

Back-up for the NYPD came by the dozens, and they were coming from both the Queens'and the Manhattan/Bronx side of the bridge.

Fuji and Kaman were suicidal. They weren't surrendering. The cop's main priorities were to get as many people off the bridge and then subdue the men. However, it wasn't long before Kaman and Fuji took hostages and held them at gunpoint.

Fuji screamed out, "Mi gwan start killin' people if police don back off!"

He pulled a woman from her car and slammed her down to the pavement violently, holding the gun to the back of her head. Pandemonium seemed to be spreading everywhere. Within an hour, the entire bridge was shut down and snipers were positioned nearby ready for a kill shot.

The news media swarmed the bridge, hoping to get a glimpse of the action, but police barricades held them miles back from the chaos. Reporters rushed to get a story and began interviewing potential victims coming from the mayhem. Within an hour after the shooting, *"Breaking News"* began flashing across millions of TV screens throughout the city. It had been confirmed that five people were dead and many injured. The media began referring to the men as terrorists, revealing to the city that they were holding hostages and there were little demands.

Two NYPD helicopters hovered over the bridge, scoping out the scene thoroughly. Fuji and Kaman thought it was just the police watching them, but they were completely unaware that two snipers had them within a kill shot.

Fuji shouted at the helicopters. He waved his gun around madly and threatened to kill a hostage or shoot at the NYPD above. However, swiftly, like a thief in the night, a single shot was heard and then Fuji dropped dead from a gunshot wound to his head.

A second kill shot was quickly fired from a sniper's rifle from above and it struck Kaman in his chest. He collapsed in front of his hostages. The Jamaicans were dead, but many questions needed to be answered and many lives have been changed.

Miranda was rushed to Jamaica Hospital. A team of doctors and nurses rushed to her aid, moving her into the emergency room. Within minutes after her arrival, there was a swarm of reporters outside the hospital lobby. They wanted questions answered and news on Miranda's daring escape from her kidnappers. It would be front-page news for a week.

NEW JERSEY

Agonizing female cries echoed throughout the bare concrete basement in Union City. Twenty naked females were lined against the cold walls. They shivered and cried loudly, and had the look of fear plastered across their faces. Four armed African men held them at gunpoint and spoke recklessly to the captured women. Some even struck the women with fists and the butt of their guns to instill perpetual fear into their minds and souls.

The men spoke in French and were hostile. They glared at each woman with a mixture of hostility and lust.

"Why are you doin' this to us?" one woman dared to ask.

She was voluptuous, with streaming long black hair that looked a tangled mess. Her body looked worn and tired, but she glared back at the men who held her captive with bravery. The surrounding women around her looked at her with pleading eyes to be quiet.

A tall and burly African man with skin like a moonless night looked possessed. He gripped the sub-machine gun he had in his hands tighter and approached the daring bitch.

"Tais-toi, salope!" he screamed out in French, which meant *'Shut-up bitch!'*

He then punched her viciously with his closed fist. The woman tumbled to her knees as blood spewed from her mouth. The other woman around cried out in horror and began to panic. They feared that the worst had yet to come.

The tall African man stood over the woman he'd punched and laughed. He continued to taunt her in French.

"Vous ne dit que votre!" he screamed.

He then carried a smirk across his black grill. He turned to look at his partners in crime and spoke out more French. The men behind him laughed. The tall darkish man then slowly unzipped his pants, pulled out his dick and began peeing on the sobbing woman.

His warm reeking piss slowly trickled down her face. She sobbed louder, as his piss sprinkled down on her like a fountain. He laughed while doing so. When he was done, he put away his tool and kicked the woman in her stomach, screaming out in French, "Get up bitch! Get the fuck up!"

The woman was too hurt, ashamed, and weak to move any further. She wanted to die where she lay. The man screamed at her again, but she remained stuck to the cold hard basement floor. Her naked and battered soul feeling somewhat of a comfort there. The man saw that she wasn't complying with his demands. So, to give her an incentive, he pointed his sub-machine directly at her face and yelled to her in French. Even though she didn't understand him, his action spoke louder, and she clearly understood that she was supposed to rise to her feet.

Once again, his commandment was disobeyed. The distraught woman, who was strikingly beautiful at one point in her life was a dancer at Sue's Rendezvous. She looked as if she'd aged ten years. Her eyes were watery and red from the constant crying. She had been forcefully imprisoned for two weeks and was raped countless times by men she wouldn't give a second look to if they were on the streets.

She stood hugging the cold ground and looking up at the barrel of a black SMG PK machine gun. The other ladies around stood unmoving and crying. They feared she would be shot if she didn't follow instructions. They wanted to call out and help, but fear held them rooted to their heartrending positions.

The African screamed out to the defiant bitch one more time. He put his muddy boot on her scarred back and trained the gun closer to her face and head. When she failed to comply, the gun went off, a quick burst exploded and the women screamed. The victim's head and face split open like watermelon hitting the concrete, leaving a contorted mess for all to see.

The shooter had no remorse. He chuckled, then wiped some of her blood off his boot using the back of the dead woman's hair. The ladies were terrified. They sobbed louder and reluctantly obeyed orders from each of the men.

More French was yelled at them and they were instructed to move further down the hallway. As the women began moving forward, something caught the goons' attention. They looked down the hall and saw their commander approaching. It was Afrika himself.

The men's attitude quickly changed. They became more like sheep than wolves. Afrika's strong presence spoke in volumes. The men respected and feared him. He was a ruthless and smart man, with political connections in over a dozen countries. The Nigerian born native was quiet for a moment. He stood in dark army fatigues, with a .9mm holstered on his right hip for all to see. His gaze held onto the naked women in front of him. They were immediately intimidated.

"You bitches belong to mi now," he spoke in his accent. "I own ya and there is no escape. You bitches bring me tons of money, and this is home to ya. Fuckin' and suckin' will be de only thing ya need to do, unless ya owners require more fo the right price."

The women sobbed. The look in their eyes showed no hope. Some women even bowed their heads in shame. They would have preferred taken their own lives than be forced into permanent prostitution. Their wails echoed louder and their futures were looking bleak with every passing hour.

Afrika locked eyes with a five-nine woman who had an eye-catching body. She lowered her head and immediately began reciting the Lord's Prayer. She mumbled it to herself, trying to find comfort from the demons and evil around her.

Shivering like she'd been caught in a winter storm, she mumbled, "Our Father, which art in Heaven, hallowed be thy name, thy kingdom come, thy will be done, on earth as it is in Heaven…"

Afrika stepped to her with an unpleased look about him. He grabbed the praying woman by her neck, causing her to jerk in fear. "What is that ya pray? Ya believe in God?"

The woman meekly nodded, with Afrika's hand still clutched around her neck. He gazed into her suffering eyes and said, "I am God down here. Ya pray to me to have mercy on ya. Ya pray to him no more…I am ya father now."

He squeezed her neck tighter, causing the woman to choke and gasp for air. She grabbed at his wrist, wanting to breathe and more importantly wanting to live.

"Mi ask ya again, who ya now pray to?" Afrika asked in a stern tone.

"You…" the woman uttered, feeling her body about to faint.

"Say de name…Afrika," he said, in a slow merciless tone.

"Afrika…"

He displayed a devious smile. "Now, get down on ya knees and suck mi dick."

When the frightened girl looked reluctant, Afrika quickly grabbed her long hair and yanked her head back forcefully, almost breaking her neck.

"Mi not goin' to ask again…mi will kill ya, bitch. Mi own ya and these bitches…ya nuthin' but me commodity now. Now get on ya fuckin' knees and suck mi dick."

The girl sobbed and slowly succumbed to her knees and unzipped his fatigues. She reached and pulled out nine inches of Afrika's dick. As she held the monstrous penis in her hand, her lips quivered. She could hear the other girls sobbing with her. They all knew that in the future, they would all suffer from the same fate…being forced into uncommitted sex or raped by men from all ethnicities and races.

The sniveling young woman slowly neared her quivering lips toward the tip of his dick and reluctantly took Afrika into her mouth. Afrika gripped her long weave and had it tangled around his fist. He forced his big dick down her throat, making the woman choke and struggle with it in her mouth. He clutched her hair tighter, causing the woman to be in great pain.

The other women around watched in horror. The girl on her knees looked like she was about to choke to death, as Afrika continued forcing his big black dick down her throat and giving her no relief for air.

As the torment went on, another figure walked down the grim and dimmed concrete corridor. This person looked total opposite from all the other grimy goons. It was a woman, clad in a stylish classic black business skirt suit, with the single-breasted three button jacket, and a tight pencil skirt. Her skin was like chocolate, with long sensuous black hair that was styled into a thick bun. She also stood tall in five-inch heels and looked as if she worked out a lot.

She approached Afrika with a sense of urgency, carrying a leather briefcase in her grip and sporting stylish wire-rimmed glasses that gave her a sophisticated persona. The men she passed gave her respect. They didn't stare too long, even though she was beautiful like the women they raped and sold into slavery.

Afrika was still getting a forced blowjob, when the woman walked up with the need to tell him something. She showed no remorse or concern to the other naked women nearby. She was as cold to them as the men were.

"Speak to me, Cymbal," Afrika stated.

Cymbal leaned near and whispered in his ear important business that he needed to hear. Afrika was stunned by the news.

"When?" he asked.

"A few hours ago," Cymbal replied.

Afrika looked upset. His face twisted into anger. He gripped the bitch's hair tighter and yanked her pleasing lips from his dick. He had enough. Cymbal simply walked away.

Afrika looked down at his poor victim, locking eyes with her again. She was still teary and hurt. He then looked at the other women around him and knew he needed to set an example. He slowly un-holstered his weapon and cocked it back, securing a deadly round into the chamber. He then spoke, "Ya bitches try to escape, and we kill ya family. We kill ya children, and then we kill ya."

With that said, he put his gun to the forehead of the pleading woman knelt in front of him and squeezed. Her body immediately crumpled at his feet. There were shouts and screams, but the panicky women remained in check and frozen in fright.

"Welcome ladies," Afrika greeted with an eerie smile.

Moments later, Afrika hurried into the great room of the building and grabbed for the remote to the plasma flat screen mounted on the wall. He couldn't turn to CNN fast enough. As the coverage on the incident played out, Afrika and his goons watched in awe.

Afrika turned up the volume to hear broadcaster, Anderson Cooper cover the breaking news. He was expecting for Fuji and Kaman to bring them a girl, but they were late. Afrika hated when a delivery didn't come on time, and when the media informed that both men were shot dead by sniper rifles, Afrika thought that the NYPD did him a favor. He was going to kill them both anyway.

He was worried about the girl, Miranda. The news reported that she was being treated and cared for at Jamaica Hospital, but they wouldn't disclose further details about her condition. Afrika wanted to know what information she could've known to give law enforcement. Fuji and Kaman had fucked up and now a full detailed investigation would be opened because the bitch was the daughter of a prominent NYPD sergeant.

One of Afrika's men walked up to him, as Afrika focused on the news.

"What you want us to do?" he asked.

"Pack de thangs and prepare to ship out. We leave da country within forty-eight hours. We have what we came for, but only a few lose ends need ta tie up."

The man nodded and walked away.

When the men were out the room, Cymbal walked into the room and approached Afrika. She locked eyes with Afrika before giving him a hard right hand slap on his face. She then pulled him closer and tongued him down passionately. When they were done lip-locking, Cymbal looked at him.

"Don't you ever disrespect me with them dirty whores again."

Afrika smirked.

Cymbal didn't like the fact that Afrika was getting a blowjob from one of the girls who was up for sale. However, she kept her emotions contained and remained professional around her man and his goons when she witnessed the act. They kept their affair private and Cymbal could be as cold-hearted as her man.

She was majority brains, but ruthless when it came to the organization. Cymbal was born in Uganda, a landlocked country in East Africa. She was raised in the states and spoke three languages. She spoke proper English and was well educated, but had an appetite for power and sex. At the age of twenty-one, she fled back to Africa after murdering a federal agent during a drug bust.

Cymbal was strikingly beautiful, having an African father and Italian mother. She was the only child and met Afrika during the Rwandan holocaust in 1994. She was part of the Interahamwe, which was a Hutu paramilitary organization and were responsible for the genocide of hundreds of thousands of Tutsi men, women and children killed in Rwanda in the span of ninety days.

Cymbal's thirst for blood, power and money attracted the attention of Afrika. The two soon were having a secret rendezvous and grew in power together over the years. Their terror reigned in numerous countries and they were soon on the radar of Interpol; wanted for human trafficking, child pornography, mass murder, weapons smuggling, drug trafficking, money laundering and computer crimes. The two together were smart and their love growing stronger every passing year.

"Don't worry Cymbal, mi eyes for you only…mi set the bitch for an example. She dead now," Afrika assured her.

Cymbal showed a smile and then forced herself against Afrika with a passionate kiss. She became aggressive, ripping away at his shirt, wanting to expose his rippling stomach and feel his large muscle thrust inside of her. Afrika scooped Cymbal into his arms with her legs straddled around him.

"I want you to fuck me, baby," she cried out.

Afrika placed her on the desk and tore apart her business skirt and panties. She unbuckled his fatigues and felt him coiled, stiff and ready to strike. Cymbal sucked and licked on his neck as he palmed her ass and thrust his dick into her creamy wet snatch. She moaned and clutched Afrika tightly, dragging her long manicured nails down his broad back with her legs pressed against his tall strapping fame.

Cymbal liked it rough, hard, and wanted it to last. She pushed Afrika from her, indicating that she wanted to switch positions. She dropped from the desk, turned from him, and placed one knee on the desk. Cymbal felt Afrika's hard dick pushed against her sides. She reached for his dick and guided it deep inside of her. Afrika spanked her ass hard and rubbed her clitoris at the same time. It drove Cymbal crazy and she cried out, while biting down on her bottom lip and throwing it back on him.

"Fuck me, nigga...oh shit!"

She felt his plunging, getting deeper and held on for dear life as he pummeled her into the mahogany wood.

"I'm cumin!" Afrika exclaimed.

He gripped Cymbal's sweet bare hips and fucked her from the back like a true porn star. He cupped her sizable tits and ran his tongue down the small of her back. Her panting was loud, her body trembling against the desk.

"I want to suck my king," Cymbal exclaimed.

After seeing Afrika's big dick pull out her dripping pussy there was no hesitation. She dropped to her knees and took his dick into her mouth with the curl of her tongue in action. Cymbal's jaws clamped his pulsing dick and her tongue teased his head until he got caught up in throes of ecstasy.

Afrika hoisted Cymbal over his shoulders and spread her across the chaise. Her skin glistened with sweat as he entered her with rapid strokes. Cymbal screamed as if she was being tortured. The way his dick slid in and out of her, made her legs quiver and her breathing sparse. She had her legs spread apart in a downward V and his big dick had her butt-cheeks wide open.

Afrika looked like a Zulu warrior as he clutched Cymbal petite sweaty frame and tore into her pussy with animal instincts. The pussy was so good that he grunted. He looked possessed with his eyes rolling in the back of his head.

"Aaaaahhh shit...baby. Fuck me," he roared.

"The world is ours, baby...the world is fuckin' ours!" Cymbal yelled.

Seconds later, she felt Afrika's dick swell up as his nut came spewing into her in several bursts.

Her body went limp and her breathing soft. Afrika was very well satisfied. He pulled up his fatigue pants and sparked a cigar. He looked at Cymbal. "We leave in two days. We take who we have."

"What about the bitch in the hospital? You think she knows anything from them two fools?" Cymbal asked.

"She done, that bitch don know nuthin'…just like Fuji and Kaman are clueless to us."

Cymbal walked up to Afrika and pulled the cigar from his lips. She took a long drag from it, enjoying the taste of a Cuban cigar and replied with, "Why take the chance. I want that bitch dead, Afrika. She escaped from us. She doesn't get to live."

Afrika smiled. "Ya more ruthless than me men, Cymbal….how ya come to be so cruel?" he joked.

"I learned from the best. I'm just a dick-less bitch," she returned.

Afrika took a pull from the cigar and smiled.

JAMAICA HOSPITAL. QUEENS

Miranda lay in her hospital bed unmoving. The doctor had performed a rape kit on her and discovered that she'd suffered intense vaginal bleeding, tearing, and also had an infection. Miranda wanted to cut herself off from everyone and everything. She lay in bed looking damn near comatose. She was being closely monitored by the hospital staff while detectives swarmed around her room like ants. They needed her to come around and remember the attack.

As her father rushed to get to the hospital as quickly as possible, the media loomed outside, wanting an update on Miranda's condition and the case. Her unfortunate incident had quickly become a high profile case.

Fifteen minutes later, Sgt Peter Monroe's pearl colored Yukon came to a halting stop in front of the hospital. As he rushed from his vehicle, he was quickly met by the press in the multitude. They pushed cameras and mics in his face and were asking him dozens of questions. However, Peter pushed through them like they weren't even there. His only focus was his daughter. As soon as he entered the lobby, he was met by several detectives.

"What room is she in?" he asked loudly.

"She's in room 402," a tall lanky detective replied, showing his condolences to a fellow officer.

Peter said nothing else. He walked toward the elevator and pushed for the fourth floor. When he arrived, a very good friend of his, Mike Canton quickly met him at the door. Mike was a federal agent and Miranda's Godfather. They grew up together in the streets of Brooklyn and always had dreams of becoming involved in law enforcement. Both men joined the Marines together and excelled in their field of service. While Peter landed a job with the NYPD, Mike exceeded his dreams and became FBI.

With a fierce look in his eyes, Sergeant Monroe walked toward Mike and asked, "Where is she, Mike? What happened to my baby girl?"

Mike had a somber expression and ran the details to his friend about his daughter before he went in to visit.

"She's stable, Pete, but it's bad. I'm gonna be real with you, they did her something terrible. She's suffering from some tearing and vaginal bleeding. She's just laying there, not saying a word to anyone, even me."

"Fuckin' animals kidnapped and raped my baby girl, Mike…they raped my baby girl," Peter cried out with tears streaming down his face.

Mike took his friend into his arms. "Peter, I'm gonna handle this. You have my word on this, my brother. I'm gonna get to the bottom of this and find out what happened to my Goddaughter. I'm pulling out all resources so we can put the monsters responsible for this behind bars for life."

"They're dead, Mike. Shot down on the Triboro Bridge," Peter replied.

"I know, but it ain't over. Go see Miranda, Peter…spend some time with her. When you come out, I need to talk to you. I have some information," Mike stated.

Peter dried his tears. He wanted to be strong for his daughter. He took a deep breath and slowly walked into her hospital room. He stared at Miranda lying still, looking distant from everything. He approached her bed, and slowly took her hand into his.

"Daddy's here, baby girl. I got you now. I got you, baby. No one else is going to ever hurt you again."

Peter spent hours with his daughter. He stayed at her bedside until dawn and talked to her, all the while trying to hold back his tears. After he was done, he walked out into the hallway. Mike was coming off the elevator just in time to see his friend leave the room. They locked eyes with each other and Mike gestured that they meet privately in the stairway.

Peter followed behind his friend, and when the stairway door closed, Mike stood quietly for a moment.

"What you gotta say, Mike?" Peter asked.

"Look, this thing with Miranda, it goes a lot deeper. I shouldn't be telling you this, but as a friend, you need to know. Miranda is lucky to be alive. For a year now, we've been heavily investigating this crime syndicate led by this vicious crime lord named, Afrika. The men killed today on that bridge, were transporters. They were delivering Miranda to this syndicate in which they capture young women for the sex trade overseas," Mike proclaimed.

"What are you telling me, Mike…that my daughter was about to be pimped to some high end perverts in a different country?"

"Look, many women have been reported missing in the past three years. This shit, it's bigger than you and me, Interpol is involved. But my agency has been investigating these women disappearing here in the states for months now. Miranda is one of the fortunate ones to escape. The women who go missing are never seen again."

It registered in Peter's mind how lucky his daughter was, even though she was distraught and raped. He couldn't even think about the worse, not seeing his daughter again, or her being dead.

"These people are wicked and out to make a profit. Afrika's girlfriend, Cymbal, we've been after her for years. She killed a federal agent during a drug bust a few years back. She fled the country soon after and was never seen again. We caught a break in the case a few weeks ago. An informant came forward and told our agency that she was back in the states and conducting her business again."

"Are you serious? I'm ready to go murder this man for fuckin' with my family," Peter exclaimed.

"You need to chill, Pete. I'm on top of this, and when the bastards came after my Goddaughter, it became personal. As a friend, I thought you should know the truth behind Miranda's kidnapping. I'm about to fly to Atlanta in a few days. I caught wind of this duo that's been on the prowl a few months back, two of Afrika's transporters. They were hitting up Atlanta's strip clubs and alluring young strippers into their web by promising fame and glory. Unfortunately, one was killed, but the friend; he survived a gunshot to the head.

"I think his name is Bay," Mike informed.

"Mike, you go after these animals, and you kill them all for Miranda. Look what they did to my baby girl. She's never gonna be the same again. Don't stop until you see a bullet in every one of those bastards' head. This is war, Mike," Peter stated with conviction.

"I'll do my job, Pete. You just stay here, take care of her, and make sure she recovers. My team is on top of it and it's become our number one priority."

Peter shook his head in understanding. He hugged his close friend and former Marine closely and cried out, "I know you will, my brother. I know you will."

ATLANTA

It had been eight months since Bay caught a shot to his head. Doctors told Bay that he would be in full recovery, and stated that he was a miracle and had God's blessing in his recovery. However, Bay had only one thing on his mind, and it wasn't his recovery or God, it was revenge.

After his rehabilitation, Bay was checked out with a clean bill of health. He had ten stacks saved up somewhere safe and he wasn't going to leave ATL until he saw Carmen and her goons again.

When Bay walked out the center with papers in his hand and

a second chance at life, he caught a cab to the nearest motel. He paid for the week, and now he needed a gun, or a few guns. He was on the hunt. He thought about his friend, Tommy who he missed a lot. Even though Tommy could be an asshole at times, he and Bay grew up together. They'd been through thick and thin since they were young.

Bay stripped away his clothing and peered at himself in the bathroom mirror. He lost a lot of weight and didn't look the same. The bullet to his head changed his features somewhat. He almost looked unrecognizable. He took a long needed hot shower and then ordered some pizza. A hot shower and food was the first thing on Bay's mind, and the next two important things were some pussy and a gun.

As Bay sat on the bed with a towel wrapped around his waist, he skimmed through the yellow pages, searching for the nearest escort service to call. He was horny. He needed his mind to drift somewhere comfortable and pleasurable for a few hours. He needed to escape from the pain he endured. He had a stack on him and needed a woman. Seconds later, Bay placed a call to this service out of Decatur, which was only a few miles from his room. When he ordered the escort, the madam on the phone assured him that his date for the evening would be knocking at his motel door within the hour. Bay couldn't wait.

Bay turned on the television and decided to see what was going on in the world. He flipped through a few channels and then something caught his immediate attention. He raised himself out of the bed and his gaze held onto the news channel, with the journalist covering the shootout that happened on the Triboro Bridge.

Bay listened and heard the details. He wasn't familiar with the names, Fuji and Kaman that were being exposed nationwide, but he knew who they had to be working for...his former employer, Afrika. Bay's heart raced as the journalist went on with the Triboro shooting and the men and women dead behind it.

Bay raised the volume and knew shit was hitting the fan for everyone, and that Afrika would be on a rampage and scrambling to clean up the mess.

"Sloppy," Bay said to himself.

He knew if it were him and Tommy, they would've never

been caught. He and his former partner were too skilled and smooth to have their cover exposed to the public. *The bitch would've stayed secured and locked down in the trunk*, Bay thought. However, that wasn't his life anymore. He was out and wanted to move on.

As the media went on about the woman's daring escape, Bay thought about the women who didn't escape from him and Tommy, and he knew that because of him, countless of women were now overseas being sex slaves to men who paid handsomely for them.

Bay couldn't worry about it anymore, everyone thought that he was dead and he had that in his favor. Bay went on to watch the news until he heard a knock at his room door. He knew it was his date arriving, but he still wanted to be cautious. Thinking about his mistake with Carmen had him a little edgy. He put on some jeans and looked for anything around the room that could be used as a weapon just in case things didn't go too well. After looking around for a few seconds, he couldn't find anything, so he quickly gave up.

Bay decided to put his fear of being set-up to the side and focus on some pussy. It had been a while since he had some ass and he needed to fuck. Bay took a deep breath and looked through the peephole of the door. He vaguely saw a woman's figure; the hole he looked through was tiny and dusty.

Bay opened the door and his eyes rested on a tall chocolate woman in an un-zipped tank dress. She had long black flowing hair that was down to her back, and stood tall in a pair of four-inch stilettos. She was curvy and voluptuous in all the right places.

"You Bay?" she asked with a smile.

"Yeah…." Bay replied.

"Well, can I come in? I can't fuck you out here," she replied sarcastically.

Bay moved to the side and the tall heavenly beauty strutted into the small motel room. She stood in the center of the room looking strikingly beautiful.

"How much?" Bay asked.

"For the first hour, five hundred," she answered.

"Damn, you a steep priced ho."

"Nigga, I'm gonna be the best fuck you ever had," she assured.

Bay quickly sized her up, and figured that she wasn't a threat to him. He was hard and horny. The woman waited to be paid first before anything came off.

"You gotta pay to play," she stated.

Bay agreed. He walked over to the weathered dresser and pulled out a large stack. He tossed her the cash and announced, "Well, I want you for two hours. It's been a minute for me."

The young woman took the cash and her eyes widened. "You was locked up or sumthin?"

"Sumthin' like that."

Once she was satisfied with the count, she walked up to Bay with the intentions to entice, seduce the shit out of him, and give him one hell of a night.

"What's your name, luv?" Bay asked.

"Sunshine," she answered.

Bay chuckled. "That's a unique name."

"Don't let the name fool you cuz of my skin color, cuz between my thighs, I got plenty of sunshine to go around that will light up any nigga's day. It's gonna be the sweetest thang you ever had," she boasted.

Bay didn't care for chatter or her name, he just wanted to fuck.

"Just get undressed," he ordered.

Sunshine began undoing her attire. She peeled away her dress and then removed her scanty thong, tossing them aside. Her Hershey brown nipples were erect and her soft black skin shimmered under the room light. Sunshine's heavenly defined legs were stretched out in her stilettos, making her naked figure look like an Amazon goddess. She stepped to Bay with an alluring smile and slowly undid his jeans. She reached into his zipper and slowly stroked Bay's growing hard-on like she was nursing it to sleep. She felt his dick growing in her fist and massaged the tip of his dick like it was play dough in her small hand. She played with it for a short moment, feeling pre-cum seep out into the palm of her hand.

Sunshine smiled and said, "Ummm, you're a big boy and ready to go."

She dropped his jeans around his ankles like a mesh. Sunshine started to kiss his nipples tenderly, circling her tongue around the tip, tasting his manly nectar. Her tongue traveled south, teasing his bellybutton, with her knees pressed against the floor, she quickly engulfed Bay's hard thick dick into her mouth like it was an icy pop. Her lips were pressed against hard flesh; she felt his dick throbbing against her jaw. She cupped his balls and began sucking his dick slowly, sampling every inch of his long length. Her tongue coiled around the tip, and she licked his hole, while sucking on the mushroom tip. Bay let out an animal like moan. He leaned back and clutched the dresser tightly, watching Sunshine suck his dick with professionalism.

Her curved tongue ran down the back of his throbbing penis, and then she chewed and sucked on his nuts, with her tongue nearing his anal. She pushed Bay back and continued to work on his hard perfection. Her head bobbed up and down on the dick like a ball on the court, while squeezing and playing with Bay's soft baggy nuts.

"Oh shit...Oh shit! Damn-it!" Bay cried out, feeling her warm wet and long tongue wetting every inch of his manhood.

Her lips were like a vacuum suction. It felt like she was magnetic and she was ready to suck all of him with a compelling force. Bay gripped the back of her head, tangling her long hair between his fingers, and allowed his manly juices to drip all over her tongue and lips. Sunshine tasted every bit of him with a smile.

"Suck that dick...yeah, you like that, right? It's good to you," Bay teased.

With her professional skills, his mind was finally away from all his troubles. Sunshine bucked, and ran her tongue between his thighs like a paintbrush against skin. Bay was positioned on the dresser, with his legs spread and Sunshine tickled his brown skin with her long warm tongue. When Sunshine ran her tongue against his nuts, it caused Bay to shiver with a strong almost endurable feeling.

Sunshine went to work on Bay's private below...sucking there, kissing him gently here, and running her tongue in there and against here, chewing on his balls like they were bubble gum in her mouth.

Bay quivered and was ready to burst into her chops.

"I wanna fuck you," he exclaimed.

"Don't you wanna cum in my mouth first," Sunshine said mischievously, being truly freaky.

She wrapped her thick glossy lips around the dick and deep-throated the sonovabitch. Her lips continued to jerk him off. Bay squirmed and turned on the dresser, with his ass cheeks rubbing against the hard wood.

He panted and screamed out, "Shit…you gonna make me cum!"

Soon, Sunshine felt the veins in his dick throbbing in her mouth and soon afterwards, a burst of semen came squirting into her open cavity like a fountain. Bay looked somewhat inflated, but he was soon ready to go again. He was extra horny and busting one nut wasn't satisfying for him.

He jumped off the dresser and pushed Sunshine against the bed. She lay on her stomach and was ready to be fucked. Bay rolled back a magnum onto his dick and climbed on top of Sunshine. He spread her ass cheeks like a book to be read and thrust his big dick into her wet snatch. He pushed against her, fucking her doggy-style. He placed a pillow under her stomach, causing her ass to arch and went in on the pussy like a hunt.

His chest began sweating against her back. Her ass pushed against his pelvis, his dick opened her pussy up like the Grand Canyon. Sunshine clutched the bed sheets tightly and screamed out from being a victim to the dick. She made her pussy contract against his constant pounding.

"Fuck me, nigga…tear that pussy up. Beat it up, nigga," Sunshine cried out. Her teeth sank into the pillow and Bay was trying to put that phat ass to sleep.

Their freaky rendezvous went on for about an hour and a half. Bay fucked Sunshine against the wall. He had her on the toilet, on the floor. He fucked her on the dresser and they even went at it in the shower. When Bay finally came, it felt like hot air was being let out of a balloon. His body went limp. His toes curled and became numb. He had definitely gotten his money's worth.

Bay lay against wrinkled, wet and stained bed sheets. His flaccid dick still exposed. He watched Sunshine get dressed. The way they fucked and went at it like animals in the wild, reminded him of Carmen. It bothered him, but he let the thought breeze by and smiled at Sunshine as she slid into her four inch clear stilettos.

She was paid and Bay got his nut, they both were happy. Sunshine grabbed her things and said to Bay, "Call me again, sexy."

Bay jumped out of the bed, his dick swinging as he approached Sunshine. Before she walked out, he needed one last favor from her.

"What's that?" Sunshine questioned.

"I need to get my hands on a gun. I got money to spend. You look like the type who can help me out," he said.

Sunshine looked at Bay for a moment. She wasn't sure about the request.

"I got the paper, luv…I just need the weapon. I'm willing to spend whateva," Bay assured.

"How much?" she asked.

"Seven hundred or more."

Sunshine nodded.

"I might know someone who can help."

Bay smiled.

A week had past and Bay caught a cab to the upscale Westin Hotel in the city. He paid the driver and stepped out into the busy streets of ATL. He looked around for a moment, taking in the scenery. The place seemed the same. High-end cars lined the cobblestone pavement to the lobby and the bellhops were busy flagging down cabs and moving customer's bags in and out of the hotel. Bay remembered when he and Tommy first arrived. They looked like rappers or some ballers in ATL to have a good time, but it was business…always business nothing personal. Bay peered at the hotel and caught a sudden chill. He had a chromed .9mm tucked in his jeans on the sly. He was dressed like a regular, denim jeans, and an Atlanta Hawks football jersey, white-ups and a blue fitted hat. He wore dark shades over his eyes and tried not to draw any attention to himself.

Bay doubted that she would recognize him. It had been almost eight months since she had set them up. He knew by how subtle and skilled the hit went down; that the bitch and her accomplices had been doing the scheme for months, maybe years and were getting away with it. He knew that every dog had its day. Bay and Tommy finally had their day catch up to them after all the dirt they did. Bay was fortunate to survive and now he knew that it was time for Michelle, Carmen and their goons to have their dog day come back on them. It was time for them to pay for their sins.

Bay took a deep breath and entered the lobby. It was buzzing with activity, and the place was huge just as he remembered. He was camouflaged amongst the dozens of guests and staff that moved around from one end to the other. He scanned the area, searching for that familiar face among the staff. When he looked at the front desk, she wasn't there. Bay started to rethink his strategy. *Maybe she quit or got fired*, he said to himself. *Or maybe she was locked up.*

Bay wanted Michelle badly, like a hard dick needing some pussy. He wanted to taste revenge in his mouth. He thought that it probably wasn't her shift, or maybe she had the day off. Bay wanted to be patient, but the anxiety raced through him like a high-speed chase.

Bay walked into the nearest bathroom and repositioned the gun in his jeans. He then looked at himself in the mirror and took a deep breath. He had Michelle and Carmen's face etched into his memory, and their faces were as clear as his own image in the mirror. He had almost gone blind in one eye and had a slight twitch in his left hand because of the injury, but he was right handed and still able to pull the trigger.

Bay walked out into the lobby and still didn't see Michelle. At that moment, he decided to stake out the place. Bay took a seat in one of the posh chairs that decorated the atrium and kept a keen eye on the front desk. Bay watched the traffic of people move by him. He only hoped that Michelle still worked at the Westin.

Bay had other options, he planned on going to Magic City and see if Carmen was dumb enough to still dance there, and if she were, it would put a nice smile on his face. He knew that with his scarring and a few facial changes, it would be hard for the ladies to recognize him behind the hat and sunglasses. They thought that he was dead, which gave him another advantage.

Bay sat in the Westin for hours. He didn't want to look suspicious and bring attention on himself, so he decided to leave and come back the next day. He couldn't ask any co-workers about Michelle because he only had her first name, no last, and he didn't want anyone tipping off the bitch in case she was still employed by the hotel.

He was kind of disappointed. However, his frown soon turned into a devious smile when he noticed the familiar face entering the grand lobby from a few yards away. She was clad in her work attire, her mind focused on her iPod. As she strutted through the lobby, Bay's eyes were fixated on Michelle the entire time.

Michelle had cut and styled her hair into a short bob, but her features were still the same. She looked like an innocent young employee moving through the lobby and on her way to start her daily shift. Little did her co-workers know, Michelle was one of the masterminds behind an elaborate theft and murdering scheme. Bay could only imagine how many victims had crossed her path.

Bay hid behind a pillar, watching her from a short distance. *The stupid bitch still works here*, he said to himself. He watched Michelle say hello to a few of her fellow co-workers and then she went into a back room to clock in. A few minutes later, Michelle was behind the front desk, greeting customers with a Colgate smile and a polite hello.

"Hello, welcome to the Westin, how may I help you today?" she would greet men and women as they approached.

Bay wanted to throw up. It was sickening to watch.

He stood watching her actions for a short moment and now that it was confirmed that she still had her job at the hotel, it was only a matter of time before he confronted the bitch and take his revenge.

NEW JERSEY

Cymbal easily tamed her two vicious Rottweilers by the leather leash gripped in her hand. She loved her dogs like they were her children. The dogs stood at alert and at attention, with their teeth sharp like razors and their black pelt shimmering like polished waxed shoes. The dogs were very threatening and had killed before, with Cymbal giving the command.

The dogs were a gift from Afrika for her birthday a few years ago. She'd received them when they were puppies and trained them to be the best bodyguards around. She fed them raw meat and even gave them a taste for human blood.

Cymbal sat in the shadowy room that was lit by candlelight only. She sat on a queen sized high-post bed with cherry headboards and black satin sheets, with the dogs positioned at the end. Cymbal was very much into S&M and had an appetite for lust, pain and sex. Her pussy throbbed for some sexual action. She was clad in a sexy black opaque body stocking with spaghetti straps and open crotch. She stood vertical in a pair of six-inch stiletto platforms with her hair wild around her shoulders.

The décor of the room was African, with its Safari surroundings, Zulu warrior statues, animal skin rugs, and voodoo paraphernalia. Cymbal was very well into her country's culture and art. There were two knocks at the door.

"Come in!" Cymbal shouted.

In stepped an armed guard clutching an M-16.

"You ready for her, Cymbal?" he asked.

"Bring her in," Cymbal instructed.

The guard nodded. He walked back out into the hallway and a few short moments later, he dragged a young pretty girl clothed in a long brown sundress and bare feet. Her eyes were stained with tears and her supposedly long flowing black hair was a tangled mess. She had rich brown skin, a slim waistline and firm B-cup breasts.

Cymbal stared at the young woman with a strong hunger in her eyes. She stood up, still clutching her dogs. Cymbal was a fierce tall striking beauty. Her deep black skin was flawless and stuck to her like paint. She had no blemishes, scars, or cellulite. Cymbal was like the perfect ten model.

"You can leave now," she told the guard.

He nodded and walked out the room, leaving his boss to play with the young girl. The door shut and Cymbal moved in closer. The woman remained rooted in her posture. She had fear in her eyes, and the dogs had her petrified. Cymbal slowly circled the young girl, sizing her up from head to toe. She kept her dogs at bay and licked her lips as she stared at the supple ass in front of her. Cymbal loved pussy just as much as she loved dick. She had any pick of the women who Afrika brought in for sale and took full advantage of the power she had.

Cymbal stood in front of the girl like a dominating overseer. She loved what she saw and wanted to do things to the girl that was devilish.

"Get undressed," Cymbal instructed in a strong commanding tone.

She looked at the girl as if she was her property. The young woman slowly pulled her dress over her head and held it in her hands and close to her chest as if it was some type of barrier. She was completely naked and her young body oozcd of appeal and sexiness. Cymbal continued to stare.

"How old are you?" she asked.

"Nineteen," the woman answered timidly.

"Were you ever with a woman?"

The girl shook her head no.

"You want to be with a woman tonight?" Cymbal asked, still circling her with the dogs in her clutch.

With teary eyes and nervousness showing through every inch of her, the young girl meekly replied, "I'm not gay."

Cymbal chuckled. "Your sexual inclination doesn't concern me. Tonight, you belong to me. You understand me?"

With tears trickling down her face, the girl nodded in understanding. She was afraid to look at Cymbal. Cymbal enjoyed the nervousness of the girl and taunted her with a wicked smile and stare. Sweat began trickling from the girls' brow and her breathing became heavier as Cymbal positioned her vicious Rottweilers closer to the girl.

"Drop the dress," Cymbal instructed.

Reluctantly, the dress fell from her hands, and she stood naked and unable to cover herself with anything.

"You have a nice body," Cymbal complimented with a smile.

The girl remained quiet. Cymbal approached her closely. She inhaled the girl's smell. She then pulled her dogs closer and allowed for the animals to sniff the girl like she was a treat. The young lady trembled and grasped herself tightly. She closed her eyes and felt the dogs sniffing and licking on her like she was a personal snack.

"Don't be nervous, they like you," Cymbal said with ease.

The girl continued to tremble. She folded her arms across her chest and just stood frozen with her feet to the floor. She felt one of the dog's tongue licked between her thighs, as an attempt to taste her pussy. Cymbal smiled, enjoying the uneasiness of the young girl in her sights. As the girl felt the moistness of the dog's tongue lick against her pussy, the girl burst into tears. It was then when Cymbal pulled the animal back with a jerk of the leash.

"You must taste lovely down there."

The girl continued to tremble and remained quiet.

"I want you to listen carefully and you'll be okay. Now, I want you to go lay down on the bed over there…lay on your back," Cymbal gestured.

The girl followed instructions, but moved slowly toward the bed. She knew the repercussions if you didn't obey their orders. She'd been held captive for three weeks and saw five women shot down dead for their unwillingness. When she reached the bed, she did what she was told. She lay down on her back, with her eyes still shut.

Cymbal moved toward the bed. She made her dogs sit near and then slowly climbed on top of the girl. She didn't know her name or cared for it. She just wanted to satisfy her own pleasures. Cymbal ran her tongue across her soft brown skin and tasted her from the belly button up. She could feel the girl shivering in her clasp, but it only made it more alluring for Cymbal. She kissed and bit on her nipples, causing the girl to wince in pain. She tasted every sweet young inch of her.

Cymbal then elevated her body over the girls face. She lowered her open crotch bodysuit toward the girl's mouth, straddling her face.

"Eat," Cymbal commanded her like she was one of her pets.

With shaved pussy pressed against her face, halfheartedly,

the girl began to eat Cymbal out. Cymbal felt the young sweet tongue enter her and clutched the headboard. She grinded her pussy against the girls' mouth and moaned.

"Eat it bitch!" Cymbal exclaimed, squeezing her thick thighs against the woman's face.

The girl licked Cymbal's clitoris and her juicy walls as tears filled her eyes. While Cymbal was truly enjoying it, the girl cried during the duration. Cymbal wanted to make things even freakier with her partner.

"Spread your legs," Cymbal demanded.

As the girl did as she was told, she felt Cymbal reach down and play with her pussy, pushing her index and middle finger inside slowly. Cymbal then exposed a heinous smile.

"Killer, Levez-vous ici…" Cymbal spoke in French.

Without hesitation, one of the dogs jumped on the bed and nose-dived between the young girls' legs. The dog began licking her pussy like it was thirsty for water. The frightened teen jumped in alarm, but Cymbal quickly restrained her by snatching her by the hair and forcing her back down on the bed, saying, "Don't you dare move."

She cried. Cymbal showed no mercy and continued to grind her pussy against the teen's face, while her dog ate the girl out with his soggy and cold tongue. Cymbal called out another command in French, and the second dog jumped on the bed. It licked on Cymbal and the girl, and before the teen knew it, a bizarre foursome had taken place. The girl eyes were soaked with tears, as the animals licked and chewed on her pussy like a fine meal.

The guard stood behind Cymbal's door and he heard a chilling scream echoed from the room he was guarding. He'd heard the screams many times from plenty of different women who Cymbal invited to her room for a night of pleasure. However, he'd gotten use to them. He never knew what Cymbal was doing to the women, but he knew from their cries and screams, that it was far from anything nice or pleasing.

An hour later, Cymbal emerged from the room donning a red sheer night robe. Her hands and mouth was coated with blood. The room she exited from was silent. She looked at the man and said to him, "Go clean up the mess. I'll be back in an hour."

The man nodded and walked into the room to see the young woman almost torn apart on the bed. Blood was splattered everywhere, and the dogs were chewing on the young teen like a tasty snack.

ATLANTA

Bay spent two days observing Michelle's actions. He had her scheduled down pack. He studied her. He knew the kind of car she drove. Bay even thought that he was witnessing Michelle set up three potential men who were checking in the hotel. They came looking like ballers, wearing stylish clothing, having high end jewelry, sporting a large bankroll of money and having an out of town aura.

Michelle flirted with them and chuckled at their jokes; while Bay stood back a safe distance and watched Michelle's scheme come into play. The men laughed and flirted back, having no idea what they were getting themselves into. Bay observed Michelle write something down and then passed it to one of the men. Bay figured it had to be the address where Carmen was working.

The men seemed very thankful and were soon on their way to their rooms. Bay followed closely behind the men. He needed to know what Michelle had written down. He stepped into the elevator right behind them. The guys were laughing and were ready to enjoy ATL to its fullest. However, Bay knew that he had to warn them without giving himself away.

"This y'all first time in ATL?" Bay asked.

"Yeah, dawg, we tryin' to do it up down here," one of the men replied, smiling.

"That's what's up. Y'all gonna love it down here. I moved down here a few months ago and I still ain't sleep yet. Where y'all tryin' to go tonight?" he asked.

"Shit, that fine ass honey at the front desk gave us this club called, Body Tap. She told us that's the spot to be with the fine bitches. She even said to check her home girl who dances there....this bitch name um…"

"Sweet Essence," another friend chimed.

"Body Tap, huh…yeah, I've been hearing about that club for a minute now," Bay stated.

"Yo, you know shorti at the front desk? She a cutie…" the third friend questioned.

Bay chuckled. "Nah, I don't."

The elevator stopped at the tenth floor and Bay stepped out, saying to the friends, "Y'all have a safe night, but if I was y'all, I would fuck wit' Magic City, the ladies are sexier and they give it up too."

"Oh word, good lookin' out my dude," one returned.

Bay smiled and watched the door close. He now had some information on Carmen. The bitch changed clubs and was now going by the name Sweet Essence. He made his way back down to the lobby and was about to make his move.

An hour later, Bay walked into the infamous Body Tap on Marietta Blvd. It was a nude strip club and the women were all fine like Beyonce. Bay left his gun in his rental car and paid the twenty-five dollar cover fee to enter the club.

Bay moved through the club with ease, as Souljah Boy's, *Turn My Swag On* blared in his ear. He looked around carefully for Carmen. Bay had on a fitted Falcons cap, a throw back jersey, and dark shades that easily made him fit in with the roughneck crowd. The place was packed with nude and scantily clad women moving around the club trying to make their tips. The stage was covered with dollar bills and had four nude ladies dancing erotically to the southern beat. Money flowed everywhere, bottles of champagne were being popped, lap dances were frequent and Bay merged in with the bustling atmosphere like he was there to have a good time.

He looked into each of the girl's faces, trying to single out Carmen. It was her type of crowd…niggas and money. He copped a drink from the bar and tried to be discreet. He tipped a few strippers to make himself look natural and got his drank on. Bay positioned himself by the bar and it was hard to scan for Carmen, when there was a sea of bitches and niggas in front of him.

He worked the club and kept a keen eye out for his target. About a half-hour past when Bay was finally on the money. Carmen had exited from a back room, clutching a wad of cash in her hand. She looked more beautiful than ever, and if Bay wasn't there to fuck her shit up, he would have fallen in love all over again. He knew that the bitch was poison and full of lies, but his vengeance for Tommy had to be carried out.

Carmen strutted through the dense crowd clad in a striped fishnet sheer dress with nothing underneath. Her nipples protruded through the outfit and her shaved pussy visible. She stood tall in a pair of seven-inch red stilettos and her skin gleamed with sexiness.

Bay watched her work the crowd with ease. She then got on stage and started her routine. Carmen AKA Sweet Essence worked the crowd like she was performing magic. A few ballers made it rain on her and in due time, she peeled away her sheer dress and was naked, twisting and turning on stage.

Carmen was working some nigga by the stage, showing him a little more attention than the others in the club. She wrapped her long legs around his neck and gave him a closer look at her moist pussy. The man had a nice size bankroll in his hand. He was dressed in a pair of black slacks, a grayish button down, wing tips and looked like he was straight of Wall Street; especially with his wire rimmed glasses. He was constantly tossing money at Carmen and she gave him one hell of a show.

Bay figured Carmen was working him; he thought that the man in the glasses had to be their next target. Bay remembered how Carmen worked him and it looked like déjà vu all over. As Bay watched the show, his left hand began to twitch, resulting from the shooting. He took a deep breath and exited the club. He had seen enough.

Once outside, Bay took another deep breath and it angered him that he had a bullet lodged in his skull. He knew that chances were he would never be the same again. Bay walked toward his car and took a seat. He looked at the time and it was a quarter to one. Bay closed his eyes and tried to relax himself. Seeing Carmen again made his blood pressure rise, and he hated that the bitch set him up because she was so beautiful and sexy as fuck.

When Bay opened his eyes again, it was nearing four in the morning and Body Tap was just letting out. People poured out into the streets and Bay caught a glimpse of Carmen strutting toward a luxurious truck with the same man in the glasses. His eyes followed them to a parked Denali sitting on 24" chromed spinners. Carmen walked around to the passenger side with a giddy smile and wore a short denim skirt and open toed shoes. The man looked eager to get with Carmen and got in the driver's side excitedly. The truck started and Bay started his rental car. When they drove off, Bay followed carefully behind them.

Ten blocks away, the Denali pulled to the side in an inconspicuous location. Bay positioned his ride a few cars down. He observed their actions closely and witnessed Carmen's head lean into the driver's seat, indicating that she was giving him a blowjob. Bay sighed. He wanted to walk up to her and just blow her brains out. But Bay was greedy; he wanted Carmen, Michelle and their two goons all to pay for Tommy's death and his injuries.

Bay waited patiently until they were finished. Fifteen minutes later, the Denali restarted and drove off slowly. Bay waited until the truck turned the corner so he wouldn't bring attention to himself. He followed them onto Interstate 85, and they traveled south, about fifteen miles down into Peoples-town. The truck pulled into a similar housing complex just like the one Bay and Tommy got set up in. However, this one was several miles away.

Bay watched the Denali pull into the parking lot and moments later, Carmen stepped out. She said a few words to her date and trotted off. The truck pulled off, and when it was out of sight, Carmen pulled out her cell phone and made a quick phone call. Bay knew that she was scheming on the man. For Bay, it was the perfect time to strike. But he held back his vendetta and watched Carmen for a moment like a hawk on its prey. She walked into one of the ground floor apartments and when he figured it was safe, Bay slowly drove by the apartment and remembered the apartment number.

"I'll see you soon, baby," Bay said to himself.

NEW JERSEY, UNION CITY

Five unmarked federal agent's cars raced toward a three-story warehouse, which were just a few blocks from Roosevelt Stadium. They were confident that their inside informant was accurate with the information he had giving them. They had received viable information that Cymbal was conducting business in the warehouse, and her partner Afrika was also in the states and was getting ready to ship over a dozen girls out of the country. It was critical that the feds moved fast. Many girls were missing and they had a warrant within the hour and raced toward the location.

Over a dozen federal agents did a jump out on the industrial sized block as morning was breaking; they were clad in dark blue flight jackets with FBI imprinted on the back. They gripped the standard issued Glock .22 in their hands, and wore their vests just in case there was any hostility. The agents moved with urgency to the elevated structure and tore down the front door with a heavy ram. They rushed into the building like a swarm, screaming out that they were FBI and were looking for many arrests. As they rushed deeper into the building, the feds knew that nobody was home. The place was deserted like school on Christmas day. The men and women only heard their echoes bounced from the walls and they stood scratching their heads and knew something went wrong somewhere.

"You sure this is it?" one agent asked.

"We sure, our C.I is always on point," another agent replied.

The warehouse looked as if there had been some activity not too long ago, and there was evidence proving that the occupants had left in a hurry. It gave the feds the impression that the suspects were tipped to their arrival.

"Damn it!" the agent in charge screamed.

"They had to be tipped by someone on the inside, sir," an agent informed.

"You mean to tell me that now we have a leak inside our department," the head agent replied with a grimace.

"Only a handful knew of our sudden raid sir…there's no

other explanation on how they knew we were coming so fast," a fe male agent chimed.

"Get Mike on the phone. Explain to him that we have nothing," the head agent instructed.

They nodded.

Within the moment, Mike's cell phone was dialed. Agents began searching through the building meticulously, hoping to find anything that would lead them to their suspects location or the missing girls before it was too late. They swept the building from bottom to top, but still came up empty-handed.

Agent Canton got on the phone with Mike. Mike was on his way to ATL to investigate someone named Bay and wanted to know what his ties were to Afrika's criminal organization. Agent Canton had a slight description of Bay and enough info to hunt for Bay. Mike was boarding a private plane to Atlanta when his cell phone rang.

"Canton, tell mc something good," Mike answered.

"We have nothing, Mike. The building's been evacuated and swept clean of any evidence," Canton informed Mike.

"What the fuck you're talking about, Canton…our C. I was sure they were there just a few short hours ago," Mike said.

"Well, it's evident that our suspects had been tipped off," Canton mentioned.

"You mean we might have a mole in our department," Mike implied.

"Yes."

"Fuck me. We were so close to catching that bitch." Mike was enraged. He wanted to toss his phone and just break things, but he checked his temper and said to Canton, "I want you to keep this with us. I want names of those who knew of the raid and I want them in my office by tomorrow morning."

"Done," Canton replied.

"If there is a leak, we will smoke him out and he will be punished," Mike proclaimed.

He boarded the private Lear jet to ATL with his mind heavy. With his goddaughter in the hospital and his best friend stressed, Mike now had to worry about a leak in his camp. He had a lot to handle, but he knew in due time, everything would get done and Cymbal would be in handcuffs by weeks end.

The plane took off from a private airfield in New Jersey and agent Mike peered out the side window having a perfect view of the NYC skyline.

NEW JERSEY

It was early morning and two U-Haul trucks sped down the New Jersey Turnpike. In the back and concealed were over two dozen girls on their way to be shipped out of the country. Afrika hated to be in a rush, but the tip he'd received about the raid from his inside source was priceless. He paid a few rogue agents handsomely to keep him informed of any investigations about him and his organization. When the call came in, Afrika and Cymbal forced everyone into the trucks and cleaned up any evidence. Afrika decided that he would be absence from the states for a few months, there were too many incidents happening and then there was the shootout on the Triboro Bridge the other day leaving two of his men dead. Now, Afrika was informed of a snitch in his crew, and he was ready to go through any lengths to smoke the traitor out and give him the gruesome slow death that he deserved.

Afrika was ready to clean up the mess and any evidence before his departure from the United States. Cymbal wanted the girl in Jamaica Hospital dead. And Afrika wanted the sole survivor from ATL dead. Bay knew too much about his organization and when Afrika got wind that he was still alive, he immediately sent a shooter to handle the problem.

Cymbal rode in the back of the stylish Yukon, with her man and king seated beside her. She turned and smiled at him. She wanted to leave the states ASAP. She knew about her being on the FBI's Top Ten Wanted list and she refused to spend her life locked away in any American prison cell.

"Mi protect ya Cymbal. No man or women will take ya from me. I will spill blood like the sea before I let anyone take ya from me…fuck da FBI. We leave tonight. We have enough what we came for," Afrika proclaimed.

"I trust you, baby," Cymbal replied.

She stared at her king and wanted to be with him forever. As the Yukon raced down the turnpike, with two U-Hauls following, Cymbal leaned into Afrika's lap and pulled out his throbbing rock hard dick. She took him into her mouth and deep-throated her man with passion. Afrika moaned and became slump in his seat and let his boo go to work on him. He loved the way her full glossy lips wrapped and curved around his dick and her tongue rubbed against his nuts.

As the couple was showing their love in the truck, following behind them were the lives of many beautiful young women ruined. They would never see marriage, family, or their kids again…or get to show their affection to a man as Cymbal was showing hers to Afrika. The dark back compartment of the U-Haul was filled with tears, panic, and heartbreak. The women were naked and headed to an East coast shipping dock where they would be hauled away like cattle.

ATLANTA

Bay followed closely behind the Denali, trying not be detected by the driver or passenger. He knew the destination of the truck. He also knew that Carmen was setting up the driver like she once did him. It was time now, Bay thought.

He came prepared. He had the .9mm on the passenger seat and he had a .380 for backup. The Denali slowly turned into the parking lot and Bay watched the middle-aged man get out with Carmen right behind him. As they walked to the same apartment that Bay staked out, Carmen walked ahead and knocked on the door. Bay watched the two walk in. The shades to the apartment were drawn tightly and it looked dark inside.

"Here we go," Bay said to himself.

He didn't make his move yet. He waited. He knew in due time that Michelle would show up, and when she did, he would be there to greet her. Bay knew that by now, the man Carmen lured in there with her, was beaten and subdued.

Fifteen minutes had passed, as Bay waited and finally the final piece to the prize had arrived. Michelle's powder blue Benz slowly made its way into the housing complex and parked. Bay chuckled. "Bitch is a hotel clerk and pushing a Benz like that," he said to himself with a smirk.

Michelle stepped out of her flawless ride looking too cute in her uniform. Bay watched her and crept from his ride with the .9mm in hand and .380 tucked securely in his waistband. With fire and vengeance burning in his eyes, before Michelle took four steps from her car, Bay was on her. Michelle unexpectedly saw Bay coming in her car window's reflection, but before she could react, Bay grabbed her violently by her hair and smashed her head against the hood of the car. Blood began trickling from her forehead and she was somewhat dazed.

"Bitch, where da fuck you goin'," Bay cursed. He still gripped Michelle by her hair and began dragging her to the doorway.

He had the gun to her temple and threatened to shoot her dead if she didn't cooperate.

"What do you want?" Michelle asked, being confused.

"I know about you and your scheme…but it ain't happening now," Bay said.

He turned Michelle around so she could face him and see who he finally was.

"Remember me, bitch!"

Michelle couldn't place his face.

"Damn, so it's been that many huh," Bay replied.

"My niggas gonna fuck you up," she warned.

Bay became frustrated and struck her in the head again. Afterward he said to her, "Now, this is what I want you to do…the same shit ya been doin'. Nuthin changes, you walk to that door and knock like everything is all good. You don't, I'll kill you right here."

Michelle looked reluctant, but she complied with Bay's instructions. Bay placed Michelle close, gun still trained on an important anatomy of her body. Michelle took a deep breath and knocked slowly on the door. She knew Bay was serious and she didn't want to die.

Bay waited for a response. He knew that if Michelle didn't

recognize him, then Carmen would.

"Who?" someone questioned behind the door.

Bay tightened his grip on Michelle and pressed the gun closer.

"It's Michelle, open up."

Knowing the person, the door began to open and when it did, Bay pushed his way in, knowing that he had the element of surprise. He knew that the room would be dark, and the men already would be cautious, so he had to be fast and accurate. Bay wouldn't have any second chances if he missed.

When the door opened, Bay pushed his way into the apartment, forcing Michelle to the floor. He quickly scanned the room and fired off his first shot.

Bam! Bam!

Two shots instantaneously struck one goon in the head. Chaos began to follow, and Bay looked around the room like a soldier behind enemy lines. He saw the second goon raise his weapon and Bay reacted just in time. He ducked; two shots flew over his head and shattered the apartment window. Bay recovered and rose up, and before the second goon could let off a second shot, Bay fired. The second goon went down with three shots into his chest.

Bay knew he wasn't out the clear yet. He noticed the man Carmen brought with her was gagged, butt-naked and bound to the floor. He quickly scanned the room and found Carmen cowering in a nearby corner. He smiled. With the two thugs dead, Bay now had the advantage.

"Remember me bitch!" he said with a smirk, his gun trained at her head.

Carmen looked up at him, panic was written all over her face. At first, there was no recognition. As Carmen's eyes stayed fixated on Bay, her facial expression said it all.

"But you're dead," she uttered.

"Nah...I know you wish I was," Bay replied.

Bay then looked at the man on the floor. He walked over to him and untied him. He then passed him his clothes. The man stood up with a relieved look on his grill.

"Get the fuck outta here...but do me this favor, wait ten minutes and then notify the police," Bay instructed.

The man nodded and ran off with his clothes in hand. Bay then focused his attention on Carmen.

"It's over bitch. You can't talk your way out of death," Bay said.

"It wasn't me. I was just doin' a job," Carmen said to him.

"Yeah, well, now I'm doing mines, bitch."

Bay steadied his weapon at Carmen's face. He wanted to shoot her directly in her lying and poison ass mug. He made one mistake that would cost him. A shot fired, and it hit Bay in the shoulder. He turned and saw Michelle holding on to a smoking .45. She fired again, but missed the second time. Bay turned and blazed her with numerous shots into her petite frame. She lay dead. When Bay turned, Carmen was already up and escaping out the back door. Bay gave chase and fired, but he missed. He cursed himself and knew he wanted to continue the chase, but he knew police would soon be on their way.

ATLANTA

Agent Mike Canton landed at Hartsfield-Jackson airport as evening came down on the city. He rushed from the private jet as his cell phone began to vibrate. He quickly picked up knowing that it was a call he had to take.

"You landed?" the caller asked.

"Yes. I'm here…" he let known.

"Good, now find him and assassinate him ASAP," the caller said.

"Consider it already taken care of. You tell Afrika to stay the fuck away from my goddaughter. How dare his thugs put their monkey ass hands on her," Agent Mike Canton barked.

"You don't need to worry about the bitch, she is already forgotten," the caller mentioned.

"You tell Afrika for that stunt that happened with my goddaughter, I want triple for this job. I'm risking everything for you people," he barked.

"You will be rewarded handsomely for your services as always…just get the job done and we want it done fast," the caller said in a calm tone.

"Just remind Afrika that I'm more of an asset to him than anyone else, so don't dare fuck me, or I swear, I'll hunt you bushwhack people down and murder everyone of y'all where y'all stand," Mike Canton exclaimed in a threatening tone.

The caller remained silent, being unfazed by his threats.

"We'll keep in touch after the hit is done," the caller said and hung up.

Agent Canton was using an untraceable sim card to a phone that wasn't registered in his name. Unbeknownst to his fellow agents, Mike Canton went rogue years ago and was the leak in the department. As he moved from the plane and walked toward the car waiting for him, Mike Canton was on a mission. Afrika's organization was paying him a lot of money to kill Bay.

Afrika firmly believed that no matter how small of a problem it was, it was still a problem. He knew that if the problem wasn't handled immediately and correctly, then it had the potential to grow into a major problem; and Afrika wasn't looking for any problems. Bay could become a possible threat in the future, so he needed to go.

Afrika knew that an FBI agent had the resources and skills to get the hit done. Mike got into the dark blue four-door Chevy and looked at his partner in crime, Agent Ronald. When Mike got settled in the passenger seat, he pulled out a Glock 17 and said to his friend, "We kill this Bay and make our move."

His friend Ronald nodded. Not known to Afrika and Cymbal, Mike had a serious vendetta against Cymbal. The agent she'd killed years ago was his first cousin and they were more like brothers. Mike figured the only way to contract his revenge and get paid while doing so was to become rogue and have Afrika trust him so he could get close enough to put a bullet in Cymbal's head and revenge his cousin's death Now, this mishap with his goddaughter made him more furious and agent Mike Canton knew it was time to push forward and fuck everybody's shit up. He was military trained and planned on using his skills to take down the head and if possible, retire from the dirty money he made over the years.

"You have a lock on this guy?" agent Ronald asked.

"I will soon. I will soon, and then when he's dead, we continue with our mission. I can taste that bitch's death in my mouth," Mike stated.

Ronald nodded and smile.

"Welcome to ATL, Mike," Ronald said with a smile.

The Chevy drove off toward the city streets and a hell waited for all parties in the city.

TO BE CONTINUED...

HOUR ONE

Dysha paced back and forth anxiously as she bit her finger-nails, watching every second of the clock pass by. Today was the day that her entire life was about to change. She was a product of Flint, MI…a city where the good die young and the bad are sucked into a world of dirty money, corruption, and greed. She was a girl with big dreams, but she was hopelessly trapped in a small city. From the day she came out of her mother's womb, she had been searching for a way out of the ghetto. She had finally found her opportunity to escape and wasn't willing to let it go. If all her plans came through, in a couple of hours she would be miles away, sipping Pina Coladas on a Mexican beach.

"Where the fuck is he?" she said out loud. "It's nine o'clock; he was supposed to be here hours ago. Something must be wrong; he should have been here by now."

With her bags packed, Dysha was ready to go. The only thing she was waiting on was her boyfriend, Trey and the money he was bringing with him. Truth be told, if she already had the paper in her hands she would have left with or without Trey, but she needed him to fulfill his end of the bargain. Their entire get-away depended on him.

Trey was a hustler, not a get money nigga with endless pockets. He was a "hustle to pay the rent and bills type of dude". A low-level worker for a hustler named, Scar. Scar was the fat cat who ran the city from afar. He didn't even live in Flint…rumor had it that he lived out west somewhere, but his magnificent coke connection allowed his power to reign supreme no matter how far away he was. Scar had a drug ring that ran from south to north and east to west. His money and influence was long. He sat back on his throne while dudes like Trey hustled day and night. Trey's job was to stand on corners. Although Dysha caught the eye of all the major players in the city, Trey had earned her loyalty long ago when she was just a little girl. Growing up poor, she didn't have the finer things in life. Her raggedy appearance and hand me down clothes caused her to be an outcast in grade school, but from the first day Trey saw her in his third grade class, he was infatuated. Standing up for her on the playground and protecting her from the cruel kids on the block, he quickly became her best friend. They had been sweet on each other ever since. Dysha knew that if he ever came up in the game he would upgrade her as well. She stuck it out with him, living in the middle of the hood because she knew that he would do anything for her. She loved Trey, but love didn't put food on the table.

She wanted to live enormous, not dormant, and when Trey moved up in the ranks from the corner to the stash house, she instantly began plotting. Her first thought was to rob him, but her love for him wouldn't allow her to be so ruthless. So, she came up with a plan for them to rob the stash house together. The 1st and the 15th of the month were Scar's most profitable days. Every crack head in the city came out of the woodworks to get high. Trey trapped it all up on the city's north side. For the first time in his life Trey was no longer hustling backwards, but Dysha still wanted more. She wanted a piece of the big pie. She was tired of watching the dopemen's wives driving around, stunting through the city. She wanted to drive big whips and buy fly shit. When she first came at Trey about robbing the stash house he was reluctant, but after weeks of watering the mental seed she had planted, Trey finally agreed. All he had to do was take a percentage of the money instead of delivering it all to Scar. There were twenty stash houses all over the city and they all dropped their paper off to Trey, who counted it up and turned it in. The operation easily cleared a million dollars every month.

There's no way they would miss the little $150,000 we're taking, Dysha thought eagerly. *By the time they realize the count is off we will be long gone.*

Every car that passed by caught her attention and she ran to the window to see if Trey had finally arrived. Time was of the essence. They had to get out of dodge before Scar's goons found out they had been shorted.

Seconds later, her cell phone rang. When she saw Trey's name pop up on the caller ID she sighed in relief.

"Where the fuck are you?" Dysha asked as soon as she picked up.

"Pump your brakes, Ma and just open your front door," Trey replied. "I'm pulling up now."

Dysha hung up the phone and hurried to let him in. As soon as she opened the door, he rushed her picking her up off her feet, and spinning her around.

"We're rich, Ma. Your man did it! We're good!" he yelled as he emptied the duffel bag full of rubber-banded stacks onto the floor.

Dysha could not contain the infectious smile that spread across her caramel face. "We did it babe!" she yelled as she wrapped her arms around his neck. He pressed his forehead against hers and pulled her bottom lip into his mouth, kissing her passionately.

"I told you I was gone take care of you," he whispered as his tongue explored her mouth, tasting the cherry gloss that adorned her pouty lips. He moved with expertise to her cheeks and her neck, eventually plucking gently on her right ear with his teeth. He knew that was her spot and her womanhood instantly grew moist.

She pulled away.

"Umm-um babe, we gotta go. We've got to get out of here. We don't have time for this right now," she tried to protest, but Trey swallowed her words as he covered her mouth with his own, seducing her into submission. Her words were a futile objection against Trey's sexual advances.

"Shh," he replied as he began to unbuckle his belt and slid out of his jeans. In no time, he had her hot and bothered. He moved with the precision of a Casanova, but his touch contained the perfect amount of roughness to let Dysha know she was dealing with a thug. His fingers found their way to her blossoming petal and her wetness saturated his hand as he worked her middle slowly. Her nipples hardened and her chocolate missile tips sticking out at him were too much of a temptation to pass up. Taking a handful of breast into his mouth, he teased them, plucking her tender nipples with his tongue and gently biting down with his teeth.

"Ooh boy stop, you're making me so wet," Dysha whispered, lust lacing her tone.

Trey smiled, but had no intention of stopping as he removed her clothing. He knew her body so well. Dysha was a certified freak. She loved sex and even the thought of a hard dick sometimes made her cum in her panties. Even more than she loved that, her greatest infatuation was money and Trey wanted to show her how it felt to fuck with a rich nigga. He loved his new status already. By pulling off the lick, he had elevated himself to the next level. With over a hundred grand in his possession, he was now a major player. He planned to celebrate by sexing his lady on top of the dough that he had stolen.

His bulging erection pressed against Dysha's stomach as they grinded and groped one another. Trey stroked his nine inches and stepped back. "Get down there and suck it for me, Ma," he ordered.

HOUR TWO

Dysha looked at him seductively. Trey had never been so demanding with her, so she knew that he was feeling himself because of the caper. The money was already going to his head. He spoke to Dysha as if he was a boss, but instead of offending her, it turned her on. She obliged, dipping down on her knees and taking her man into her mouth. His hands were wrapped up in her thick cinnamon colored locks as he pumped in and out of her gently. His head fell back in ecstasy. Dysha used her throat like a pro, making use of her luscious lips and slippery tongue as she sucked him in and played with his mushroom shaped tip. Humming slightly, the vibration from her melody caused Trey's toes to curl. She smirked as she felt his manhood begin to pulsate. She knew that he wanted to explode. Her head game was out of this world. Although she didn't bless him with it often, he had earned this one. This blowjob was worth one hundred fifty stacks.

Easy money.

Lovely money.

Dirty Money.

As Trey's orgasm was building, he looked down at his girl to admire her work. She was licking him like a lollipop, paying extra attention to the sensitive vein that ran along the underside of his shaft.

"Ooh," he yelled out from the intense feeling she bestowed upon him. Her suction was tight like a vacuum and just as he was about to explode she stopped.

"Yo' what's up Dee-Dee? Why you stop?" he whined, calling her by her nickname. She put her finger to his lips and smiled as she arose to her feet. Her voluptuous body bared nothing but a red lace Victoria's Secret panty and bra set.

"You know I'm gonna get mine before I let you get yours babe," she said. Dysha quickly took off her panties and straddled him. A moan escaped Dysha's lips as he entered her. Their bodies were like two puzzle pieces. He was a perfect fit and she rode him like a jockey while sweat glistened on her body. If sex were a drug, she would surely be addicted. Dysha's eyelids lowered as the rapture of their lovemaking took her to a new high.

"Oh my…" Dysha opened her eyes and frowned when she noticed the tiny, red dot that was roaming around the room. She froze when the dot landed in the middle of Trey's forehead.

"What the…?" before she could finish her sentence, a bullet whistled as a silenced, hollow point ripped through the air and hit its intended target. Trey's body jerked and the foul stench of him releasing his bowels filled the room. He never even saw it coming.

"Aghh!" Dysha screamed as she clumsily dismounted Trey, crawling backwards until her back was against the wall.

The man she had loved lay dead with his brains on the floor beside him. She covered her mouth and shook her head in disbelief. Her heart pounded furiously as her eyes darted around the room. She could see two men approaching her house through the window and she began to panic. *It's them…they know we stole this money,* she thought frantically as she stood to her feet. She crawled over to the pile of money and began stuffing it back into the duffel bag before stepping back into her jeans. Her hands were so shaky that she could barely zip them and her nerves were shot as she grabbed Trey's jacket and put it on. It was the first thing she saw to cover her body. She didn't give a damn what she wore as long as her ass was covered so she could get the hell out of there.

BAM! BAM! BAM!

The banging on the door terrified her because she knew that it was only a matter of time before the door came crashing down.

"Bitch, we know you're in there, so open the fucking door! All we want is the money," a voice called out.

Dysha's tears blinded her as she scrambled to collect the cash. The grim reaper was at her door, but she refused to run until she had every dollar in her possession. She forced herself to look away from Trey. His soulless eyes haunted her as if he was blaming her for his death. She couldn't stomach the sight of his dead body. *This is all my fault. He would've never taken this money if it weren't for me,* Dysha thought to herself. She stood to her feet just as the men burst through the front door and ducked as she ran toward the back of the house. She purposely kicked over the lamp that illuminated the room. It was the only light on in the entire house, which gave her a small advantage. Dysha knew her home better than anybody and didn't have a problem navigating through the dark.

"Fuck, find a fucking light!" one of the intruders called out as he bumped into her coffee table.

Suddenly, the sound of gunshots rang out causing random bullets to fly in her direction. She ran upstairs taking them two at a time, but the goons were hot on her trail. Dysha was almost to the top when she felt a hand grab her foot, causing her to fall. Her face struck the steps with such force that she was in a complete daze.

"Bitch I'ma kill you," the goon threatened.

"You got her?" another man called out.

"Yeah, hurry up and find a light," the man responded.

"Please don't hurt me," Dysha pleaded.

"Thieving ass bitch.... should have thought about that before you and your man got sticky fingers," the goon replied.

As light suddenly appeared in the two-story home, Dysha looked up into her assailants eyes. His wild, locked hair and crazed eyes scared her shitless and the bright flashlight and chrome 9mm he held in his hands threatened to end her existence at any moment.

"This bitch bad as shit fam. I might have a little bit of fun with her before I rock her to sleep," the wild hair dude said.

The other assailant sucked his teeth and replied, "Man, dead that bitch, get that bread and let's go."

A fear stricken Dysha panicked as she saw the goon's trigger finger begin to curl. Without thinking, she lifted her foot and kicked him backwards, sending him tumbling down the staircase, which immediately caused the gun to discharge and a bullet flying in her direction.

"Aghh!" Dysha screamed as the bullet nicked her arm. She knew that she had been shot, but didn't have time to react to the pain. At that moment, she jumped to her feet and sprinted to her bedroom, then locked the door behind her. *I've got to get out of here,* she thought as she grabbed her duffel bag and pushed a dresser in front of the door to slow down the two men. There was only one way out of the room and as she walked over to the window, her stomach began to turn over. Dysha was deathly afraid of heights, but she didn't have a choice but to use it as her exit. Lifting the window, her world began to spin as she looked down. The ground seemed so far away, but the banging on her bedroom door urged her to move forward.

Just jump! Just get the fuck out of here, she told herself.

Dysha inhaled deeply as she stepped out of the window and onto the roof. She put the duffel bag strap around her body and without thinking; she leapt. Luckily, the neighbors' car cushioned her fall, but it knocked the wind out of her lungs as she rolled onto the ground. Her neighbor came out of his house, cursing her out and demanding that she pay for the damages.

"I'm sorry," Dysha said, peeling herself off the ground. "Please…someone's after me."

POW! POW! Bullets flew from her upstairs window and she scattered to avoid being hit.

"The bitch jumped! Go get her!" a male voice yelled.

Dysha took off running at full speed, through her neighbor's back yard and hopped over a fence that took her to the next street. She ran until her lungs felt like they would explode, all the while never letting go of the bag of money. It was her only escape. She was in too deep now. There was no turning back. She was either going to leave Flint rich or die trying because there was no way she was returning the money willingly.

Them mu'fuckas gone have to pry this shit out of my dead hands, she thought.

However, Dysha had no idea that if she was caught that's exactly what Scar intended to do.

HOUR THREE

Dysha ran until the bottom of her feet hurt. She was sure that she had shaken Scar's goons, but since Scar ran the entire city, she knew it wouldn't be long before he found her. Not to mention, he had so many eyes watching over Flint that Dysha knew she couldn't trust anybody. The only person she could depend on now was gone. She was on her own. The throbbing in her shoulder reminded her that she'd been shot, so she rushed into a gas station to see what kind of damages had been done.

Tears flowed relentlessly down Dysha's face as she stared at herself in the mirror. She had a small bruise on the side of her face. When she raised the sleeve on her shirt to see her arm she sighed in relief. It was just a flesh wound. It was more like a deep cut and she was grateful because things could have been much worse. Completely overwhelmed, she gripped the sink and stifled her cries as agony gripped her heart.

What the fuck have I done? she asked herself as she envisioned Trey's face.

He'd been the only person in her life who'd ever shown her unconditional love and in return, she traded him in for the chance to make a quick buck. She had known what the repercussions for their actions would be beforehand, but she still urged him to go through with it.

"It's too late for regrets Dysha," she whispered out loud in an attempt to relieve herself of the guilt she felt.

Suddenly, the sound of a ringing phone startled her. She jumped slightly before realizing that the sound was coming from her jacket. She had dressed in such a rush that she had put on Trey's jacket. His cell phone was still inside. When she searched the pockets and retrieved the phone, the caller ID read *BLOCKED*. Dysha reluctantly answered the call, but did not speak. She listened as the caller simultaneously listened to her. Seconds later, a raspy voice finally spoke.

"Bitch I know you've got my money." The voice on the other end of the phone was calm, but stern. Dysha knew it had to be Scar and she trembled in trepidation as he continued. "When I find you I'm going to make you wish you were dead. Trey didn't see me coming, but you will. Every nigga in this city is looking for you. I got a $50,000 bounty on your head. When I finally catch you, I'ma make you pay...slow."

CLICK!

Dysha put the phone back in her pocket and stared into the mirror. She could feel tears burning her eye ducts as fear paralyzed her body. She couldn't even think straight, because she'd often heard of the slow deaths that Scar had administered to many a nigga. Now, it seemed that her fate would be the same. Scar had already put the word out in the streets that she was a wanted woman. Everybody in Flint was trying to get their paper up by any means necessary and turning her into Scar would be somebody's payday. Every stick up kid, hustler, hood rat, and dope boy was going to be on the lookout for her now.

I've got to get ghost and kiss this mu'fucka goodbye. I don't have a choice. I have to leave town, she thought. Dysha rinsed her face with water in the stores bathroom and purchased peroxide, band-aids, and Tylenol along with a pair of knock off oversized Chloe glasses. She then nursed her injury as best she could before calling a cab. Her disguise was mediocre, but it would have to do. She waited impatiently inside the store until her cab arrived. Dysha walked with her head down, hoping and praying that no one noticed who she was. She was at a gas station in the middle of the hood, so taking chances wasn't an option. Once inside the car, she finally relaxed a little bit.

"I'm going to the Greyhound station on Dort Highway," she instructed the driver before leaning back in her seat. She then closed her eyes and exhaled as the cabbie pulled off.

When the cab pulled up to the station a few minutes later, it was unusually crowded for a Friday night, but Dysha was glad because that meant she could get lost in the sauce. After paying the driver, she exited the cab and quickly walked into the building to purchase her ticket. Dysha was so close to escaping she could feel it. All she had to do was choose a destination and ride out then all of her problems with Scar would disappear. Even though he had a lot of pull, Dysha planned to make herself drop off the face of the earth, so hopefully finding her whereabouts wouldn't be easy. She would leave Dysha Simmons behind and become someone completely new. A new environment and a new life were in store. $150,000 wasn't the type of cash that could have her set for life, but she could at least move away and be comfortable for a while without worry. If she made the right moves and was smart with the money, then she would be okay. Once Dysha stepped foot on new ground she didn't have plans to look back, not even for Trey. He would be a distant memory. She appreciated him for all that he meant to her, but she needed a clean slate. She couldn't hold onto Trey without holding onto the bullshit that forced her to run away. Trey was directly connected to betraying Scar. He was the one who had taken the money. Dysha couldn't claim him if she wanted to. She had to forget that her life in Flint ever existed.

"Can I help you?" the lady behind the glass partition asked.

"I need to purchase a ticket," Dysha said, in a hushed tone. She didn't want anyone in her business. She needed to stay low key.

"Where you going?" the woman said cheerfully.

Dysha gave her a weak smile. She wished that her world could be so simple. It was always a difference in the white people and black people who resided in Flint. They viewed the small town in completely different ways. White folks called it home, but to Dysha and many others it was hell. The Murder Capital of the Midwest…and Dysha was on the list of those to be murked next. She looked up at the destinations.

"Cali…I'll take a ticket to L.A.," she responded.

"Roundtrip?" the woman asked.

"One way," Dysha said surely. After paying the woman, Dysha took a seat in the back of the station and waited patiently for her bus. The bus wouldn't be leaving for another two hours and her leg bounced uneasily in anticipation. As soon as the bus carried her outside the city limits, she would be safe. All she had to do was make it through the next two hours alive.

HOUR FOUR

Goosebumps arose on the back of Dysha's neck. Suddenly,

she turned around to see what had her so on edge. She felt unsafe as if someone was watching her and her suspicions were confirmed when she saw a man nod his head to another guy across the room. The movement was supposed to be discreet but Dysha caught on to it immediately. When she turned her head to look at the other guy, he diverted his eyes away from hers and quickly looked down at the newspaper in his hands. Dysha's palms began to sweat.

He doesn't have any luggage with him, she thought as she took deep breaths. Her anxiety was on high. *You're just being paranoid. That nigga ain't worried about you,* she tried to tell herself.

However, when she strained her eyes to see the date on the newspaper he was reading, her suspicions were confirmed. The paper was a week old. Her heart kicked into overdrive instantly. *Okay, they can't do anything to me with all of these people in here,* she thought. The bouncing of her knee grew more rapid. *Damn it! I can't just sit here though. They probably heard me say where I was going. They'll know where to find me.*

Dysha turned around to look at the guy behind her. She felt trapped. They had her closed in and there was no doubt that they were going to get at her. They were just waiting for the perfect opportunity. Dysha stood to her feet and gripped the duffle bag as she walked toward the handicapped restroom, a place where she could be alone. After locking the door, she paced back & forth. *Think...think!*

Dysha was at a loss. She was so frightened that she wasn't thinking logically. Her usual, slick wit was out the window. She took deep breaths to calm herself down. She couldn't let her emotions override her intellect. *I've got to get rid of these niggas and get out of here. I could always take a train or flight out of the city.*

Dysha shook her head and bit her fingernails as she played devil's advocate to her own plan.

Nah that won't work. If Scar has niggas guarding the bus stations, then I know he has people watching the airports, too. I just need to get out of this bus terminal. I can figure the rest out later.

Suddenly, a knock at the door startled her. She didn't respond.

"Ma'am its security. Is everything alright in there?"

Security! Fucking security! This rent-a-cop mu'fucka won't scare them off, but the real police will, she thought happily.

"Everything is fine!" Dysha responded. "I'll be out in a minute."

She reached into the jacket and retrieved Trey's phone. She hated the police and felt like a snitch as she dialed 911, but she had to do what she had to do.

"911 what is your emergency?"

"There are two gentlemen at the Greyhound bus station carrying drugs and weapons. They're trying to transport them on the bus. Both are black males. One is wearing a red shirt with a baseball cap. The other is wearing light jeans, and a white t-shirt," Dysha stated.

"And what is your name Miss?" the dispatcher asked.

Dysha hung up the phone without saying another word. Speaking with the police put a bad taste in her mouth, but she figured since she was lying she wouldn't be considered a snitch.

Maybe they'll hold them up long enough for me to get away, Dysha thought as she exited the restroom.

Both dudes looked her way as she walked back over to her seat, but she felt real smug and had a smirk on her face. As soon as the police came through the door asking questions she was going to make her exit with the money still in her possession and her middle finger in the air.

After ten minutes, four officers finally arrived. The two dudes immediately tensed up and looked at each other. The officers entered the building with their authority swag on high, holding their hands near their service weapons and nodding at certain individuals as they passed by. They quickly located the two thugs.

"Gentlemen put your hands above your head," they called out.

As soon as the officers went into action so did Dysha. She stood to her feet and walked past one of the guys. She shook her head and wiggled her finger as if to say not this time. The dude looked at her in shock before shouting to the cops, "Man I aint got nothing!"

Dysha high tailed it out of the building as fast as she could. She stood outside and exhaled. Scar was too close for comfort. She didn't have much time before the police realized that the call had been a prank. Looking around, she spotted a pearl white Lexus sitting across the street with the hazard lights on. Without giving it too much thought, she jogged over to it. Flint wasn't the type of city where you picked up hitchhikers, but at this point her options were limited. She had to try it. She tapped on the passenger window. They were tinted so she couldn't see inside.

"What's up, Ma?" a sexy, brown-skinned dude asked; as he rolled down the window and leaned his down to look her in the face.

His attractiveness threw her off, but she quickly recovered as she looked over her shoulder in paranoia.

"Look I know you don't know me but can I get a lift?" she asked.

Dysha gave him a smile, hoping that her goddess looks would win him over, but she doubted it. She was all battered and beat up from running for her life. She knew that at this moment, she was definitely not eye candy.

"What?" he asked with a frown.

In a city like Flint, the only people asking for free rides were prostitutes and crack heads. He was about to roll up his window when he noticed the tears building in her eyes. She looked over her shoulders again and shifted her stance desperately.

"I'll pay you. I just need a ride," she said with urgency.

"You're for real?"

"More than I've ever been in my life," she responded with stress-raised eyebrows.

He reluctantly popped the locks, instantly turning her frown into a smile.

"Get in."

Dysha quickly glanced in the rearview to make sure no one saw her get into the car. Her heart pounded rapidly as she tried her best not to show her nervousness. She glanced over at the guy who was driving and gave him a quick smile.

"How you doing, Ma?" the man asked, as he released a slight grin. He looked to be in his early twenties and he had a dark smooth completion with perfect white teeth.

"Hey, thanks for picking me up. My ride is a couple hours late," she said, as she glanced in the rearview mirror once again.

"No problem. Is everything okay?" he asked.

A confused look grew on his face when he noticed how jittery she was. When he looked in his rearview to see what she was looking at, he saw three men rushing out of the terminal and scanning the area. Dysha knew what the guy had noticed and decided to come up with another lie.

"I'm not going to lie to you. I have a crazy-ass boyfriend. I'm just trying to get away from his ass. Can we go?" Her hands began to sweat as one of Scar's henchmen came closer to the car, still looking around frantically for her.

"Say no more," the man replied as he put his car in drive and slowly pulled off without the henchmen noticing them.

Dysha clenched the bag full of money tightly as she stared in the rearview mirror. Scar's goon had his head on a swivel, searching for where she may have gone. She slightly sunk into her seat as the car drove further away from the terminal. The man driving also looked in his rearview mirror and somewhat grinned.

"So, what's your name?" he asked as he glanced over at Dysha who still hadn't taken her eyes off the mirror.

She wanted to make sure no one was following them. When they got at a comfortable distance from the terminal, she loosened up and looked over at the driver. It was the first time she had gotten a good look at him. She noticed how handsome he was. His dark skinned complexion and strong facial structures were very attractive. Not to mention, his diamond earring sat perfectly in his ear. Dysha looked him up and down and saw how fresh he was. He wore a white linen shirt with crisp Roc jean shorts; he definitely knew how to dress.

"I'm Dysha," she said, as she sat up and looked around nervously.

"Well, hello Dysha. My name is Cameron, but my friends call me Cam," he said, as he extended his hand. Dysha noticed his bright, perfect smile and shook his hand. Cam continued, "It seems like you having quite a day," he said sarcastically.

"Tell me about it," Dysha replied as she pulled back her hair and used the rubber band around her wrist to tie her long mane back.

Her beauty instantly hit Cam and he smirked as he looked at her beautiful face. She had a rough, hood swagger about herself that attracted him, but her beauty also added innocence to her tough exterior. Dysha looked around the car and noticed that Cam's inside was plush, obviously custom made. He had the letter "C" engraved in his dash and on his steering wheel.

Dysha smiled. "So, where were you on your way to?"

"I was taking a little road trip to Ohio for a couple of days," Cam said as he kept his eyes on the road and switched lanes.

A light bulb instantly went off in Dysha's mind as she began to put a plan together in her head. She knew that if she didn't get out of town soon, Scar would eventually find her. With $150,000 of his dirty money, he wasn't gonna spare her any mercy. Dysha quickly unzipped the duffle bag and sifted through the bills. She grabbed two stacks of money that contained ten thousand dollars a piece. She was about to make Cam an offer that he couldn't refuse. Dysha tossed the stacks in Cam's lap and positioned herself so she was facing him as she leaned against the window.

"Look Cam, that's yours if you let me roll with you to Ohio. No questions asked. What do you say?" she asked, hoping that he would agree to her proposition.

Cam looked down, saw the big faces, and couldn't believe what she'd hit him with. He never expected to see a woman with that much money. He was impressed by her bravery. She wasn't even scared about him robbing her, which he could've done with the .45 he had tucked under his seat. To him, it was kind of sexy how courageous she was. He respected her gangster. It was attractive.

"Are you serious?" he questioned, as he picked up the bills, giving them a look-over. He had the trained eye of a hustler, so he already knew that it was about twenty thousand in his hands by how thick the stack was.

"I'm dead serious. I will part ways with you after we get there. I just need to get out of town quick and in a hurry," Dysha said desperately as she tried to read Cam.

"No questions asked, huh?" he commented with a slight smirk.

"That's right," she answered, knowing the least Cam knew, the better it would be for her.

Cam sat the money in his lap and began to think. He had $50,000 worth of goods hidden in his trunk and figured that an extra twenty in his pocket wouldn't be a bad idea. Being a true hustler, he couldn't turn down the offer. Cam was moving weight and now he had someone along with him for the ride.

"You got a deal, Ma," he said, as his deep dimples emerged. He then held out his pinky.

Dysha took a deep breath of relief and returned his smile with one of her own. She locked pinkies with him. The deal was official. Cam turned on I-75 south going toward Ohio with a new friend riding shotgun with him.

HOUR FIVE

Dysha clinched her bag tightly as she rode comfortably in the luxury car, sinking into the plush leather seats. At that moment, she began to think about Trey and how he was murdered right in front of her. *Damn Trey*, she thought to herself as if she was talking to him. *Why couldn't we just leave*? She went through the scenario a hundred times in her head, thinking about how they could've played the situation totally different and that way Trey would still be alive. A single tear slid down her cheek and before it even reached chin; she wiped it away knowing that crying wouldn't bring him back. His body lying slumped would be forever etched into her brain.

She glanced over at Cam, who was slowly bobbing his head to the music and seemed to be in his own world. For some odd reason, she felt safe with him. Something about his swagger screamed power as she watched his mannerisms. They had been driving nearly an hour and neither of them had said too much to one another. Since, they both were profiting from the trip, it was obviously strictly business on both of their parts. Dysha wanted to get Trey off of her mind for the time being, so she decided to spark a conversation.

"So, what were you doing there?" Dysha asked. She leaned her seat back to get even more comfortable.

"What?" Cam said, with his eyebrows raised. He looked at her with his big brown, kind eyes.

"The terminal, where you picked me up?'

"Oh, I was in my own world," Cam replied, when he realized what Dysha was talking about. "I just dropped my baby sister off. She was on her way back to college," he said lying. He didn't want Dysha to know that he'd come to Flint to pick up a shipment that would give him his biggest payday ever. What was in his trunk was enough for him to live comfortable and set him up for a while.

"Oh, okay," Dysha said. "How old is she?"

"She's eighteen," Cam said, not lying totally. He did have a sister that was attending college. In fact, he had dropped her off at the station, but it was a week ago.

"And how old are you?" Dysha asked being curious.

"You said no questions asked," Cam said, playfully referring to her stipulations.

"Uh uh homeboy, I said that you couldn't ask me any questions, not the other way around."

Cam couldn't help but to chuckle at her wit as he continued to focus on the road.

"I'm twenty-four…if you must know."

"Well, you're doing well for yourself to be only twenty-four," Dysha said, as she glanced around the car once again. It had the smell of a car, fresh off the lot.

"I'm doing well? How do you know how well I'm doing Miss Dysha?"

"Well, you got you a Lexus, and I know it's new because it has temp plates on the back, like you just bought it. That watch you got on your wrist cost ten stacks at least. I'm up on my game," she stated proudly while smiling.

Cam liked the way Dysha was so sharp, and peeping her surroundings. She was definitely a character, a character he liked. "I ain't complaining," he confirmed as he alternated looking at the road and then back at Dysha. "But you're not doing so bad either. You look about twenty or twenty-one. You got a duffle bag full of money and a plan. That's not bad at all."

Dysha blushed, not knowing that Cam saw the rest of the money in the bag when she discreetly opened it up. She clenched down on her bag tighter and remained quiet.

"Don't trip, Ma. I'm just observant, too. I saw the money when you opened up the bag earlier. But that's your business, not mine. All I'm saying is that you're not doing so bad yourself."

Before Dysha could respond, she felt Trey's cell phone buzzing. It was Scar's number again. She picked up the phone and pressed the talk button. She just listened closely while the phone was up to her ear.

"Listen and listen close. I'm going to find you. Believe that. Your time is running short Babygirl," Scar said in a deep, sinister tone. He had hatred in his voice, which made Dysha's heart begin to race. She quickly flipped the phone down. Cam noticed how her demeanor had changed within a matter of seconds. He grew concerned.

"Everything good?" he asked, placing his hand on her lap. Dysha jumped at his touch, but quickly gained her composure.

"Yeah. I'm good," she answered, lying through her teeth. She wasn't good and she wouldn't feel safe until she crossed the state line.

"Whatever you worried about, don't be. You're safe with me," Cam said confidently as he pulled into a truck stop that had a restaurant connected to it.

For some reason Dysha believed him, but she still wouldn't tell him what was really going on for fear that he would ditch her. Nine times out of ten, he would know who Scar was just by the mention of his name. Especially since Scar was feared by all and loved by few. Cam would have to have been living under a rock for the past five years if he didn't know of Scar, the biggest boss Flint had ever seen. Although Scar wasn't from Flint, he made it snow there. That was just as good as living there for his presence to be felt.

Dysha grew more nervous as Cam pulled into the food stop, knowing that they weren't far enough from Flint for her to feel safe. They were just on the outskirts of Detroit, well within Scar's street jurisdiction.

"Why are we stopping?" Dysha asked as the anxiety was evident in her shaky voice.

"We gotta eat right?" Cam said, as he turned off the car and looked in Dysha eyes. "I told you, you're safe with me." He smiled and reached under his seat then pulled out his chrome pistol. "I got you," he confirmed as got out the car.

Dysha had no choice but to trust him as she got out with the duffle bag over her shoulder. She refused to let it leave her possession. That money was all she had and she wasn't going to let it out of her sight under any circumstances.

HOUR SIX

Dysha was finishing her salad as she kept a close eye on the door. She kept glancing at the tinted truck that had pulled up shortly after they entered the restaurant. She was nervous, but tried not to show it to Cam. Since the windows were tinted, she couldn't get a good look at who was inside the car. Cam and Dysha were seated near the back exit and she had already had her escape route in mind if something popped off. Cam followed Dysha's eyes and looked back noticing the truck too.

"Are you okay?" he asked, chewing his turkey sandwich.

"Yeah I'm good," she answered.

Cam grinned at her. "Then why you keep eyeing that truck out there?"

"Am I that obvious?" Dysha forced a smile.

"Actually you are," he said playfully. "But if I was you I wouldn't worry about that truck, unless you have beef with a square," he said, looking into her eyes.

"What?" She had no idea what he meant.

"I see you looking at that truck, trying to see who's in it, but I peeped it when he pulled up. Look at the license plate," he instructed without even looking back. "The truck has *WWJD64*. WWJD means 'What Would Jesus Do' and I'm assuming sixty-four is the year he was born. I say it's a he because Land Rovers are vehicles that men tend to like, more than females, right. So, if I had to take a wild guess, it's a male in his late forties, a church going type nigga. Is that the type of cat you scared of?" he asked with assurance.

Just as the last word left Cam's mouth, an older man with a Bible in hand, stepped out of the mysterious car. Obviously, he'd been reading the word while waiting in the car. Dysha couldn't believe what she'd just encountered. Cam had identified the guy without even seeing him.

"That's crazy. How did you know?" she asked in amazement.

"I'm a street nigga. It tends to give you a sixth sense," he replied, as he waved over the waiter to bring him the bill. "This one's on me." Cam pulled out a wad of cash and left a twenty on the table. Feeling more comfortable, Dysha finally began to relax. The church man walked in as Dysha finished her salad, but she didn't see the guy come in right after him. Without Dysha even knowing, the dark skinned short man raised a gun aiming straight for her head. The gunman obviously didn't care that he was in broad daylight; he just wanted Dysha dead so he could collect the contract money that Scar had put on her head. Anyone who knocked her off would get paid, and the gunman looked as if he would do anything to make that bread. He'd been following them since they left the bus terminal and was waiting for them to stop to make his move. Without warning, loud gunshots erupted as he tried to empty the clip, sending bullets whizzing past her head, just barely missing her. However, an elderly woman who caught bullets in the back of her head wasn't so lucky. Cam instantly pushed Dysha to the ground, all the while reaching for his own gun. His gun was already cocked and loaded, ready to bust. He quickly let of two rounds that hit the shooter in his mid-section, dropping him instantly. The entire restaurant went into frenzy, trying to run and duck for cover.

"Come on!" Cam yelled knowing that the man probably wasn't dead. He grabbed Dysha's hand as they quickly ran out of the back entrance. They hurried out of the restaurant and jumped into Cam's car. They didn't see the Chevy that was next to the Land Rover that the gunman pulled up in. Just as Cam was starting up his car, he heard the thumping sounds of bullets hitting his back doors. The "church man" was loading up the car with hollow-tip bullets with his black glock. Cam ducked down, along with Dysha as they dashed off. It was all a set up.

"Fuck!" Cam screamed as he pulled onto the street and hit the gas, escaping the scene. "What the fuck did you get me into?" he asked. Once they bent the corner, he finally sat up.

"I don't know!" Dysha screamed. Everything happened so fast; she couldn't catch her breath. She placed her hands on her chest, breathing deeply and at a fast pace. Cam quickly pulled into a parking lot of an abandoned building and threw his car in park. His adrenaline was still pumping, going into overdrive. He took a couple of deep breaths to calm himself as he gripped the steering wheel tightly.

"Fuck that! Tell me what's going on? I want the truth!" He couldn't believe that he'd just been shot at in broad daylight.

"Okay, okay. My boyfriend took a lot of money from someone that he wasn't supposed to. Now, he's sending his goons to try and kill me," Dysha admitted. She kept looking in the rearview hoping that the shooters wouldn't catch up with them.

"What?" he asked not believing what she was saying?

"Yeah, this nigga named Scar…" she said.

"Scar! Oh, hell naw. That's Scar's money?" Cam looked down at the duffle bag that she had in her lap.

"Yeah," she admitted.

"I don't want anything to do with this. Get out," he said, in a calm voice. Cam looked forward, not wanting to face her. He clenched his jawbone, showing the muscles in his face. He then hit the unlock button, signaling to her that it was time to go.

"Are you serious?" Dysha asked, with fear in her voice.

He nodded to confirm his decision and still didn't look at her, he couldn't.

"Fuck you nigga!' she yelled before getting out the car. Dysha slammed the door with all her might as Cam pulled off in a hurry, leaving her in the parking lot alone.

"Fuck!" she yelled as she watched his car disappear down the street. She was stranded with nobody to turn to and an entire city after her. Dysha didn't know what to do next.

HOUR SEVEN

Cam hit his steering wheel repeatedly as he began to feel bad about leaving Dysha. "Why am I about to do this?' he asked himself as his conscious played see-saw with him. He rode down the street then suddenly did a u-turn to go back for her. His guilt had taken over. He couldn't leave her. Cam rolled up on her a few minutes later as she walked down the street with the bag over her shoulder. He slowed down and drove along side of her.

"Dysha, get in," he ordered. Cam then leaned over toward his passenger side and yelled out of the window. "We had a deal, right?"

Dysha stopped walking and looked at him. She put her hands on her hips while eyeing his white teeth and pretty eyes. "That's right; we had a deal," she said, walking toward the car. She was relieved as she sat down in his comfortable leather seats once again. "Now can we get the fuck out of here, before we get shot?"

"Sure," Cam said, as he put his hand on her lap and gently squeezed her inner thigh. She was growing on hi

Scar got a call from one of his goons letting him know that

Dysha had slipped away and the attempt on her life was unsuccessful. Pissed, he hung up the phone, sat back, and smoked his blunt. He was well over 300 pounds and had a full beard, similar to the rapper Rick Ross. At that point, he didn't even care about getting his money back, he just wanted revenge. He couldn't sleep at night, knowing that Trey and Dysha had taken money from him. He put a bulletin out to the hood that whoever bought them to him, dead or alive, would get the prize money and he was waiting patiently for someone to catch up with Dysha.

"One down, one to go," he said, in between pulls of the kush weed. He couldn't wait until one of his goons caught up with her. They had informed Scar that she was with an unknown man who'd helped her escape and in Scar's eyes; whoever was helping her was a dead man, too.

HOUR TEN

Three hours passed and Cam had just crossed the state line, entering Ohio. Dysha couldn't help but smile because at that point, she knew she was home free. She and Cam talked about everything under the sun within the three hours and in some sort of strange way felt like they'd known each other for a lifetime. Dysha told Cam the entire truth about Trey and what had happened in the past twenty-four hours. Cam didn't judge her and just listened closely as she told him the story in its entirety along with some other things about herself.

He was coming up to his exit and wanted to stop at a bar to get a drink.

"You game?' he asked Dysha as he got off the highway and checked his mirror to make sure no one was following them.

"I guess. Fuck it!" she said, shrugging her shoulders. Besides, Dysha needed a drink. She was about to start from scratch and had to figure out her next move now that they were in Ohio.

HOUR ELEVEN

Dysha and Cam were at a low-key, red neck bar, having shots of Patron, and enjoying each other's company. Dysha had almost forgotten about the hardships that had just occurred. Cam was a good dude and a step up from what Trey was.

"You ready to go?" he asked with a shot glass in his hand.

"Yeah, I think I've had enough for tonight," she replied as she threw the faithful duffel bag over her shoulder and stood up. While leading the way out, Cam walked behind her noticing how thick she was. He watched as her plump cheeks shifted from side to side and his manhood began to harden. *Damn*, he thought as he gripped his rock hard pole that was hidden in his jeans. He couldn't take his eyes off of her cantaloupe type ass cheeks. His eyes stayed on the beautiful view that Dysha's ass was providing, all the way until she reached his car. He pushed the unlock button on his keys and walked over to the driver's side and got in. As he sat in the seat, his head began to spin, letting him know he had downed one shot too many.

"Whew," he said, as he blew out air. He glanced over at her with drunken eyes.

"Thank you Cam," Dysha said, feeling drunk as well. "You a real nigga." Her eyes drifted to the dick print that was forming in his jeans. His pole looked so thick, so juicy to her. She felt her clitoris began to thump and the Patron had her getting wet, wetter than usual.

"Ooh," she whispered involuntarily.

She couldn't hold her gasp in. The sound escaped her lips without her consent. Cam knew that sound oh-too-well, which made his dick even harder. He started up his car and pulled onto the street trying to take his mind off of Dysha's pussy.

"I will drop you off at a hotel if you want. My stop is just up the road," he said, trying to keep his eyes on the road and off Dysha. He was moving weight and wanted to stay focused, but it was very difficult to do that. The sexual tension was at an all-time high and both of them were ready to go for it. The only thing he kept thinking about was how it would feel to smack her ass cheeks while she rode him. Eyeing the tent he'd formed in his jeans, Dysha couldn't wait anymore. She had to taste him. She leaned over onto his lap and unbuckled his pants to release his beast. Cam couldn't believe what was happening. Off Patron, any girl could be unpredictable and Dysha was no exception. She hummed as she saw Cam's nine-inch, thick pole standing tall in front of her. He had veins throbbing out of his joint, which drove Dysha crazy. She gently grabbed his sack and then massaged them as she took him into her mouth. Cam tried his best to stay straight on the road while Dysha slobbed him up. Her mouth was so wet and hot; he nearly popped only thirty seconds in. Cam slowly grinded her mouth as if it was a vagina, then threw his head back in complete bliss.

Cam drove while getting slow dome and temporarily took his eyes off the road. All of a sudden, he felt the car rumble and he quickly put his eyes back on the road.

"Damn, what happened?" Dysha asked. She jumped up and looked toward the road.

"I think I hit an animal or something," Cam said, as his rod stood erect. He quickly pulled to the side of the road and pulled down his pants. Dysha followed his lead and she took her clothes off too, almost ripping them off. She was hot and horny ready to flex and sex. She took off her bra and exposed her big brown nipples. They were erect and sensitive to the touch. Cam instantly took her left breast into his mouth as his hand drifted down to her southern lips. Dysha was so wet that she was sitting in a small puddle of her own juices. Her clitoris was swollen to the maximum. She threw her head back and moaned loudly. Dysha slowly rotated her hips as Cam's warm fingers went in and out of her. Dysha felt herself about to orgasm and couldn't wait any longer; she had to feel Cam's thickness inside of her. She pushed Cam over in his seat and straddled him as he slid straight into her ocean. She slowly grinded as his width filled her up. Dysha grabbed the back of Cam's head and rode him like a jockey rode a prize-winning stallion.

"Oh, my God," she screamed as Cam used his thumb to slowly stroke her rock hard clitoris.

Feeling a gigantic orgasm approaching, Dysha placed both of her hands on her breast. She rubbed her own nipples and moaned loudly and she sped up her rhythm. The sounds of her ass smacking against his balls enticed both of them even more as they both reached their sexual peak.

"Oh, shit!" Cam yelled as he released himself inside of her.

Moments later, Dysha exploded and squirted juices on Cam's pelvis area then shook feverishly. Both of them breathed heavily while Cam remained inside of her. They sat there, trying to catch their breath. They'd both just experienced the best orgasm of their lives and the quickest.

Dysha eventually got off of him and when the smoke cleared, she began to feel guilty for having sex with a complete stranger. *Trey ain't even in the dirt yet and I'm already fucking the next nigga,* she thought as reality set in and instantly began to sober her up. She put back on her clothes and remained silent as he drove to a hotel. He offered her a place to sleep for the night when he got a room. She agreed, knowing she was too tipsy to do anything else.

THE 24ᵗʰ HOUR

Cam and Dysha woke up the next day, with banging headaches. Dysha was so ashamed of herself for sexing Cam and knew that the drinks played a big part in her decision. She was ready to get to Ohio's bus terminal and get away forever. *Maybe I'll go to New York with my cousin;* she thought trying to put a plan together in her head. She just wanted to get away from Cam, Scar, and her past.

"Can you drop me off at the bus station?" Dysha asked, watching him get up and put on his belt and gun. She grabbed her duffle bag and peeked inside. It seemed to be all there. Cam knew that she was ashamed at what happened the previous night and he was ashamed of himself. More so, because he didn't use protection, rather than the actual, sexual act itself.

Cam checked out of the room and was on his way to his connect to drop of the goods. They both remained silent. Nothing was said. Not even as much as a glance. They both tried to avoid eye contact with each other. But eventually, Cam was the first to break the silence. "I have to stop at one of my cribs before I take you to the terminal. Cool?" he asked.

"Yeah that's fine," she agreed. Suddenly, Dysha began to smell a horrendous odor. She scrunched up her noise in displeasure. "What the fuck is that smell?" she asked, putting her hand over her nose.

"I think I hit something last night. Got my shit stinking," Cam replied, then rolled down the window. He had to let some air in to try and get rid of the smell.

Minutes later, they were pulling into a gated house. Dysha's head was practically hanging out of the window trying to escape the smell. When Cam's car reached the gate, it opened giving him access.

"This is your house?" Dysha asked in amazement. The house was nothing short of extravagant. The long drive way was at least a hundred yards away from the entrance, and the big pillars made the property resemble the White House in D.C.

Cam didn't answer her; he just smiled modestly as he drove up. When they approached the main entrance, he began to talk.

"You can come in for a minute. I might be a while." Cam turned off the car and hopped out. Dysha followed him to the front door with the duffle bag on her shoulder. When Cam approached the door, a doorman with a suit on opened it for them. Dysha was impressed and shocked. She began to wonder why he didn't bring her to his house the previous night instead of getting a dinky hotel room.

"This is nice Cam," she complimented as he led the way into the marvelous house. The entire front room had marble floors and it seemed like a museum more than a place of residence. "You out here balling and didn't even let me know," she continued.

When she looked at his face, he had a stone cold expression and his demeanor during the last twenty-four hours seemed to be different.

"Cam, what's'…" Dysha stopped mid-sentencing when she saw who was sitting behind the desk as they entered the den.

It was Scar…Cam's boss.

"Hello Dysha," Scar said, puffing on his cigar. Dysha heart seemed like it skipped a beat as she looked into the eyes of the man Trey had betrayed. She never thought that he lived in Ohio; she just knew that he didn't live in Flint. She'd just walked right into his house, willingly. Cam had been playing her the entire time. Dysha tried to turn and run, but two men with guns were standing behind her.

"What you been smelling is that nigga, Trey. He's in my trunk," Cam said, as he snatched the bag away from Dysha and walked it over to Scar.

When he sat the bag on the desk, Scar opened and looked at his own money. The entire time Dysha thought Cam had drugs in the trunk; and all along it was her dead boyfriend, Trey. Scar told anyone that if they brought Trey and Dysha to him that they would get fifty thousand a piece; and that's exactly what Cam did. He brought one back dead and one alive. He was the one who'd killed Trey, sniper style, but he couldn't get a good shot on Dysha.

Dysha's whole world crumbled as she looked at Cam in disbelief. "But you shot the niggas who was trying to kill me," she said, thinking back to Cam saving her at the restaurant.

"Yeah, that was another crew after you, trying to get the contract money. You were a hot commodity in the streets, a walking meal ticket. Niggas was trying to get that money. I left my crew at the terminal. Who do you think was the getaway driver when they were looking for you? Yo' dumb-ass came straight to me. Easy as 1, 2, 3," Cam bragged. He thought about how he wouldn't have to share the money with his crew. He and Scar shared a chuckle. Scar reached into the bag, pulled out ten stacks of money, and threw them to Cam.

"Nice doing business with you fam." Cam said, as he stuffed the money in a bag. Dysha was heated, and knew he'd betrayed and deceived her to the fullest.

"Fuck you, you bitch-ass nigga!" Dysha yelled with passion.

She tried to lunge for him, but one of the men guarding the door grabbed her and put a gun to her head. Cam didn't even pay her any mind. It was all business to him. He walked out with his contract money smiling from ear to ear.

"It was just business Ma, never personal," he said, as he walked passed Dysha, leaving her alone with Scar and the killers. He heard a loud gunshot blast as he reached his car door and knew that Dysha had just been rocked to sleep. Karma is real. It was a dirty game and Cam was just a player in it.

FRUSTRATED

"Yes, yes, yes, oh baby yes," Maleka Tidwell cried as she made love to her husband Kevin. "Oh, God don't stop."

"I'm, I'm cuming, I'm cuming!" Kevin panted as his face contorted with pure ecstasy. He placed his final stroke deep inside of her and just like that, it was over. Exhausted, and breathing heavily, Kevin rolled off of her and over to his side of the king sized bed.

Maleka just laid there, frustrated and sexually deprived. Maleka, 31, was a pretty, petite woman who'd been married to her husband ten years. He was only two years her senior and hadn't been able to achieve an orgasm with him in nine.. She began to wonder whether he reached his sexual peak, or was it hers. Nonetheless, she was still raging with sexual desires. She grew tired of getting the best out of sexual toys, and she wanted more, much more. The fact that his penis, she estimated, was only five inches long, didn't really matter to Maleka. What did matter was that under any circumstances, Kevin would never go down on her; something she craved.

Kevin was more reserve and traditional in his love making. He was thinly built and muscular who worked out at the gym four days a week. When they got married, they both didn't have a lot of sexual experience and it didn't matter much to Maleka. However, as years went by, she often heard stories from her best friend, Dana regarding her sexual exploits and realized that something was missing in her marriage. Dana was brown-skinned with a vivacious body and still single; someone who dated several men a week. She would often tell Maleka that she wanted to settle down, but all the good men were married or taken, and the rest was full of shit and didn't want commitments. Despite her complaints, Dana was happy with her lifestyle and would hint to Maleka about getting her swerve on at times if she wasn't happy with Kevin. Though Maleka would never cheat on her husband, she turned over and buried her head in her pillow and began to fantasize about making love to other men as she cradled herself to sleep.

TWO WEEKS LATER

Dana, who was very attractive and well endowed in the chest area, would often stop by Maleka's house to hitch a ride with her to her job since they worked in the same downtown Manhattan area. Dana and Kevin never saw eye to eye, often treating each other as a cordial guest at best. Kevin never trusted Dana and was insecure whenever the two friends were together. He felt because Dana was single and a bad influence, Maleka shouldn't be associating with unmarried women. They would argue about this matter often, but Maleka refused to part with her friend that she'd known since high school, just because her husband said so. She had to draw the line somewhere. But today was a special morning, it was Maleka's birthday and Dana wanted to get an early start of the day she had planned for the birthday girl. They both sat and ate cereal and talked about the plans Dana had scheduled for that evening.

Kevin walked in the kitchen fully dressed and ready to walk out the door. Kevin was an investment banker who worked on Wall Street and often got to his job before 8 a.m. to get a jump on the market. His six figure salary enabled them to live very comfortable in a downtown Brooklyn townhouse.

"Oh, yeah, babe, the real estate agent is coming by tomorrow to show some potential buyers the house. Do you think you can be home by six to show them around?" Kevin asked.

Maleka nodded. "Yes, honey, I'll be home by then."

They had their house on the market for six months now and were ready to move to a bigger house in Brooklyn. Because their agent would bring potential buyers around with little to no notices, Kevin wanted one of them to be home at all times. He was anal when it came to strangers in his house for some reason.

Kevin kissed his wife on the cheek. "Okay, honey, have a good day."

"Kevin, don't you see we have a guest?" Maleka inquired.

"Don't worry Maleka, some people are rude like that," Dana replied.

Kevin stood for a moment with his briefcase in his hand and corrected, "I'm sorry Dana, good morning. Are you enjoying *my* food?"

"Funny," Dana responded, "but, what's funnier is that you probably don't know that it is your wife's birthday."

Kevin's smug smile suddenly turned into a surprise, and begged, "Honey, oh damn, happy birthday baby, I forgot. Let me make it up to you over dinner tonight."

"Oh, sorry honey, I already made plans to go out tonight with Dana. I hope you're not mad."

Kevin gained his composure. "Fine, but what time will you be out till?"

"Not late," Maleka said uneasily. "We're just going to have some dinner and some drinks afterward." There was an uncomfortable pause until Maleka quickly added, "If would you like to come with us, we don't mind if you tag along, right Dana?"

Dana looked at Maleka to see if she was really serious, but didn't answer.

Kevin got wind of the blatant hint and quickly said, "No, no, you go out and enjoy yourself, and I'll be here with a surprise waiting." He looked at his watch and edged forward and gave her another kiss on the cheek and was out the door.

As soon as he was out of ear shot, Dana mocked, "I'll be here with a surprise waiting, please, that's just his way of saying don't stay out late."

"And what's wrong with that?"

"C'mon, Maleka, he's trying to keep tabs on you, and not let you have fun."

"Again…and what's wrong with that? That's just his way of saying he loves me."

Dana sucked her teeth. "Girl, you only thirty-two. Y'all act like y'all in your sixties."

"No, we don't, we act just fine. You just mad because you don't have what we have…love."

Dana giggled and shrugged Maleka off before rebutting. "If you call having sex every other month and staying home like a good housewife 24/7 fine, then you can keep that shit. But me, I got a life and I can fuck everyday if I choose too."

"You're nasty," Maleka responded.

"Yeah, I may be nasty, but I'd rather be nasty and satisfied than miserable and frustrated any day that's for damn sure."

Maleka waved her off and asked, "What about when you told me you don't want to grow old alone, what about that?"

"I'm not gonna grow old by myself."

Maleka decided to change the subject. "You didn't tell me what we were going to do after we eat dinner?"

Dana displayed a mischievous smile and answered, "I'll tell you in due time my dear, in due time."

IN DA CLUB

When Dana and Maleka entered Club Ozone on 21st Street and 5th Avenue in Manhattan, Maleka was surprised by the amount of women who were in the club. At that moment, she paused and said, "Dana, I know you didn't bring me to a gay club."

Dana smirked. "Now, you know me better than that. We got a reserved table up front and I'll tell you when we sit down."

They made their way to the front where a u-shaped makeshift stage was. The music was blaring so loud that they had to lurch forward and scream into each others ear just to talk.

"So, what is this place, Dana?" Maleka wondered.

Dana gave her a wicked smile. "It's an all male strip club."

Maleka was taken back a moment then repeated, "All male strip club?" Dana had a wide smile as she shook her head rapidly. "Girl, if Kevin finds out I went to a strip club he will kill me."

"Stop worrying about your husband and try to live for the moment and enjoy yourself for once in your life."

"But…" Maleka uttered.

"But, nothing," Dana quickly replied, "all you got to do is sit back and enjoy the show. Catch a feel or two if the moment arises."

"Oh, no, I'm not touching any of these men, trust me. I'm a married woman," Maleka reminded her.

"So, are most of the women in here," Dana advised.

"I don't care what you say. I'm not having none of these men humping on top of me like I'm a dog."

Just as Dana was about to speak, the D.J made an announcement that the show was about to start. All the women suddenly began to scramble to the front with stacks of money in their hands waving it in the air excitedly.

"Ladies," the D.J announced, "put your hands together for your first dancer, Maximus." Then the booming sound of Jay- Z's *I'm A Hustler* filtered through the speakers as Maximus came out dancing in a Roman Gladiator costume. The women erupted when he unbuckled the attachment on his waste revealing a huge bulge in his trunks. All the women vied for his attention as they waved and threw dollar bills in his direction. He worked the crowd then walked up close to the women who grabbed a quick feel of his protruding penis as they stuffed loads of dollar bills in his waistband. Moments later, he backed away and threw the multitude of bills in his waist and crotch to the floor. He slowly got on his knee's and began simulating a sex act as he thrust his hips and pounded the floor whipping the ladies in a frenzy. After he finished, he stood and grabbed a microphone and began looking into the crowd as if he was looking for someone.

"I'm looking for a special lady tonight. Someone who want to CUM up to the stage and get your freak on. Someone who loves it big, black and long."

The women in the crowd went crazy as they began jumping up and down waving their hands. Maleka and Dana looked at all the women and were amused at their reactions. Finally, Maximus pointed to a rather large woman and extended his hand.

"Would you like to get your world rocked by Maximus?"

She shook her head violently and walked up on the stage and extended her hand to him. When he asked her what her name was, she responded nervously, "Keisha."

"Well, Keisha, looks like this is your lucky day. Are you married?"

Again, she nervously answered, "Yes."

"Well, tonight, I'm your husband." He began to thrust his hip into her and continued, "I'm also your daddy, and your lover."

Suddenly, the D.J put on a record and the crowd went ballistic "Slooooooowwwwwwwwww dance," R.Kelly's silky smooth voice filtered out of the speakers causing everyone to melt.

"Now, what I'm about to do to you wont hurt a bit okay?" Maximus spoke in a sexy tone. As Keisha nodded, he immediately wrapped his arms around her and began to grind deeply into her body. Without warning, he grabbed Keisha by her thigh and lifted her off her feet and began pounding her into his hips. Everyone went crazy as he began thrusting in and out without mercy when suddenly he lowered her to the floor. Maximus stood over her like she was a wounded animal and he was her prey. He then began pulling off his trunks and exposed a full view of his large long dick. At that moment, a man walked on stage and passed him a Magnum rubber and a small pack of lubricant jelly.

After taking the two items, Maximus, stared down at Keisha and asked, "Are you ready to experience the power of Maximus?" When she shook her head, he then asked her, "Now, all you have to do is pull off them panties from under your skirt."

Surprisingly, she followed his instructions to the letter and pulled up her skirt, spreading her legs wide open. Maximus ripped open the condom and slowly began to roll it over his penis. Maleka could hardly believe what she was seeing as she put her hand over her mouth.

Slowly, Maximus ripped open the pack of lubricant jelly and began massaging his dick until it got rock hard. "Now, what I want you to do is to open your legs wide," he instructed.

Keisha followed his orders without hesitation. Moments later, he got down on his knee's and put some lubricant on his fingers and slid it slowly up her pussy, massaging it. When Keisha began leaking her juices all over the stage, he asked her, "Are you ready for the pain?"

She nodded for him to enter her and Maximus quickly obliged. He wasted no time thrusting his dick deep inside of her as she shook violently. He pumped faster and faster as she moaned in both pain and pleasure when suddenly, Keisha let out a loud sheik.

"Oh, my God, oh, my God!" The louder she screamed, the harder he began to thrust until finally she reached her peak and let out a lion's roar. She'd reached a climax within five minutes.

Maximus was sweating profusely, but it was no way near how BAD Keisha had soiled her skirt from her orgasm. After winking at the crowd, Maximus helped Keisha to her feet. He then handed Keisha her panties and hugged her before gathering up his money off the stage and walking off.

Maleka still couldn't believe what she just saw as Dana kept saying, "I told you. I told you that you would enjoy yourself."

Maleka could hardly respond as she uttered, "What the hell kind of strip club is this?" Before Dana could respond, Maleka continued. "I don't believe this."

"Well, believe it. This is a world you don't know anything about. That girl on stage was married, but she was able to let that shit go for a little while and get her shit off in what, five, six minutes? You gotta learn to live a little. Everybody else is living out their sexual fantasy except you. But don't worry, your girl got your back."

For the first time in her life, Maleka didn't know what to say. If she could admit it, she would tell her friend that she was turned on from the antic that had just taken place on stage. For the next hour, they saw pretty much the same thing and it became normal to Maleka to see so many women willing to perform a sex act on stage with a total stranger. She was even more impressed with the size of the men penises who flaunted them openly. Although she didn't admit it, Maleka was turned on in a way she never knew was possible and had came at least seven times throughout that night.

The last act of that night was supposedly the best they had to offer, the star of the show, who went by the name, The Punisher. He was reportedly to have a fourteen inch penis and was equally large in girth. He was only twenty-five years old, and had gained a big reputation of a show stopper.

"Ladies and some gentleman," the DJ joked, "cumming to you live up next, straight from Club Ozone, we give you our final dancer of the night, the eighth wonder of the world, The Punisher!"

"Oh, shit!" Dana yelled. "This is the one I was telling you about. This nigga got fourteen inches of limp dick and it's fat, too. Damn, there is a God!"

Maleka smiled. "You sound like you want some yourself."

Dana looked at her and frowned, "You crazy, that shit inside me? I just got my coochie back in shape too, girl please."

"You so stupid, Dana."

"I'm serious. Remember I told you I was dating this young boy?" Maleka shook her head. "Well, shorty was packing something awful. The lil nigga was built like a quarter horse; straight Shaka Zulu dick." Maleka laughed. "Seriously," Dana continued, he had this pussy stretched like Play Dough." Maleka couldn't believe her ears as she laughed uncontrollably.

The DJ put on Big Pun's song *Still Not A Player*, Punisher hit the stage. He was dressed in only a red piece of cloth that was specially designed to cover his hanging penis. The women all marveled at the length of it as it hung nearly down to his knees. He swayed it back and forth as he danced to the beat of the music. Maleka and Dana looked at each other in total disbelief. Never in their lives had they seen a man with a dick that size. Women by the stage stared like zombies as her performed with ease flexing his glistening muscles on his well oiled body.

Then the time came when he removed the cloth, giving everyone a full view of his freakish sized penis. The women could hardly contain themselves. As Maleka watched him dance and sway his huge dick back and forth, she suddenly got a guilty pleasure when her panties became soaking wet. The stage suddenly became littered with hundreds of dollar bills as he allowed women a quick feel or stroke of his dick. When the music stopped he took the mic and addressed the women,

"Is everybody having a good time?" There was a loud roar of approval. He nodded back and continued, "Well, I got a message that it's a special lady in the house and it's her birthday."

Maleka suddenly lost her bluster as she looked at Dana who was clapping and pointed to at her for all to see. "That's right bitch, this is my surprise that I set up for you. I paid for him to call you out for your birthday," Dana said with excitement.

In disbelief, Maleka said hysterically, "Dana, why you do this. I'm not going up there to fuck him."

"Yes, you are. Just relax, and let nature take it's course."

Maleka was so angry she wanted to run out the club right then and there.

"Where she at?" Punisher asked. "I'm think her name is Maleka. Maleka, where you at?"

Dana began jumping up and down waving to him. "Here she is. She's right here!"

Maleka tried to stop her, but it was a pointless effort. Instantly, they put a spot light on her. She was so embarrassed at that moment, Maleka wished she was invisible, but it was nowhere for her to hide. She wanted to kill Dana.

"Oh, she's the shy type. I love them shy!" Punisher shouted. He then walked off the stage and over to where Maleka sat with her hand buried in her face. As he stood over her, Maleka couldn't believe this was happening. "Don't be shy baby. I just want to take you up on the stage and give you a special dance, is that okay with you?" He took Maleka by the hand and tried to get her to stand up but she wouldn't budge. At that point, Dana took matters in her own hands and helped her friend to her feet. When Maleka stood, Punisher whispered in her ear.

"I won't do anything that you don't want me to do, so just relax, okay?"

His voice was smooth, which instantly made Maleka feel relieved. She felt much better and let him lead her up to the stage. All the women started to applaud as they walked toward the stage. He led Maleka to a tall stool where he told her to sit down.

"So, since you're the birthday girl, I got a big, fat gift for you. Do you want it?" The ladies in the crowd began to coach Maleka on with loud screams and yells. When she didn't respond he continued. "So, do you want it?" By now, Dana was by the stage and yelled for Maleka to take it.

Reluctantly, Maleka said yes, then the man who brought out the condoms earlier, brought out a big brown teddy bear, which Maleka accepted.

"Okay, I got one more gift for you and that's a dance and feel session. Can you handle that Maleka?" Punisher asked. Maleka once again looked at Dana who was nodding her approval and caved in and said yes.

"Okay, stand up and let me put on the right grinding song." Suddenly the DJ put on *Butta Love* by Next. It wasn't long before, he took Maleka in his arms and pressed his flesh against her body. An instant jolt permeated through her body as she felt his penis touch her pussy lobe. She suddenly found herself grinding back and her juices began to pour out of her body like a faucet. She buried her head in his chest as he guided her hand down to his thick dick. It was so fat, she couldn't wrap her entire hand around it. She could feel her panties getting moist again.

By the end of the song, Maleka was drained and could hardly stand on her feet. Punisher thanked her for the dance and kissed her good night. Everyone applauded loudly as she exited the stage and was met by Dana, who gave Maleka a big hug.

"I told you that you would enjoy yourself. That was only the second part of your birthday. The third part is on its way."

Maleka, already exhausted said, "Please, I had enough."

Dana took her Coach bag when suddenly Maleka was tapped on her shoulder, it was Punisher, who had quickly changed into a pair of jeans and a wife beater. "Hey, Maleka, I'm ready to take you upstairs to you personal male Masseuse."

Maleka looked at Dana who responded, "Go ahead, and enjoy yourself for once in your life."

When The Punisher extended his hand, Maleka reluctantly took it and allowed him to lead her to the back and up a small staircase. When they got to the top of the landing, only a red light bulb illuminated the hallway. Punisher walked to the end of the hall and opened the door and let her enter. "You can change inside that room here's a towel for you to change into. Your Masseuse will be with you shortly." After that, he closed the door behind him.

Maleka looked around the sparse room where she saw a table, an entertainment system, oils, lotions, and white towels neatly stacked. After changing, Maleka sat down in one of the chairs for about ten minutes when suddenly, a well-built man with dread locks walked in. He smiled, flashing a set of perfectly white teeth.

"Hi my name is Marcus and I'll be your masseuse for this evening."

"My name is Maleka," she blushed

"Maleka, what I need you to do is get up on the table, relax and let me do all the work, okay?" Maleka blushed again as Marcus continued, "Is there any particular music you'd like to listen to while you enjoy your massage?" She shook her head and laid down on her stomach on the table. He went over to the music console and put on a mix tape of R&B and grabbed some oils off the counter. He then pulled down the towel from off of her shoulders and slowly began to work the oils soothingly to her back and shoulders.

Maleka had to admit that it felt good and her tension was being relieved. His powerful hands worked its way down the small of her back, creating millions of tingles throughout her body. After another fifteen minutes of bodily pleasure, he asked her if she was ready for an oral massage. Perplexed, Meleka didn't know what he meant and asked, "What is that?"

Marcus smiled. "Let's just say anything that you want me to do. Your service has already been paid for."

Maleka had finally gotten what he meant and blushed again. "I…I just don't know what to say."

"You don't have to say a word, just let me do what I do best." Marcus slowly began taking off her towel and lifted her off her stomach and on to her back. He then stood back and slowly began to disrobe himself. When Maleka got a birds-eye view of him nude she began to shake. His penis was just as big as if not bigger than the Punisher's manhood was. The mere sight of it made her shake and decided to back out of it.

"I'm sorry, this is all wrong… I have to go."

"Just relax a minute, I'll take everything slow," Marcus advised. Part of her wanted so badly for her to do it, and the other part knew it was plain wrong. "You'll see," he said affectionately.

Maleka submitted to her desire and eased back down on the table. He then took some lotion and slowly applied it to her stomach and the side of her ribs, hips and in between her legs. Then suddenly, without warning he spread her legs like an eagle and slowly began to kiss around her inner thighs. The anticipation build up was killing her as he slowly licked around her neatly trimmed pussy until she began to convulse. Finally, his hot, wet tongue touched her clit, and just like that her juices began to flow. The deeper her delved the more began to cum and began to moan. It was too much for her to handle as reality set in as she thought about her husband.

"Wait, that's enough, that's enough!" Maleka jumped off the table and wrapped her towel back over her and ran back in the dressing room to change.

Ten minutes later, Maleka came out the dressing room fully dressed and noticed Marcus standing by the door. "Listen," Marcus stated, "forget about what just happened. When can I take you out for a cup of coffee or something?"

Maleka was flattered and eyed the floor. "I'm sorry Marcus, but I'm married."

"I understand that. Pretty women like you are always taken, but I just want to take you out and get to know you a little better."

"Thanks, you're a beautiful man as well but, I should really be getting home to my husband."

Marcua nodded his head. "I respect that, but in case you ever want to go out or something I would love to be in your company. Here's my number and call me even if you just want to talk."

Maleka reluctantly took his card and bid him a good night.

FANTASIZE SURPRISE

When Maleka arrived home the first thing she noticed was that the lights had been turned down and candles were lit throughout the house. The second thing she noticed was the red rose petal trails that lead down the hallway and into her bedroom, which she quickly followed. She opened the door to find her husband smiling widely with a small aqua blue box in his hand.

"Happy birthday, honey."

Maleka was clearly flattered as she dropped her teddy bear and ran up to her husband and hugged him. They kissed for a moment before he handed her the gift. Like a kid on Christmas, Maleka opened the box and revealed a Tiffany's key quatrefoil pendant with diamonds on a beaded chain. She was exasperated by her gift and gave him another long kiss and hug.

"Here, let me put it on you," Kevin said. When he fastened the clasp, Maleka walked over to the dresser mirror and marveled at it's beauty. "You like it?"

"Like it?" Maleka blushed, "I love it!"

Kevin wrapped his arm around her from behind and said in a sexy voice, "The night's not over. I got some champagne on ice in the kitchen and I'm feeling horny."

Maleka's heart began to race, as thoughts of her panties being drenched in her juices from the incident earlier entered her mind. She panicked. "Baby, I want to get out of these clothes and take a shower real quick, okay?"

Kevin nodded and asked, "Where did you get the teddy bear from?"

"Oh, that, um, I got it from Dana."

"Dana? Why would she give you a teddy bear?"

Maleka's head began to spin as she quickly thought of a lie. "Well, um, at the restaurant, she arranged with the waiters to wish me a happy birthday with a song, cake and a complimentary teddy bear as a gift."

"Oh, okay, that was nice of them."

"Yeah, but let me take a quick shower and I'll be back lover man."

When Maleka got into the bathroom the first thing that she did was scrub out her panties and threw them in the hamper. She then took a long hot shower and reminisced of the evening she'd just experienced and thought about the number she received. When Maleka finished showering, she entered the room in a satin robe. Kevin had her champagne glass ready. After touching glasses and taking the drinks straight to the head, they began to kiss. Kevin immediately disrobed her and laid her down. It wasn't long before he entered her. Maleka was uncomfortable about the lack of passion on her birthday, but went along with it like she always did. She decided to fantasize that it was Marcus inside of her. Without much thought, she found herself thrusting her body into his harder. It caused Kevin to thrust harder as he moaned and groaned.

"Oh, baby, oh, baby," they both cried out.

"Don't stop, please don't baby, punish me, punish this pussy," Maleka said in return, and suddenly, just like that, she had the biggest orgasm she'd ever had in her life. About the same time, Kevin shot his load too and it was over.

He kissed her one last time and asked, "Was it good to you baby? Did you cum?" Maleka nodded her head and said with a smile, "Yes, big daddy, yes."

This made Kevin feel magnificent as he laid back in his pillow feeling like the man. Maleka picked up the teddy bear that was on the side of the bed and held it tightly. She couldn't stop thinking about what she experienced that night. What was even more interesting, was how she finally achieved an orgasm by just thinking of Marcus inside of her and thought about the card she had stashed down inside her purse for the rest of the night.

ONE WEEK LATER

All that week, Maleka couldn't get Marcus out of her mind. Everyday she would come home early and masturbated as she thought of him inside of her. She became obsessed. A day wouldn't go by without her pulling out the card trying to get the nerve up to call him until finally that day came and she did it.

"Hello…can I speak to Marcus."

"Yes, this is Marcus."

"This is Maleka. You probably remember me from last week at Club Ozone. You gave me a massage and asked me out for coffee."

"Oh, yeah, how could I forget? So what's going on?"

"I was just calling to thank you for the massage on my birthday and to see if I can take you up on your offer for some coffee."

"Fantastic. When do you want to meet up?"

"Are you available tonight?" There was a slight pause and Maleka quickly redeemed herself, "If that's too soon we can make it tomorrow."

"No, tonight or tomorrow isn't good because I have an appointment at eight and ten. Hey, why don't you come out for the show? We could have coffee afterwards."

Maleka thought about it for a moment. "Okay, I'll just meet you after your last massage."

"Great, I'll see you there."

Maleka hung up the phone and fell back against the wall with her eyes closed. She couldn't believe what she just did, but an uncontrollable urge just came over her as she ran to her bed and ripped off her clothes and decided to feed that urge with Hercules, her ever ready dildo. When she finished, she quickly got back on the phone and called Kevin to tell him she would be working late that night. After she hung up, she rushed to the bathroom and took a quick shower and was out the door. Maleka met up with Dana at her apartment to tell her the news and she was floored.

"Bitch, you are a sneaky hoe trying to act like a goodie-goodie. You knew all along you were going to get with him."

Maleka blushed. "No, it wasn't that. I just couldn't get this man out of my mind and I can't help myself, I'm just going to talk."

"Talk my ass," Dana countered, "You want the big dick, plain and simple and I don't blame you. If you aren't getting it at home you might as well stray a little once in a while."

"I told you, we're just going to talk and have coffee."

"Believe what you want, but before this night is over, you gonna be having your legs in the air while he make that dick shift in your uterus," Dana joked.

CREEP

The night was brisk when Maleka arrived at Club Ozone 10:45 p.m. that night. She wanted to wait as long as possible outside, to save herself the awkwardness of seeing him with another girl. As the women began falling out of the club, Maleka made her way in and waited by the bar area. After waiting about fifteen minutes, Marcus arrived from out of the dressing room and over to the bar where Maleka sat. They greeted each other with a light hug.

"So, you made it," Marcus said.

"Yep, just like I said I would."

When Marcus extended his arm, she took hold and they walked out like a certified couple. Ten minutes later, they sat in Joe's Diner on 25th Street and Lexington Avenue drinking coffee and chatting.

"So," Maleka said, "do you like what you're doing for a living?"

"Well, it pays the bills and that's what it's about as far as I'm concerned."

"I hear that. I bet you love your job, having all those nude women throw themselves at you."

"Well, in the beginning, I thought I was having the time of my life, but I've been doing it so long it's just a job now. However,

I don't give special treats to every woman. Your friend Dana hired me and assured me that you were safe and was only with one man these last ten years."

Maleka was surprised Dana had told him that. "Dana paid you to do that?

"Yep, and paid well. So, what do you do for a living?" Marcus asked.

"Oh, I'm into advertising."

"You're one of those rich advertising executive's, huh?"

Maleka chuckled. "Something like that. I'm just a junior executive at The Winbrook Agency here in Manhattan, but I'm working my way up."

"You'll be the president in no time cause I see you're the smart type, that's actually what attracted me to you."

Maleka blushed and asked, "Where are you from?"

"I'm originally from Philly, but now I live in Newark. I'm in New York just about every day though.

"Are you married, have a girlfriend or what?"

"None of the above. It's too complicated to be in a relationship doing what I do for a living. It's just easier to remain single. You know what I mean?"

Maleka nodded. "But, a handsome man like you must be able to find someone who understands you…"

Marcus cut her off mid sentence. "Let me ask you a question, are you happy in your marriage, I mean, is he pleasing you in bed?"

Maleka was caught off guard by the question and stuttered, "Wha…what?"

"Is your husband pleasing you sexually?" he asked point blank again.

"Well, forgive me for not being candid with you, but I don't think that's any of your business," Maleka snapped.

"Listen, I'm sorry if I came off so harsh, but most of the women that I meet are looking for a good time."

"Well, I'm not like most women."

"I know. That's why I gave you my card, because I saw something different about you. But I figured you must be lacking something in your love life because you called me."

Maleka waved her hands and said, "I actually think I made a mistake and should be leaving now. Sorry if I misled you or something." She stood up and fished through her purse to pay the bill, but he stopped her and said that he would take care of it. Maleka thanked him and made her way into the night.

12 PLAYS

Maleka was just coming out of a meeting when her secretary made it known that a delivery person had a package for her.

"Why didn't you just sign for it?" Maleka asked.

"He said that it was a person to person delivery and he was to hand it only to you Mrs. Tidwell. It must be something expensive," her secretary added.

Maleka thought of her birthday that had just passed and thought that Kevin was somehow still feeling guilty about forgetting it. "Send him into my office please, Gail."

"Right away, Mrs. Tidwell."

Moments later, Maleka heard a knock on her office door. "Come in."

When Maleka turned around, she almost collapsed in shock from seeing Marcus standing in the doorway holding a small colorful package. Before she could open her mouth he closed the door behind him and he was right on her like an animal attacking his prey. His strong hands embraced the back of her head as he stuck his tongue deeply down her mouth. She tried to fight him off, but the passion was too overwhelming. He suddenly lifted her up off her feet and on her desk as he swatted away any object that was in his way. He forced her Donna Karan dress up over her hips then forcefully ripped her panties off. With one hand, he unbuckled his pants and pulled out his huge, throbbing dick and slowly eased it into her vagina. Maleka knew it was so wrong, but her body craved him to go on as he eased his dick in and out her pussy slowly.

"Take it out. It's too big," she pleaded, but he didn't listen.

She lost her breath with every inch he put in her, she thought her pussy would explode, but soon the pleasure came down as she began to ride it in and out. Her grunts grew louder as he plunged in and out of her faster and faster, deeper and deeper, until finally she felt an eruption flow through her entire body. Maleka shook as if she was being electrocuted, as thick white cream formed a puddle on her desk. She experienced one last jolt as he pulled his shiny penis out of her and zipped up his pants and walked out the office without saying one word. Maleka felt dizzy as her pussy began to throb and her love juices continued to flow. In an instant, she regained her bearing, rushed over to the door and locked it. She found her panties, put them on and cleaned her desk and floor. Maleka plopped down in her chair not really wanting to believe what had just happened. She eyed the tiny box she received and decided to open it. Inside, was an expensive white gold ring. She blushed at the gesture, sat back in her chair and reminisced on the short-lived moment.

Later that night, Maleka played out the incident over and over again in her mind. She couldn't believe the amount of risk that she took by having sex in her office because anybody could've just walked in on them. But, she also couldn't help but fantasize how that was the single greatest moment of sex she'd ever had in her life. She had to take a long bath and douche to try to get her pussy back in shape. Maleka couldn't believe she took Marcus' whole dick and knew she couldn't have sex with her husband that night. After getting out of the tub, she even threw on some unattractive pajamas and quickly got in bed early just in case he planned on asking. As soon as Maleka's head hit the pillow, she replayed the office moment over in her mind a million times and eventually fell asleep that way.

The next morning, her husband was about to leave for work when he asked, "Honey, are you okay?"

Maleka was caught off guard by the question. "What?"

"You were talking in your sleep all night, like you were having a nightmare."

In a panic, she asked him, "Did I say anything crazy?"

"Well, something like, *get out or get it out!* I tried to wake you, but it didn't work. You just kept gripping that damn teddy bear as if your life depended on it."

"Oh, I must've been dreaming about rats' again," she lied.

"I see," Kevin replied, "Okay, I gotta go, I'll see you tonight." He gave her a kiss goodbye just as the doorbell rang. It was Dana. Kevin opened the door without saying a word.

"Good morning, Kevin," Dana said with sarcasm.

"Good day, Dana," Kevin responded flatly and closed the door behind him.

"You know your husband got problems Maleka. Every time I come here he gets more disrespectful."

"Don't pay him any mind, girl. That's just his way of saying he likes you."

"Well, if that's his way of showing me, I would never want to be on his bad side," Dana joked.

"Girl, guess what," Maleka said excitedly.

Dana quickly took a seat at the breakfast counter. "Go, ahead, tell me."

When Maleka quickly ran to the window and saw Kevin getting into his car, she quickly ran back over to where Dana sat before continuing. "Guess, who came to see me at my job yesterday?"

"Don't tell me," Dana asked in astonishment.

"Yep...Marcus."

Dana could hardly contain herself. "Get the fuck out."

"Yep, and guess what else?"

"It's more?"

Maleka paused a moment to build up her anticipation then came out and said, "We did it."

Dana put her hand over her mouth. She was speechless…for a moment. "When…how?" was all Dana could utter out of her mouth.

"My secretary told me I had a delivery and I thought it was from Kevin since he'd forgotten my birthday. But when the delivery person came in, it was Marcus…with his sexy-ass self."

"How did he know where you worked, I thought you said you walked out on him the other night."

"I did, but during the conversation I told him where I worked. I guess he looked me up."

"So, what happened next?" Dana asked, nearly out of breath.

"Girl, he just came in my office and grabbed me. Then we started getting it on right there."

"On your desk?" Maleka nodded. "And you took all that dick inside you?" Dana continued to ask.

"Almost. I felt like I was having a baby it was so big, but I rode that shit like a cowboy."

"And you waited till now to tell me?"

"I'm sorry, but, it was so surreal. I couldn't believe that it happened like that."

Dana stood up and gave Maleka a hug. "I can't believe my girl is finally getting down with the program. I'm proud of you, girl. So, what are you gonna do now?"

"I didn't think about that yet," Maleka answered

"What do you mean you haven't thought about it yet? You got to take that young buck to the hotel and get the full version now. You just had a snack, now it's time for the whole entrée."

"I don't know," Maleka confessed.

"What the fuck do you mean you don't know? You gotta have the man give you mouth to mouth resuscitation on the pussy to bring that shit back to life."

"I don't know."

"So, give it a couple of days and call him back to set up a little midnight rendezvous this weekend."

"You think I should?" Maleka coyly asked

"Hell, yeah, you should have at least one chance to go all out."

Maleka thought about it for a second. "What should I tell Kevin if I spend the night with him?"

"Just tell him that you're staying with me for the night," Dana quickly interjected.

Maleka looked at Dana and extended her a high five. "I'll set it up for this Friday."

SEEMS LIKE YOU`RE READY

Maleka thought Friday would never come, as she marked off the calendar each day. She'd already told her husband days in advance that she would be staying at Dana's house for the weekend. She told him that Dana's boyfriend had broken up with her and she wanted to look after her friend for a day or two. He didn't take it too well at first, but after the third day he calmed down and let her be. As Maleka packed her clothes, her husband hovered over her suspiciously while she packed. "What is it with you and Dana lately, Maleka?"

She rolled her eyes not wanting to hear the same thing all over again. "What do you mean by that?"

"I mean, you two have been acting strangely ever since your birthday, that's what I'm talking about."

"Why don't you tell me what's really on your mind Kevin instead of beating around the bush."

"You want the truth?"

"Yes, I want the truth." Maleka answered.

"Okay, is Dana gay or something?"

Maleka looked at Kevin to see if he was joking then let out a loud laugh. "Are you serious?"

"Yes, I'm serious."

Maleka giggled once again. "Hell, no. Dana loves men just as much as the next woman. What made you think that?"

"The way she acts when I'm around."

"Trust me when I tell you, Dana has her share of men."

"Just make sure she doesn't try to get you to share with her."

"I told you, she doesn't get down like that Kevin."

"Okay, just don't come home all funny on me," he joked.

"If you ever try to get to know her, you would feel different."

"Yeah, maybe one day."

Maleka stood outside the Park Merriam Hotel at 11:40 p.m. that Friday night waiting for Marcus to arrive. Finally, he pulled up in a yellow cab ten minutes later and got out and gave her a big hug. They proceeded inside the hotel that was already paid for by Maleka and went to the elevator. Minutes later, they were inside the room, 1169. Maleka had already set up through the hotel's room service to have champagne in the room… on ice of course. They sat and talked for nearly an hour as the expensive champagne flowed through their bodies. Maleka was feeling horny and Marcus knew it. He didn't hesitate taking off his shirt to display his chiseled chest and abs. Maleka's juices had already began to flow, but before they got started she wanted to take a shower first.

"Listen, I'm going to take a shower. Call down to room service if you want something else to drink or eat."

"I got all the things I want to eat and drink right here," Marcus replied.

Maleka suddenly had to restrain herself before rushing to the bathroom. While Maleka showered she heard the door to the bathroom open and suddenly the curtain slid opened. It was Marcus standing in front of her completely naked. She stared at his dick for the first time in the light and it looked like a baby elephant's trunk up close. She staggered backwards as he stepped in and embraced her with his tongue in her mouth. To feel his body next to hers made her melt as his hands exploded her entire body.

With each touch, she felt electricity shoot throughout her body as she stood helplessly while his fingers explored her insides.

A few minutes later, Marcus turned off the shower and carried her out of the tub and to the bed. He used a towel and slowly patted her dry as she laid there in anticipation. He tossed the towel aside and stood over her at the foot of the bed then spread her legs open. It didn't take long for him to lightly prowl around her bush with his tongue. Maleka shivered in anticipation as he plunged his tongue deep inside of her. This was Maleka's second time having oral sex performed on her and she felt like she was in heaven as her juices flowed like a water faucet. Kevin would never have done anything like that to her. He thought that it was against nature to perform oral sex on a woman. His tongue darted in and out as he worked on her pussy with expertise and passion. Just when Maleka thought she couldn't take anymore he began giving pleasure to her anus. Bolts of electricity convulsed her body as she screamed with passion. Then finally, he stood to his feet and turned her over. The moment had finally arrived for her to get 'The Dick' and her body began to shake from fear and passion. He reached over on the nightstand, took two packets of KY Jelly off, then ripped them open with his teeth. He slowly poured the mixture on his penis until it glistened. Marcus then eased down on the bed and stroked his penis as he put the head inside of her. Her body began to quiver out of control as he pushed deeper inside of her. Once again she began to strain from the pressure of his fat dick inside of her, it felt as if she would pass out.

All at once the pain turned into pleasure as she yelled out loud, "Fuck me, fuck me. Punish this pussy, give it to me!"

The more Maleka screamed, the more he began to pound her until the whole fourteen inches was inside. She gripped the sheets and bit down on her bottom lip as she released a mega orgasm. She continued to scream at the top of her lungs as she felt her uterus shift to and fro. Marcus pounded faster and faster until finally he let out a roar and pulled his penis out and jerk his sperm all over her bush. Maleka was immobilized, unsure if she could walk as the pain traveled throughout her body sending her into a complete frenzy.

"I love you Marcus, I love you. I've never had anyone make me feel the way you do." She reached for him to hug her.

"I love you too, baby," he confessed as they cuddled up next to each other, "So what do we do now?"

"I don't know? We could still see each other from time to time."

"What do you mean see each other from time to time?"

Maleka was surprised by his response. "I mean, I'm still married so this will just have to be every now and then when we see each other." Marcus lay back in his pillow and rubbed his eyes. "What's wrong, baby?"

He hesitated before answering. "Why is it every time I get with a woman she just wants me for what's just between my legs?"

"No, it's not like that baby."

"Well, then what is it about? After you leave here you are going home to your husband, right?"

"Yes," she replied

"Well, what about me? What do I go home to?" Maleka was speechless and remained silent. "See, I thought so, but I'm not going to let you use me, no, not this time. I want to get paid for my services."

Maleka couldn't believe what she was hearing. "What?"

"You heard me. I want to get paid for my services both times I been with you."

Maleka finally saw that she was being played and wanted suddenly to get out of it. She reached for her purse and pulled out some bills. "Fine, what is it that you want?"

Marcus smiled. "You don't have enough money in your purse to pay me the amount that I want."

Suddenly, the realization of her being extorted finally entered her mind so she challenged him. "How much do you want?" Maleka asked again.

Marcus seemed to enjoy the game and looked toward the ceiling before responding. "Well, we fucked twice, and my fee is five thousand dollars an hour, I would say ten thousand dollars would do it."

Maleka thought she was in a bad dream when he said the

amount. Her heart began to pound. "I'm not giving you ten thousand dollars are you insane?"

Marcus smiled again. "Well, just a little bit. But one thing you should know is that I had you taped the night at the club, and if that tape should ever fall into the wrong hands your investment banker husband Kevin wouldn't like seeing it."

Maleka was completely shocked and dazed at just the mention of hearing her husband's name.

"Yes, I know about Kevin. I know about the townhouse you two own on Henry Street in Brooklyn."

Maleka's mind began to race so fast that she could hardly think anymore. She knew she was being set up from the very beginning and wondered how he knew so much about her. But it didn't matter, she would protect her family at any cost. "Okay, okay, I'll pay you the money, just don't go anywhere near my home or husband."

"Now we're talking. I want the money in three days, that's on Monday. Meet me at Club Ozone before the show at 5 o'clock with the ten thousand dollars in cash. Do you understand?"

She nodded and began to dress and headed out the door. Maleka decided to go home instead of Dana's house like the original plan. She even cried all the way home which also wasn't on the agenda. Maleka cursed herself constantly for being so stupid in the first place. But, she knew one thing and one thing only, she wouldn't allow anyone to break up her marriage at any cost. She called Dana to tell her everything and said that she wouldn't be coming back to her house that night. After she wiped away her tears, Maleka entered her home and was greeted by Kevin who looked surprised to see her.

"What are you doing back so soon," he asked.

"Oh, one of Dana's boyfriends came by and I felt like the third wheel so I left."

Kevin hugged her. "You did the right thing."

"I just want to take a bath and fall asleep in your arms. Is that okay with you?" Maleka asked.

"Of course, baby, I'll run the water for you."

"Thank you, boo."

Ten minutes later, Maleka laid in the tub in a daze as she replayed the entire event over and over again in her mind, even though nothing made sense. She knew she was wrong for messing with a total stranger, but she couldn't help but to cave into the allure of the circumstances. She was looking for love in all the wrong places when she had everything she needed at home. At that moment, Maleka promised herself that if she got past this, she would never, ever go astray again.

DOUBLE DIPPIN`

Maleka had a long weekend and couldn't wait until that Monday had finally arrived to get everything over with. She was so lucky that she and Kevin always kept separate savings account and that he wouldn't know anything about her stash being ten thousand dollars lighter. She had planned to meet up with Marcus with the money at 5:00 p.m. so it would be over forever. Kevin had scheduled another view of the townhouse for that day and asked her to be home, so she needed one more excuse to get out of the house and once again called on Dana.

"Hello, Dana," Maleka said on the phone, "I need you to do me a favor. I need you to house sit for me today so the real estate agent can bring by some buyers. You know how anal Kevin is. He doesn't like the realtors and the buyers to be at the house alone. Kevin should actually be home a half hour later, but I need you there in case they come early."

"Girl, you know I got your back. I'll pick up your keys when I meet you this morning, okay?"

"What time should you get here?"

"About eight."

"Okay, I'll see you then."

The day was going by tremendously slow for Maleka as she sat at her desk and watched minute by minute go by. Finally lunch time came and she went to the bank and withdrew the money out of her account. As soon as she walked out of the bank, her cell phone rang.

"Hello."

"Hey, baby, what's going on?" To her surprise, it was Marcus.

"What do you want?" she said with disappointment

"It's been a change of plans."

Maleka stopped in her tracks. "What change in plans?"

"Well, it looks like my fee just went up due to the economic crisis that we're in. The new fee has doubled to twenty thousand dear."

Maleka was beyond furious. "Listen, you bloodsucking son of a bitch, I'm not paying you a penny more then what we agreed upon and that's it."

"Oh, you're going to pay it my dear or else."

"Or else what? I'll go to the police and tell them that you're extorting me. You've probably done this shit before and you probably have a criminal record, so try me."

"So, is that the way you want it. I can still show your husband the tape."

"You go ahead and try it. As a matter of fact, I changed my mind, I'm not paying you a dime. So if you come near me or my husband I'm going to the police and tell them about your extortion attempt." Maleka hung up.

Maleka thought long and hard about what had transpired earlier and no longer felt the same way. She decided that it wasn't worth the trouble of Marcus ruining her life for a mere twenty thousand dollars and had a change of heart to give him the money and went back to the bank and withdrew ten thousand more. She tried in vain to reach him, but he wouldn't answer his phone. After leaving nearly twenty five messages she gave up and decided to meet him at Club Ozone anyway.

When she got to the club, the owner said that all his scheduled dates to perform were over. Maleka waited around for thirty more minutes. When he didn't show, she was kind of relieved and hoped he was gone out of her life forever. She got home around 6:30 p.m. and when she walked through the door and up the stairs, her heart nearly dropped to the floor. It was Marcus.

Maleka wanted to run for her life, but her husband said, "Good, honey, you're home." Kevin's smile threw her for a loop, then she noticed a third man, who Kevin quickly introduced. "Honey, this here is Mr. Brooks. He's looking to purchase our home."

When Maleka saw Marcus, she froze instantly. Dana was in the background with fright in her eyes as she put her finger to her mouth as to say, "keep quiet." Maleka simply nodded.

"Well, Mr. Brooks," the real estate agent said, "you saw every inch of the house except the kitchen. Are you ready to see that?"

Marcus smiled. "Maybe the appropriate person to show me that is the woman of the house."

Kevin smiled in return. "That's a great idea, honey do you mind?"

Maleka quickly gained her composure and shook her head. "No, I don't mind at all. Follow me Mr. Brooks." Marcus followed Maleka into the kitchen and when they were out of ear shot of her husband, Maleka turned to him and said through gritted teeth, "What the fuck are you doing in my home?"

Marcus only smiled and stared at her with a wicked glare. "You know goddamn well why I'm here. I want my money and I want it now."

Maleka reached in her purse and ripped out the money that was in an envelope and threw it in his face. "Now, get out my house!"

Marcus picked up the money and turned to walk out the door before turning around and winking. "It was a pleasure doing business with you. Maybe next time you shouldn't go around sleeping with strangers." He let out an eerie laugh and walked off into the night twenty thousand dollars richer.

Maleka walked back upstairs into the living room to face her husband. When they saw that he wasn't with her he asked,

"Where's Mr. Brooks?"

"Oh, he told me to thank Mr. Davison for his time, but that the place was too small for him." Both Kevin and the realtor thought her response was strange, but accepted it.

"Okay," Mr. Davison said, "thank you all for your time and Mr. and Mrs. Tidwell, you'll be hearing from me soon. Goodnight." They all bid him a good night and he was out the door.

"Does anybody want some coffee?" Kevin asked.

"I would love some," Dana replied.

"Coming right up," Kevin added with a smile.

They sat around the dining room table and chatted for the next hour when Kevin said, "You were right about Dana, honey. She's not such a bad person. When I came home she was here and we got to know each other better." That was music to Maleka's ears. She wanted so badly in the past for her best friend and husband to get along and it finally seemed to happen. Maybe this wasn't the worst day of her life after all.

Maleka walked Dana to the door and briefed her on the events that went down that night. Maleka was so exhausted that all she wanted to do was sleep. Dana told her not to wait for her the next morning because she had to run a few errands. Afterwards, they gave each other a hug and said good night.

When Kevin got in bed a few hours later, he told Maleka, "Honey, I won't be going into work tomorrow. I'm feeling a little under the weather. I think I'm coming down with a cold or something."

"Can I get you some medicine?"

"No, I've already taken some I just need some sleep."

Okay, baby, good night."

"Good night, baby."

The next day after work, Maleka stopped off at the drug store to buy her husband some more medicine just in case he needed it. When she arrived home, she found it strange that the chain had been put on the front lock. Maleka banged on the door for nearly ten minutes until Kevin finally came down. However, he opened the door with the chain still blocking her entrance and peered through the narrow opening.

"What do you want?"

Maleka was completely perplexed. "I want to get in. What's your problem?"

Kevin unlatched the door without saying a word and walked up stairs. Terror started to fill her heart as they walked up stairs in silence. In a panic, Maleka grabbed Kevin by the arm and demanded him to talk to her.

"What's wrong with you Kevin? Talk to me!"

"You know damn, well what's wrong with me."

"No, I don't know what's wrong, tell me."

Kevin chuckled. "A friend of yours came by the house today and we had a little talk." Maleka's heart dropped at that moment and knew she had made the biggest mistake of her life by trusting Marcus. "I know about the massage, they even showed me a video in case you decided to deny it." At that point, Maleka wanted to die as her head began to spin not knowing what to say or do. "That tape showed my wife doing a disgusting act on stage with a man in front of a whole lot of people."

"But, honey…" Maleka managed to say "that was just for my birthday and…"

"Was it also for your birthday to fuck another nigga too in your office?" She was caught and she knew it as she lost all the bluster she had in her body. "Go ahead, try to lie some more. How could you do this to me after all we been through, huh?"

Maleka just stood there in silence. She knew her marriage was over. Kevin looked at her in disgust. She attempted to make one more final plea when suddenly out of the corner of her eye; someone came from out of her bedroom. Her heart stopped when she saw that it was Dana. She walked right up to Kevin and handed him her cell phone which he showed to Maleka. She had recorded the whole event at Club Ozone without her even knowing it. Dana then gave Kevin a kiss on the cheek.

"I'll call you tomorrow, baby." She turned to leave. Maleka

stood dazed and speechless.

"Hold on Dana" said Kevin, "I need a place to stay for awhile, can you put me up?" Dana looked at Maleka and said with a devious smile. "As long as you want, baby." Dana extended her hand for Kevin and he walked over and took it. Before they walked down the stairs, Kevin turned towards Maleka and said, "I suggest you find a place to stay soon because my realtor made the deal to sell our house today. So you got about a month to move out." Maleka couldn't believe this was happening and just wanted to beg for his forgiveness but it was too late.

"Oh, yeah, my lawyer will be contacting you with the divorce papers soon, so you and Marcus can have a nice life." Maleka heard the door close as she dropped to her knees and screamed at the top of her lungs as she cradled herself and cried the rest of the night.

THE BREATH TAKER
DASHAWN TAYLOR

Saturday July 18, 2009
Newark, New Jersey
3:24 a.m.

Don't be shy honey. Move your web cam lower so I can see between your legs!

Twenty-seven-year-old Brenda Owens smiled at her computer screen as the bold request popped up on her instant messaging window. She looked around her apartment and quietly removed her panties. Brenda had been daydreaming about this chat session all day and she knew she was just minutes away from putting on a show for her online friend.

A devious smirk came to her face when she noticed how excited she was. She'd been chatting online for only a few minutes, but her panties were already soaking wet.

"Whoa," Brenda mumbled tossing her underwear to the side. She reached for the webcam and quickly put it under her desk. The excitement of showing off her body to a total stranger was turning her on even more. She playfully nodded her head and began typing on her keyboard.

"One second I'm doing it now," she typed.

Brenda reached under her desk and seductively spread her legs. It only took her a few seconds to position the camera just right to show off her wet pussy to her new online friend.

"Can you see that?" Brenda typed.

She leaned back to give the voyeur a better look at her body. A few seconds later, a smiley face icon appeared in her chat window. Brenda giggled. She knew her online friend was getting a good look at her moist private area. The thought made her even more energized.

"So, what's your name?" Brenda typed.

"*The Breath Taker*!"

Brenda smiled at the reply. "I know that silly. I mean what's your real name?"

"*Why do you want to know my real name? Are we getting married*?"

"We might," Brenda typed as she began to feel extra flirtatious.

"*Oh, yeah*? *So, when is the honeymoon*?"

Brenda smiled at the screen. "When do you want it to be?"

"*Tonight*!"

Brenda smiled even wider. Her friend's response made her nervous and horny at the same time. She felt a tingle between her thighs and thought for second. It had almost been eight months since she felt the warm touch of a man on her body. She was hopelessly lonely. Chatting on the internet and finger-popping herself was becoming more than a hobby for her. It was undoubtedly becoming an addiction. Brenda stared at the blinking curser in the chat window and smiled. She decided to flirt with her new friend a little more and see where the offer would lead.

"Tonight, huh? And how would we celebrate our honeymoon if I say I DO?" Brenda leaned back in her chair again and waited for the response.

"*You have a pretty pussy*."

Brenda blushed as she read the screen. "Why thank you, Breath Taker. But you're avoiding my question." She waited again for the response.

"*If we got married tonight I would eat it for you baby.*"

"Sorry Mr. Taker, but you gotta come better than that. I got plenty of guys that can eat this pussy tonight. What makes you different?" Brenda finished typing her reply and giggled to herself. She shook her head as she thought about the white lie and waited for another response.

"*Darling, you don't understand. I can be really creative when it comes to eating your pussy.*"

"Tell me more."

"*Well, if you met me tonight, I would wait for you to knock on the door.*"

"Umm hmm..."

"*I would yell for you to come in and join me in the bedroom. Once you walked into my bedroom, you would see candles lit everywhere and there would be soft music playing.*"

"Okay…that's romantic," Brenda typed.

"*But when you looked over to the bed I would be there laying butt naked with a hard dick waiting for you.*"

"Hmmm. I like that." She was getting more and more excited. The words on the screen made her envision the scene ever so clearly. She kept reading as more messages continued to pour into the chat window.

"*I would stroke my dick slowly for you and make you hotter and hotter. But I won't stop there.*"

"Oh, no?" Brenda typed. "What else would you do?"

"*I would ask you to come over and join me near the bed. My head would be hanging off of the edge of the bed and I would ask you to take off your panties for me.*"

"What if I didn't have any on?"

"*Even better! That way you can just sit on my face right there and ride my tongue, baby.*"

"Oooo…you're bad." Another tingle hit Brenda right between her thighs as she thought about the last message.

"*I want you to start off slowly baby. Gently place your clit right there on the tip of my tongue and let me get a small taste. I want to tease it first and make you want me even more.*"

Brenda slightly squirmed in her seat as she read the message. "Damn boy you got a way with words." She was getting hornier by the second.

"You don't know the half baby. I got a way with this tongue, too. After I tease you a little bit, I'll gently grab your ass and work your body on my face. Forcing my tongue to go deeper and deeper inside of you. I want to make you scream in pleasure!"

"You're making me want to scream now!" Brenda typed.

"And the best part is…I won't stop until you cum in my mouth."

"OMG!" Brenda covered her mouth in shock. Her heart started racing as she got more excited. She looked around the quiet apartment once again. She felt almost embarrassed that she was so horny just from chatting online.

"Have you ever done that before?"

"Done what?"

"Had someone eat your pussy while you stood over them?"

"I haven't yet. Why? You want to try it?"

"Yes, baby. I want to try it tonight."

"Tonight, but it's so late."

"I know. But this is the best time to sexually explore each other."

Brenda playfully put her index finger in her mouth. She thought about the offer for a moment and looked at her watch. It was almost four in the morning, but the excitement made her alert. Another message popped up into the chat window.

"Baby I'm so hard for you right now. Trust me, we will have a great night together."

Brenda moved her hand from her mouth and slowly slid it down her neck. She felt herself becoming warmer from the excitement. Another slick grin came to her face as she decided to make a decision.

"You know, a little excitement would be good for me right now," she typed. "It's
been such a long time since I had a good orgasm."

"Baby I will be your sex slave tonight if you give me the chance. Trust me honey, I'm not going to hurt you. I just want to

Take Your Breath Away!"

Brenda smiled at the computer screen again. She was ready for some action. "Okay baby. Let's do it, but I'm not coming to your house. We have to go to a hotel."

"*That's fine. I have the perfect place on Route 1 in Rahway. It's called the Rodeway Inn!*"

"Sounds good to me. You just make sure you bring that stiff dick with you, baby."

"*I will honey...can't wait to meet you. Believe me. This is going to be a night you will never forget!*"

II

Saturday July 18, 2009
Newark Police Department (4ᵗʰ Precinct)
9:47 a.m.

Detective Crystal Wilson let out a primitive growled as she hastily shuffled through a mountain of paperwork on her desk. Her stern yet gorgeous face was twisted with anger and agitation. The eight-year veteran continued to make funny noises as she dumped loads of papers into a wastebasket next to her chair.

"Where the hell is that report?" Crystal barked as she began to fling loose papers everywhere. "I can't believe this shit! And where the hell is Mark?" She stood up from her desk and looked around the disheveled office. She then scowled at the empty chair across from her that was usually occupied by her partner of three years. "You better have a good reason as to why you're late Mark," Crystal mumbled to herself and walked over to her partner's desk.

She looked at a few papers that were scattered about and shook her head. Crystal shoved the papers around in search of the missing report. After a few moments, she sat down at his desk in frustration. She booted up his computer and began to mumble to herself again. "I know you gotta have it saved on your desktop

Mark," she whispered. "This is insane."

Crystal looked at the clock on the wall and waited for her partner's computer to come on. Another frustrated look came to her face when the machine prompted her to enter a password. "Goddamnit!" She was clearly angry now. "I don't know the goddamn password!"

Crystal angrily typed a few guesses, but none of them worked. She slammed the mouse and cursed the computer again. Before she could take another guess at the password, a male voice startled her from behind.

"Whoa, whoa, whoa DC. Easy on the computer," the male voice said.

Crystal turned around just in time to see her partner Detective Mark Jones. "Everything okay DC?" Mark asked, as he walked in the office.

Crystal stood up and walked away from the desk. "Everything is fine. I just need the Gibbons Report. Captain Reilly is up my ass for it."

"Okay no problem I got it on my desktop," Mark said, as he sat down.

Crystal walked over to her desk. She sat down in her chair and looked at Mark. "You know you never gave me that damn password to your computer," she snapped.

"No, no no DC," Mark joked. "I can't give you the password to my computer. That right there is a secret."

"So, why are you so late today Detective?" Crystal asked as she quickly switched to another subject. "Were you with one of your bitches last night?"

Mark shook his head and laughed at the statement. He looked over to Crystal who was still staring at him. She tilted her head and gave him a strange look.

"Something's different about you partner," Crystal said, as she twisted her face again. "What did you do different?"

"I got some new contact lenses. I had to buy some new ones."

"What? You lost the old contacts?" Crystal questioned.

"Nope. Just wanted to get some new ones. That's it."

"Okay Mark. I see you player," Crystal joked as a smile came to her face. "I see the difference now. These contacts are lighter than the old ones."

"Yup. I figured I'd changed the game a little bit and buy some stylish ones." Mark laughed at himself. "That's why I was late. Had to make sure I had them before I came in today."

"Okay…any luck on that report?" Crystal tried again to change the subject.

"Yes, I found it," Mark answered. "I'm going to print it out now."

Crystal grabbed the papers from the printer and walked toward the door. "You coming?" she asked turning around.

"I wouldn't miss this for the world." Mark jumped up and followed Crystal into the hallway.

The 4th Precinct of the Newark Police Department was buzzing with activity that Saturday morning. Patrolmen, detectives and suspects were all making a ruckus in the already noisy building. Crystal and Mark quickly approached Captain Reilly's office and knocked on the door.

"It's open!" a burly voice yelled from behind the frosted glass door.

Crystal shook her head expecting the worse as they entered the office. Both detectives instinctively painted fake smiles on their faces as they sat down in front of Captain Reilly's desk. He stared at both detectives with a look of worry. Captain Shane Reilly was a twenty-year veteran on the Newark Police force. Being one of the first high ranking African-American officers in Newark was causing him to age a lot faster than he desired. His emotional and physical scars could be seen plainly on his face. Captain Reilly grabbed a manila folder from his drawer and tossed it to Mark.

"Detective Mark, look at this file and let me know what you think," Reilly continued. "DC, do you have the Gibbons Report?"

"I sure do sir," Crystal said, handing the five-paged report to Captain Reilly. "Seems like the tip we got last week paid off. Terrance Gibbons is the last of the family that's involved in high risk crime. So his arrest will mark the end of the Gibbon's family reign in Newark. Everyone else in the family is involved in petty crimes; auto theft and simple assaults. But once the head is cut off, everyone else will falter."

Captain Reilly looked over the report and nodded his head. He placed the paperwork on his desk and looked at Crystal. "Good work DC," Reilly said. "This is great news. And it's coming at a really good time." However, something in Reilly's tone wasn't matching his expression.

"What's the matter Captain?" Crystal asked. "You don't seem pleased with the results."

"I am pleased DC," Reilly indicated. "But the truth of the matter is that I have some bad news."

"What is it Captain?" Mark questioned lifting his head from the notes.

"Corzine is coming down on us pretty hard these days," Reilly replied. "As you know, the overall crime rate is down in Newark, but the violent crimes are up. And of course he wants to make some changes."

"What kind of changes?" Crystal asked. She was becoming more concerned as Reilly continued to speak.

"Looks like they're trying to force me out," Reilly advised. "They want some new blood in here. Seems like the old way of doing things is not the best way anymore. So, they're looking to hire a new Captain in this Precinct soon. They want me to take an early retirement."

As Mark's eyes lit up at the news, Crystal put her hand on her chin and shook her head.

"No shit, Captain?" Mark asked.

"No shit, Mark," Reilly replied. "But I'm not going down without a fight."

Reilly handed Crystal a manila folder with the same information that he'd given Mark. He waited for her to look over the material and continued to speak. "What you have there is a case we've been working on for a few months. Looks like there's a sociopath on the loose and he's targeting young women on the internet. His screen name is The Breath Taker and we found his page on a few websites including Ebony Sex Partner.com."

"He's a child sex predator?" Crystal asked.

Reilly shook his head. "Not quite. He seems to be targeting women from the ages of twenty-four to thirty-eight. He meets them online, chats for a few days and meets them at various locations. The only problem is, a few of the women that he's chatted with have ended up dead."

Both detectives raised their heads at the news. Crystal felt herself immediately becoming angry.

"The latest victim was found this morning in Rahway," Reilly stated.

"So, Rahway should be on the case," Mark added.

"They are, but I want you guys to go check the scene out and report back to me," Reilly said. "This new victim is from Newark and I want to get ahead of this prick and shut him down. This collar will help bring some credibility back to this department."

Crystal nodded his head and looked at Mark. She couldn't place his expression as he looked at Reilly.

"So, how close are you guys to catching him?" Mark asked.

"We're close," Reilly responded. "He hasn't slipped up yet, but he will. They all do eventually. And we he slips, we'll be right there to clean his grimy ass up and send him to prison. And we can show Corzine that we mean business out here."

Mark nodded his head and stood to his feet. Crystal followed suit and proceeded to the door.

"We're behind you Captain. We're going to get this guy," Crystal assured.

"Just remember guys," Reilly said. "Any information on this case comes right to me. Don't pass off any information to other people in this department. Is that clear?"

"Yes sir," Crystal and Mark said in unison. They nodded toward Reilly and left the office.

III

Saturday July 18, 2009
Rahway, New Jersey
10:58 a.m.

Detective Crystal pulled out her cell phone as she sat in the passenger side of a white Chevy Caprice. The loud engine of the unmarked police vehicle didn't faze her as she started to send text messages through the phone. Detective Mark remained quiet as he sped down the congested highway. Crystal noticed he had something weighing heavy on his mind and decided to break the silence.

"What are you thinking about partner?" Crystal asked, as she kept her eyes on the cell phone.

"It doesn't add up," Mark stated.

"And what exactly is supposed to add up?" Crystal mumbled as she turned to Mark.

"If the Captain is so hell bent on catching this guy, why won't he let us share information with anybody else?"

"Well," Crystal answered. "Put yourself in his shoes. If you knew you were going out, wouldn't you want to go out in a blaze of glory?"

Marked turned to her. "A blaze of glory?"

"Yeah…I would. I guess he figures if we catch this guy and he gets the credit than he can feel adequate in his retirement."

"I guess so," Mark continued. "But something doesn't feel right."

Crystal decided to drop the conversation. She retreated back into her text messages and remained silent. Mark looked over to her again.

"What are you doing?" Mark asked as he shifted his eyes to her cell phone.

"Trying to get me some dick tonight." Crystal laughed to herself.

"You're such a lady," Mark sarcastically mumbled. "No

120

wonder I never took a shot at you. All the guys must be beating down your door."

Crystal waved him off and continued to type on her cell phone. "I don't see where you have room to judge me, Mr. Five Girls in Three Nights. Isn't that what you told me?"

An embarrassing grin came to Mark's face. He shook his head as he reflected on Crystal's statement. "You right. I can't lie about that. But I was going through something then."

"Is that right? Well, I'm going through something right now. It's called RCS."

"What the hell is RCS?" Mark asked.

"Restless Coochie Syndrome!"

Both Detectives busted into a boisterous laughter in the car. Mark shook his head and turned his attention back to the road.

"Oh man DC, you're a piece of work," Mark said, trying to hold back his laughter as the white cruiser pulled up to the parking lot of the hotel. The crime scene was already buzzing with police and news vehicles as they battled for position. Mark pulled around to the back of the hotel and parked the car in the first available spot.

"Okay here we go," Crystal said, as she reached over and opened the door to the vehicle. Mark stayed in the car as she got out. He grabbed his cell phone and began to make a call.

"You're not coming in?" Crystal asked.

"I'll be in there in a minute. I have to make a call really quick."

Crystal gave Mark a strange look and headed to the building. She felt an all too familiar knot form in her stomach as she approached the hotel lobby. Although she had been on the force for almost a decade, Crystal never got use to the anxiety of seeing human destruction. She slowly approached the lobby door and was immediately greeted by a Detective from the Rahway Police Department. A Hispanic male in his mid-thirties approached her with his hand extended.

"How are you? My name is Detective Roman."

"How are you?" Crystal responded as she shook his hand.

"Your Captain called and said we should be expecting you

guys," Detective Roman said. "If you would follow me this way."

Crystal followed Detective Roman down a long hall until they approached an opened door to one of the rooms. It didn't take long for her to notice that the crime area looked more like a social gathering than a place where someone just got murdered. The Rahway officers were talking and laughing among themselves and only a few of them were actually investigating the scene. Detective Roman invited Crystal into the room. She immediately noticed a young woman lying naked on her stomach across the bed. Her dark skin was still glowing despite the fact that she'd been dead for a few hours. Detective Roman walked over to the woman and pointed at her.

"Well, this is the deceased."

Crystal gave Roman a sarcastic glance and walked over to the body. She knelt down beside the bed and began to investigate the area. "How did she die?" Crystal inquired.

"Looks like some sort of suffocation. There's no blunt trauma or visible injuries that we can see."

Crystal focused in on the dead woman's back, shook her head then mumbled, "Oh wow."

"What is it detective?" Roman asked.

"Just caught a chill when I saw the tattoo on her back," Crystal replied as she pointed to a black rose tattooed on the back of the victim's shoulder. "I have the same tattoo of a black rose on my arm."

"Oh wow," Roman replied. "That is eerie."

"And we have a positive I.D. on her right?" Crystal asked as she focused her attention to the nightstands.

"We do. Her name is Brenda Owens. We found her purse with her identification in it. Her debit cards and cash are still in the purse, so it doesn't appear to be a robbery. And her car is still in the parking lot."

"And the front desk?" Crystal asked, as she stood up and walked toward the bathroom. "What's his story?"

"The front desk clerk said he didn't see the man clearly," Roman responded. "This is one of the last hotels that don't require an I.D. to rent a room. Trust me…our guy knew what he was doing. We can't find the hotel key and none of the towels. He probably took it all with him. And he paid in cash."

"What about surveillance?"

"There is none. Camera system hasn't worked in a year, and the owner is too cheap to replace it."

"What an asshole," Crystal blurted shaking her head.

"Hold your applause," Roman said. "You're really going to love these people after this. A few of the other guests thought they heard some unusual noises coming from this room and called the front desk. But they couldn't get through. Come to find out that the hotel clerk was too busy getting a blowjob from a prostitute and didn't investigate the noise."

"Wow."

"Wow what?" a male voice asked interrupting Crystal. It was Detective Mark. Crystal and Roman turned around.

"Hey Mark, I was just getting the bad news from Detective Roman here," Crystal said.

Mark walked over to Roman and shook his hand. "What's the bad news DC?" Mark questioned.

"DC?" Roman asked, with a confused expression. "Are you referring to me?"

"No, he's actually talking to me," Crystal replied. "DC…short for…Detective Crystal."

"Oh, okay," Roman said. "I'm sorry for the mix up."

Mark ignored Romans apology and turned his focus to the dead body. He looked at the young woman for a moment. Crystal walked over to Mark and stood beside him.

"The bad news is that there's no surveillance and right now no prints," Crystal said. "The most we can hope for is DNA or some other slip up from this guy."

Mark didn't say a word. He continued to stare at the woman.

"You okay, Mark?" Crystal asked.

"I'm okay. She's just so damn young and beautiful," Mark responded.

Crystal was taken aback by the statement and looked over at her partner. He stared at the woman for another brief moment and turned to leave.

"Okay we are done here," Mark said, as he headed for the door.

"Wait hold up," Crystal said. "We just got here."

"This is bullshit DC and you know this," Mark blurted. "What did the Captain expect that a clue was going to fall out of the sky? I'm going back to the office and do some real police work. This is a wild goose chase."

Crystal was shocked by Mark's tone. She watched him leave as he headed for the lobby. Crystal turned to Detective Roman who witnessed the entire scene.

"It's okay Detective, I understand," Roman indicated. "We'll take care of this."

"Okay. That's fine," Crystal replied. She reached in her pocket and pulled out a business card. "But if you find anything that you want or need to share with the Newark PD, please call me. That is my cell phone number on that card."

Roman took the business card and placed it in his pocket. "Sure thing, Detective. Once we get some pieces to the puzzle figured out I'll contact you."

Crystal nodded her head and left the room. She couldn't figure out why Mark was acting the way he was and decided to confront him. When she got outside she noticed he was leaning against the trunk of the police cruiser waiting for her to come out.

"What the hell is your problem Mark?" Crystal questioned as she approached him.

"I'm sorry DC, but something is just not right about this case. The Captain knew that we weren't going to find damn thing."

"Mark, we were in there for two minutes," Crystal said. "How could we find anything?"

"Think about it for a second. There's something not right about this."

"So, tell me Mark. What do you think? What's on your mind?" Crystal asked. Mark walked away from the rear of the car and over to the driver side door.

"Give me some time DC," Mark said. "I'm going to take the rest of the day off and I'll tell you about it later. I need to make a few more calls and get to the bottom of this."

"What the hell?" Crystal mumbled to herself. When Mark got into the car and started the engine, she decided to drop the subject. She then walked over to the passenger side and got into the car.

Crystal turned to her partner. "So, what the hell am I supposed to do with the rest of my day while you're getting your head together?"

"What about that Heidi Kachina case?" Mark asked. "You still working on that?"

"Hell no! That bitch is delusional," Crystal barked. "I wish she was still in that damn coma. I gave the case back to Detective Williams so he's on the job."

"Well, in all seriousness I need to figure this out," Mark said. "Do you want me to drop you off at the Precinct?"

"Yes," Crystal quickly answered. "That would be perfect. I think I have an idea to catch this guy."

IV

Saturday July 18, 2009
Newark Police Department (4th Precinct)
4:01 p.m.

A few hours later, Crystal was feeling excited about her idea. She spent most of the morning developing a plan and even doing some research to catch the infamous Breath Taker. After writing everything down Crystal decided to meet with her boss to deliver the news. Crystal quickly jumped up from her desk and headed straight for Captain Reilly's office. She was moving so fast that she never noticed that Captain Reilly's office door was closed. Without a thought, Crystal grabbed the doorknob and rushed right into the office.

"What in the hell?" Captain Reilly yelled. He scrambled to

pull himself together.

Crystal watched as he slammed his laptop closed and threw some papers to the side. "What the hell is wrong with you DC?" Captain Reilly stuttered. "You don't knock anymore?"

Crystal tried to retreat out of the door. "I'm so sorry Captain," Crystal pleaded. "I didn't know you were busy." She backed out of the office.

"No, no no!" Reilly yelled. "It's okay. You can come in. You just startled me. That's all."

"I didn't know Captain…really," Crystal said. "I apologize." She slowly walked back into the office and took a seat across from his desk. She suspiciously watched him as he pushed his laptop to the side and removed a few notes from his desk. He seemed to be coming back from another world as he tried his best to come back to reality.

"I guess you wanted to see me about something DC?" Reilly sternly asked. He was still looking around his desk in a daze.

"Umm yes," Crystal responded. She was also trying to bring herself back from the awkward moment. "After thoroughly investigating the Rahway crime scene and doing some thinking I want to go deeper into this case."

"Deeper?" Reilly was clearly confused. "What in the world are you talking about DC? You *are* on the case already. Remember, I put you on it this morning."

"Yes, I know Captain. But follow me." Crystal moved closer to the edge of her chair. "I want to go undercover on this one."

"Okay," Reilly replied without hesitation. "How's this going to work?"

"Now, this guy is preying on women on the internet," Crystal said. "And according to the report, it appears that he never meets the women until the night the crime occurs. So, let's set him up. I already went on Ebony Sex Partner.com and created an account. I'll make sure to hit his page up and see if we can get a bite."

Captain Reilly started to nod his head. He looked at a few

papers on his desk again as Crystal continued to speak of her plan.

"If I get him to bite I want to set up a visit," Crystal continued. "And once he agrees to meet me we will get the bastard."

Captain Reilly looked at Crystal. "Are you sure you are up to this?"

"I think this could work," Crystal responded. "I know this guy will bite. I think I'm sexy enough to bait him in." Crystal smiled to herself and did a shimmy in her chair.

Captain Reilly was not amused. "This is not a game DC," he firmly said.

"No sir," Crystal said, as she erased the smile from her face.

"This is a very important case," he reiterated. Reilly sat back in his chair and looked at Crystal. "This is it DC. I'm out the door after this. So, you have to take this one serious.

"Absolutely sir," Crystal said, as she nodded her head. "Serious as cancer Captain."

"That's more like it."

"But trust me boss," Crystal continued. "You have been like a mentor to me and I will make sure that your legacy stays in tact."

"You got it DC," Reilly said. "The minute he agrees to meet you call me. I want to know where it's going down and how long I have to get there. Okay?"

"Yes sir. The minute I know, you'll know, sir."

"Okay," Reilly said. "Now, get the hell out of my office and knock the next time you see my door closed. You scared me half to death with that nonsense."

Crystal smiled and left the office. She jogged to her office and jumped in front of her computer. She was excited about the opportunity to put her idea to work.

A few minutes later, Mark walked into the office and sat at his desk. Crystal gave him a hard stare and sat back in her chair.

"Where the hell were you?" Crystal asked. "I tried calling you for about the last hour."

Mark took out his cell phone and waved it in the air. "Blame it on the phone, DC. It doesn't ring when I'm on the internet."

"You were on the internet for that long?" Crystal questioned. "Doing what?"

Mark shook his head in frustration, but decided to answer Crystal's question. "I had to research something."

"Research what?"

Before Mark could answer the question, Crystal's cell phone started ringing. She picked it up from the desk and answered it. "Detective Crystal, Newark PD how can I help you?"

A familiar voice answered from the other line. "Hello, this is Detective Roman from the Rahway PD. I didn't catch you at a bad time did I?"

"No, not at all," Crystal said.

"Good. I wanted to inform you that we got some preliminary test back from the lab," Roman informed.

Crystal was shocked. "Already?"

"Well, again this is preliminary and it will take another week or so to confirm this information," Roman continued. "But we think we found a trace of Hemlock in the victim's system."

"Really?" Crystal asked.

"Yes," Roman responded. "Are you familiar with the poison plant Detective?"

"I think so," Crystal stated. "But how would she get that into her system?"

"It's fairly easy actually," Roman replied "It could've been in her food, in her bottled water or even a glass of wine. But as you know, it's very potent and it attacks the throat and can cause…"

"Suffocation!" Crystal yelled cutting him off. "Yes, this is interesting."

"Well, that's all we have at this time, but I wanted to give you some information." Roman said. "If there's anything else we discover out of the ordinary I will surely give you a buzz."

"Thanks Detective," Crystal replied.

"Have a good day," Roman said before hanging up.

Crystal hung up the phone and looked at Mark who was logging into his computer.

"Was that Rahway?" Mark asked. "Do they have anything

worth hearing?"

"That was Rahway, Mark. But I'm not done with you," Crystal said. "Why didn't you answer your phone? I wanted to tell you something before I took it to the Captain."

"Okay, so, tell me now."

"Well…I'm going undercover on this Breath Taker case," Crystal informed.

Instantly, Mark slammed his computer mouse on the desk and looked at Crystal. She was shocked at his reaction.

"What the hell is wrong with you DC?" Mark yelled.

"What?"

"What do you think you're doing?"

"My job," Crystal snapped. "I really want to catch this guy."

Mark began to shake his head. He was clearly disappointed by the news. "You really don't know what the hell you're getting your self into."

Mark stood to his feet and began to pack his desk up. Crystal watched as he shut his computer down and grabbed his jacket.

"What's going on with you Mark? Where are you going?"

"I'm about to do some undercover work on my own," Mark responded. "I need to find out what the hell is going on with our so called Captain."

Crystal twisted her face up and stared at Mark. He wasn't making any sense to her. Before he walked out the door she stopped him. "Wait Mark. What exactly are you saying?"

"Give me a few hours," Mark said. "I need to look into something. This whole thing really seems out of place."

Crystal simply shook her head as Mark stormed out of the office. Before she could call him back, her cell phone started ringing. She quickly picked up the phone noticed it was her friend Quinten calling.

"I've been trying to call you all day Q," Crystal said, as she answered the phone.

"My bad, Mami," Quinten replied from the other line. "We still on for tonight?"

"Hell yes," Crystal said. "Be at my apartment by ten.

Okay? I'll be there."

"Say no more," Quinten responded.

"Okay…see you later baby, and don't forget to bring condoms." Crystal hung up the phone and turned her focus back to Ebony Sex Partner.com.

V

Saturday July 18, 2009
Newark, New Jersey
10:25 p.m.

Later that night, a loud moan could be heard coming from Crystal's apartment. Even with the smooth music playing on her stereo, Crystal's voice could be heard clearly moaning with sexual pleasure as her friend Quinten lay firmly on top of her. The two missed each other so badly that they decided to get undressed and make love on her living room couch instead of wasting time trying to make it to her bedroom.

"Oh, damn Q…please…just a little bit harder baby," she moaned.

Crystal felt Quinten grabbing her tightly and she reacted to every tingling sensation. Lying on her stomach was Crystal's favorite position and tonight she was loving every second of it.

"Hurt this pussy baby!" Crystal demanded.

The sensuality in her voice was making Quinton more excited with every moan. Crystal's back suddenly jerked when she felt the hot sweat dripping from his naked body.
She couldn't help but smile to herself as his forcefulness made her seductively bite her bottom lip. Crystal knew he had missed her, but she could tell that Quinten was extremely excited tonight. She felt him going deeper than ever before as he slowly, but forcefully grinded her from behind. As he pushed harder into her wet pussy the pain was almost heaven-like for Crystal.

"You like that baby?" Quinten whispered as he began to

stroke her faster and faster.

"I love it!" Crystal responded. Feeling his voice vibrating in her ear turned her on even more. "Put it deeper baby…I really wanna feel it!" she moaned again.

Crystal almost screamed as she felt Quinten hit a spot deep within her that she never felt before. Not wanting to yell too loud, Crystal quickly buried her face in the pillows. Quinten noticed her reaction and began to relentlessly stroke the same spot. Crystal let out a louder sexual moan and tightly grabbed his arm. Her body started shaking uncontrollably as an explosive orgasm was just seconds away. Quinten felt her excited pussy tighten around him and knew she was climaxing.

"That's right, Mami…cum for me!"

Hearing his voice was all she needed to let go. Quinten watched with delight as Crystal's entire body seemed to tremble like an earthquake in ecstasy. She almost sounded like she was whimpering as the sensation of the orgasm shot from her thighs to the back of neck.

"Oh my God….that was wonderful," Crystal moaned as she felt Quinten collapse on top of her. "I needed that so bad."

"I know you did baby," Quinten said. He slowly kissed her on the back of her shoulder. "I'm sorry I have to run now."

"I know," Crystal mumbled. Her mood quickly changed as she felt Quinten slide out of her. She listened as he stood up and began to get dressed.

"Tell your wife I said hello, okay?" Crystal sarcastically said. She grabbed the nightgown from the floor and slowly covered herself. Quinten never responded to her as he got dressed. He grabbed his keys from the floor and kissed her on the cheek.

"Next week?" Quinten calmly asked.

"Maybe baby," Crystal mumbled. "Just answer my call when I call."

Quinton nodded his head and left the apartment. Within a few minutes, Crystal felt herself getting lonely again. As a few images from the sexual episode began to flash in her mind, Crystal realized she was still horny. She decided to take her sexual energy to cyberspace.

Crystal stood up and walked over to her computer. Within a few minutes, Crystal found herself logging onto her computer and navigating directly to Ebony Sex Partner.com.

"Okay," she whispered to herself as the screen prompted her to log in. "Let's see what all of the hype is about."

Crystal was amazed to see so many users on the website. She'd never witness anything like it before. Photos of ordinary men and women alike posing naked were posted everywhere on the website. It didn't take long for Crystal to find herself answering dozens of friend-requests and chat-invitations.

"This is insane," she whispered. "What a bunch of sex-a-holics." Crystal chuckled to herself again. The irony in her last statement made her smile as she realized she too was on the website for sexual stimulation.

After twenty minutes of chatting with a few users, Crystal decided to take her experience to another level. She turned on her webcam and started broadcasting live from her living room. Although her viewers could see her body clearly, Crystal was very careful not to show her face on the website. More messages poured into her inbox. She smiled as the compliments flooded her computer screen. She was contemplating giving her audience a more provocative show when an instant message hit her computer screen that made her heart drop.

"Have you found your first sex partner yet?"

Crystal anxiously looked at the message. Despite its harmless nature, her heart raced as she read the sender's name.

"The Breath Taker," Crystal unconsciously mumbled. She leaned back in her chair baffled at the odds of drawing her mark on the first night. She thought about calling her Captain and running a trace on the user, but decided to go at this challenge alone. She took a deep breath and sat back up in her chair. After pulling the keyboard closer, she began to type her response. A sense of excitement came over her as she began to realize the gravity of her decision. Before she could send her reply to the user another message abruptly popped up on her screen.

"I'm sorry to bother you. Maybe I can reach out another time."

Crystal immediately responded to the message. "Oh, no don't leave. I was just closing some other windows."

"*So, where are you from?*"

"I'm in the North Jersey area."

"*Okay, that's good to know. I'm in the North Jersey area also. So, what's your name?*"

"Debbie!" Crystal quickly typed. She chuckled at the innocent lie.

"*Okay...nice name. So, Debbie what brings you to Ebony Sex Partner?*"

"That's a silly question," Crystal typed. "Sex...of course!"

"*Of course Debbie...but what kind of sex? Straight sex? Bi-curious sex? Tri-curious sex?*"

"Ha...what the hell is tri-curious sex?"

"*That means you will 'tri' anything!*"

Crystal giggled at the silly response. "Hmmm....okay I like that." She smiled and continued to type. "So, to answer your question...I guess I'm here looking for you." Crystal couldn't help but chuckle at the double meaning of her last response. "And you...what are you doing on this website?"

"*I love sex.*"

"Don't we all?" Crystal responded.

"*Not like me. I'm very gifted at what I do. I can really make a woman's body scream.*"

Crystal pulled her face away from the computer screen. Although his last statement made her feel uneasy, she was focused on setting her trap and decided to pursue the conversation further.

"So...you think you can make my body scream?"

"*If you give me a chance to.*"

"Hmmmm."

"*I hate to be so forward, but looking at you on this webcam is making me want you even more.*"

"So, I take it that you like what you see?"

"*I do. I love that are mocha brown skin. It's almost like sweet chocolate.*"

Crystal instinctively smiled at the compliment. "I see you're a charmer, Mister...?"

"You can just call me The Breath Taker."

"You don't have a real name?" Crystal typed.

"Not on here...too many psychos out there. But back to you...is that a tattoo on your arm?"

Crystal noticed that he quickly changed the subject and decided to play along. "Yes, this is my first and only tattoo."

"What is it? It's coming up a little blurry on my screen."

"It's a black rose," Crystal continued.

"Wow, what a coincidence!"

"Why do you say that?" Crystal responded.

"A friend of mine had that same tattoo. But it was on her back."

Crystal's heart skipped a beat as she thought about the woman lying in the hotel room with a black rose tattooed on her back. The irony of the evening was becoming thicker and thicker by the second. Crystal pushed forward.

"You speak of her in the past tense. Why is that?" Crystal inquired.

"Oh, she's gone now."

"Gone?"

"Yes, she and I had to take a break from each other. I guess I took too much of her breath away and she couldn't handle it."

A cold chill rushed through Crystal's body as she read the statement. She was momentarily frozen. Thinking of the dead woman in the hotel made her emotional. She felt a streak of anger piercing throughout her body. After a brief moment Crystal realized that this was definitely her mark. She sat up again in her chair and decided to bait him in further.

"Whoa...so you must be really gifted if you are putting that thing on these chicks like that," she typed.

"You better believe it Debbie. Some of these girls are dying to get next to me."

Crystal balled her lip up as she continued to type. The arrogance of this murderer was making her more upset.

"So, what about me? How can I get you to take my breath away?"

"Just ask me to."

"Well, you got me all hot and bothered over here and now I'm curious to see what you got."

"*Do you want me to send you a picture?*"

"Hell no!" Crystal typed "I'm a grown woman. I need flesh!" A few seconds passed and there was no response. Crystal impatiently stared at the blinking curser on her screen and bit her bottom lip. She was praying that she didn't scare him off.

"Did I lose you honey?"

"*No, you didn't lose me. I was just calling the hotel to see if they have any rooms available for tonight.*"

"Good. Because now you have me horny and wanting to see what you got."

"*Nice. Trust me sweetie, you will see everything I can do tonight. What are you going to wear?*"

Crystal thought for a second and began to type. "I might wear some leather. Or I may wear some lace. Or I may wear nothing at all. I'll surprise you."

"*Sounds good to me. Can you meet me at the Motor Lodge on Route 46 in Fairfield? Is that too far for you?*"

"That's not too far. I can meet you there. I want to come wherever you feel comfortable baby."

"*I will be there at 2 a.m. Don't be late sexy. When you get there just go to the front desk and pick up the key. The password is ESP.*"

"Okay, but what is ESP?" She was confused.

"*Ebony Sex Partner baby. I use that code to be discreet.*"

"Okay great. See you at two o'clock mister Breath Taker. Don't be late."

"*I won't.*"

Crystal noticed the chat session was immediately shut down. She felt herself becoming nervous as she closed out of the computer windows and grabbed her phone. She quickly called Detective Mark and waited for him to pick up. There was no answer after the first attempt, so Crystal tried again. After a few rings Mark finally picked up the phone.

"DC do you know what time it is?" Mark uttered. He sounded tired.

"I'm coming to pick you up," Crystal said excitingly. "I think I found our guy!"

"What?" Mark stuttered.

"Don't worry about it. I'll explain on the way. I'll be in front of your house in an hour, be ready."

Before Mark could respond Crystal hung up the phone and rushed to her bedroom. She quickly got dressed and prepared herself to catch this internet predator.

VI

Sunday July 19, 2009
Fairfield, New Jersey
1:42 a.m.

"He's still not picking up?" Crystal yelled as she continued to speed down Route 46 en route to the Motor Lodge Hotel. Between the roaring engine and the loud police siren it was hard for Crystal to hear. Detective Mark was in the passenger side of the police vehicle using his cell phone. He repeatedly dialed a few phone numbers, but was having no luck reaching the other party.

"No!" Detective Mark yelled. "I don't know why he's not answering his calls. I called his house and his cell phone, but there was no answer at either one of them."

"Well, forget it then!" Crystal barked. "Captain Reilly told me to call him when I made my move. He's probably sleep."

"You want me to call for some backup?" Mark asked as he looked over to Crystal.

"No!" Crystal yelled. "I don't want to scare this guy off."

"And you sure this is our guy?" Mark tucked his cell phone away and checked his weapon.

"I'm sure. He knew things that only the real Breath Taker would know."

Crystal's last statement caused Mark to look up and turn to her. "Like what?"

"I'll brief you on it later," Crystal snapped. She turned off the sirens and slowed the car down as she approached the hotel. With the exception of the flickering of a neon light, the hotel parking lot looked quiet. Crystal noticed that the rooms looked like single-floor row houses. Each room had a separate entrance from the parking lot. Although this particular hotel was known to be popular among truckers and prostitutes, the empty parking lot indicated that this was a slow night for the establishment.

"Okay, this is your show, DC," Mark said. "What's the game plan?"

"This guy left a key at the front desk for me, so I'm going to get the key and go into the room. I should be able to cuff him without incident. Then we can find out if he is our guy or not."

"So, what do you want me to do?"

"Find a good spot to see the room and keep an eye on the parking lot," Crystal said. "When you see me go into the room, give me five minutes. That's it. Five minutes. And if I'm not out by then haul ass in that room and back me up!"

"Okay, DC," Mark replied. "I got it. Five minutes."

"Yes, five minutes. That should give me enough time to get him comfortable and bag him up."

"Let's do it," Mark said.

Crystal checked her weapon one more time before both detectives got out of the car. Mark jogged in front of Crystal to get a head start on finding a good hiding spot to lay low. Seconds later, Crystal looked at her watch and picked up the pace. She groomed herself one last time as she approached the entrance to the hotel. She tried her best to ignore her butterflies, but was clearly nervous and didn't really didn't know what to expect. She took one final deep breath and exhaled slowly as she walked over to the check-in window. Crystal could see an old lady watching television just beyond the thick glass. She rang the bell and summoned the attendant.

"How can I help you?" The old lady asked walking over to the window.

Crystal could barely here her weak voice. "Yes, someone was supposed to leave a key for me."

"Your name?"

Crystal raised her voice hoping the elderly woman would hear her. "Actually it should be under ESP."

"Esp…esp…esp," the old lady repeated as she looked for the hotel key. After a few seconds she found a small white envelope and slipped it under the window.

"Okay, Ms. ESP, here is the key. It's Room #18 around the back. Have fun."

Crystal gave the old lady and gentle smile and dropped her eyebrows. The old lady's words were out of place, but Crystal decided to ignore the omen. She took the small key and headed for the room.

"Okay…here we go," Crystal whispered to herself and took a deep breath.

She reached around her back and checked her weapon again as she approached Room #18. Now, with everything in place she was ready to apprehend her suspect. Crystal slowly walked in front of the hotel door. Most of the lights were off in the room which made it difficult for her to see inside.

After a brief moment, Crystal nervously knocked on the door. When she thought she heard a noise come from inside the room, she waited for a second, but couldn't hear anything else. Moments later, Crystal took the key from inside the envelope and slowly placed it in the doorknob. A funny feeling came over her, but she ignored it and walked inside.

"Hello?" Crystal gingerly whispered as she stepped into the dark room. "Is anyone here?"

She reached for the light switch and turned it on. Crystal noticed some clothing and a pair of shoes tossed in a corner, but there was no one in the there. Suddenly, she heard a noise come from the bathroom that startled her. Crystal reached for her gun. A shadow from under the door indicated that she was not alone in the hotel room. Crystal's heart skipped another beat. She raised her gun and pointed it directly toward the bathroom. Crystal then squeezed the weapon tighter when she noticed the doorknob on the bathroom door turning. The killer was about to reveal his face. Crystal put both hands on her weapon as the door opened up.

"Put your fucking hands in the air right now!" Crystal yelled at the man who was coming out of the bathroom. Her adrenaline kicked into overdrive as the man stumbled into the bedroom.

"Whoa…whoa...hold on!" the man yelled as he put his head down and raised his hands in the air. The man continued to plead as he stood nervously near the bathroom entrance wearing nothing but a pair of boxer shorts. Something about his voice was very familiar to Crystal. She continued to yell commands to him as she moved closer to the middle of the room.

"Wait a minute!" the man yelled. "I'm a police officer."

"Shut the fuck up and keep your hands raised!" Crystal was about to walk over to him when she recognized his face. Crystal stopped dead in her tracks. "What the hell? Is that you Captain Reilly?"

The man slowly raised his head in embarrassment. Crystal's jaw dropped at the sight. It was her boss, Captain Reilly with his hands raised standing just a few feet from her.

"What are you doing here Captain?" Crystal angrily barked.

"Oh, my God this is all wrong," Reilly mumbled. For the first time in her career Crystal saw fear come to his eyes. "I can explain this," he continued as he frantically looked around the room. "Something's not right here. I was supposed to meet somebody here. What are you doing here?"

"I need you to stay still Captain," Crystal commanded. "The question is what exactly are you doing here?"

Reilly noticed Detective Crystal was becoming more agitated by the moment. Reilly kept his hands raised. He was clearly shocked at the situation that was unfolding before his eyes. He decided to obey her, but Reilly also needed to plead with her.

"How did you know to come here?" Reilly questioned. He kept his hands raised.

"I'm following up on a lead," Crystal replied. Her adrenaline was still pumping, so she kept her weapon raised on him. Reilly opened his mouth and was about to speak when a loud crash came from the front entrance. It was Detective Mark rushing into the hotel room.

"Keep your hands up you son-of-a-bitch!" Mark screamed as he entered the room. He quickly looked at Crystal as she turned to him. "Is this our guy?" he yelled. Mark turned to the man near the bathroom and almost choked on his own air. "What the fuck is going on here? Captain Reilly is that you?" Reilly didn't say a word.

"I don't know what the fuck is going on here Mark, Crystal said. "I came into the room and he was here. So, I guess he's the Breath Taker."

Captain Reilly's eyes grew as wide as headlights as he stared at both detectives. All the blood in his face seemed to disappear as the fear mounted. "What? Wait!" Reilly pleaded. "You guys got this all wrong. What? You think I'm the internet predator? You guys got this all wrong. We need to work this out another way!" Reilly made an unexpected move toward the other side of the room.

"Wait Captain...don't move!" Crystal yelled. She raised her gun again.

"Don't do it Captain keep your hands up!" Mark commanded. "Don't you fucking move!"

Reilly ignored the commands and reached into the corner. Crystal tried to plead with him as she pointed her gun directly at him.

Bang...Bang...Bang...Bang...Bang...Bang! Six loud gunshots rang out in the hotel room. Crystal screamed in horror as she watched four bullets enter into Captain Reilly's chest area.

"JESUS CHRIST! NO!" Crystal yelled. She rushed over to Captain Reilly, who was now slumped over in the corner near the bed. She turned around to Detective Mark and noticed that he still had his gun raised. She could still see the smoke slowly disseminating from the barrel.

"Why the fuck did you do that?" Crystal yelled. "Are you crazy?"

"Holy shit!" Mark grunted. "He was going for his gun. You saw him! He was going for his gun!"

Crystal quickly turned around and turned her focused on Reilly. He was barely breathing when Crystal laid him flat on his back and lifted his legs.

"Reilly hang in there," Crystal whispered. A few tears came to her eyes as she watched her Captain suffer from the hot gunshots. "It's not that bad Captain," Crystal whispered. She turned around and looked at Mark, who was standing in the middle of the room emotionless. "Call an ambulance Mark! Why are you just standing there?"

Mark grabbed the radio from his hip and went outside. Crystal could hear him radio in for an ambulance to be rushed out to the Motor Lodge.

"Captain, hang in there." Crystal grabbed his hand. The fear in his eyes was unimaginable. She noticed Reilly's body was barely responding. His blood was leaking heavily now as the bullets continued to cause massive internal damage. Reilly looked at Crystal and tried to speak.

"I was going…" Reilly whispered.

"Shhhh…. Shhh…." Crystal whispered. "Save your strength Captain."

"I was going … for ...my clothes," Reilly mumbled. "My clothes…. I was …trying to…trying to put my clothes on."

Mores tears began to flow from Crystal's face as she watched Reilly battle for his life. She squeezed his hand tighter. Mark was still outside on the radio and Crystal turned around to find him.

"It's okay Captain," Crystal whispered as she continued to look for Mark. "Hang in there. You're going to be okay."

"ESP," Reilly whispered.

Crystal quickly turned back to Reilly. "What did you just say Captain."

"ESP," Reilly repeated.

Crystal eyes lit up when she heard the letters. "Where did you get that from Captain?"

Reilly couldn't answer her as he began to have trouble breathing. His body began to shake uncontrollably.

"Hold on Captain," Crystal frantically said.

Reilly couldn't hear her. The bullets were doing irrevocable damage to his body and Crystal could sense it. She watched helplessly as his eyes rolled into the back of his head and Captain Reilly took his last breath. She squeezed his limp hand tighter but there was no response. Crystal knew he was dead. She sobbed and stayed by his side until the ambulance arrived at the hotel.

VII

Wednesday August 12, 2009
Newark Police Department (4ᵗʰ Precinct)
3 Weeks Later
11:08 a.m.

"Welcome back Crystal it's good to see you," a fellow officer said, as she walked into the door.

It had been almost twenty days since Crystal stepped foot into the 4ᵗʰ Precinct in Newark. But to the melancholy Detective it seemed like a lifetime. Crystal's mood was sinking near the depths of outright depression as she walked through the quiet hallways of the police department. Losing her mentor, confidant and boss was a hard fact for Crystal to accept. But after a mandatory paid leave of absence, she was unsure of what her future would be as a Newark Police Officer.

"Wow, I didn't expect to see you back in here so soon," a familiar voice said just off to the side of Crystal. She turned around just in time to see her partner Detective Mark walking toward her. "How are you holding up?" he asked.

Crystal was surprised to see him. She'd only heard from Mark a few times since the incident at the Motor Lodge. She nervously smiled at him and gave him a hug. "I'm doing much better. It's been tough for me these past few weeks."

"I know it has," Mark somberly agreed.

Suddenly, a loud ring came from Crystal's cell phone startling the detective. She quickly reached for her hip and grabbed the phone. She noticed it was Detective Roman calling from the Rahway Police Department. She had no clue as to why he was calling so she decided to ignore his call. Crystal put the phone back on her hip and turned her attention back to Mark, who was staring at her closely.

"So, have you made up your mind about moving forward with the department?" Mark asked.

"I have," Crystal mumbled as she purposely looked away from Mark. "I have decided to leave the force."

Mark was shocked. "Are you sure? That seems a bit extreme DC. You're a good cop."

"It doesn't matter really," Crystal said. "With Reilly gone, I really don't have a lot of trust in the badge anymore. So, I'm giving my one week notice today."

Mark started to shake his head. He was visibly baffled by the news. "I don't know DC, this seems to be rushed. But listen I have to go into this meeting right now. We can talk when I get out. They're considering promoting me."

Crystal turned back to Mark. "Promotion?" She was stunned.

"Yes," Mark continued. "It's all a shock to me, too."

"To what?" Crystal quickly asked. "Promoting you to what?"

"Captain," Mark proudly answered.

A cold chill shot through Crystal's body. She was beyond words. Mark picked up on the strange reaction and decided not to pursue it. He looked at his watch again.

"I should be out in fifteen minutes," Mark said. "I hope you're still here when I get out. If you need me I will be in the conference room."

Crystal watched as Mark quickly shuffled off to his meeting. The news of the promotion was almost a smack in the face to her boss. The man that killed him during a botched arrest was now considering replacing him at the helm of the department. Crystal felt sick to her stomach. She headed to her office and quickly took a seat behind her desk.

"I have to get away from here," Crystal whispered to herself as she sat back in her chair.

The look and smell of the office began to bring back many

memories of her time as a police detective. Memory after memory flashed into her mind like movie scenes. Crystal tried her best to focus on the good times, but the images of her Captain invaded her mind. Her emotional trip down memory lane was abruptly interrupted by a loud knocking on her office door. She quickly came back to reality and turned her attention to the visitor.

"Come in…it's open!" Crystal yelled.

She was shocked to see a familiar face walk into her office. It was Detective Roman. When Crystal saw the detective her face lit up. She stood up to greet him.

"Oh, wow, this is a surprise," Crystal said, as the two shook hands. "What brings you all the way up here to Newark?"

"How are you?" Roman asked as a wide smile grew on his face. "I called when I was outside, but your phone went straight to voicemail."

"Yes," Crystal said, recalling how she ignored his call. "I was talking to my partner Mark about something important."

"Speaking of Mark," Roman continued. "That's who I was coming to talk to. He has been bugging me about bringing him some evidence from the Brenda Owens' case. So, I decided to bring it up here before we closed her file."

Crystal tilted her head and stared at Roman. "When did you talk to Detective Mark?"

"We've been corresponding now for about two weeks," Roman replied. "He asked me to specifically contact him if there was any other evidence found on the crime scene."

"Is that right?" Crystal questioned as she walked back to her desk. "Mark didn't tell me that at all when I spoke to him."

"Oh, I didn't know that."

"It's okay," Crystal replied as she sat back in her chair. She offered Roman a seat and watched as he sat behind Mark's desk. She began to think about Roman's last comments. Something seemed out of place as more angles about the case entered into her mind. Roman watched her drift into thinking mode and decided to proceed with his conversation.

"If you want, I can give you the remaining articles from the scene," Roman said, breaking the silence in the room.

"Oh yes…sorry. So, what type of evidence do you have? Is it a large package?"

"Not at all," Roman replied. "To the contrary, it's actually only a few items left. The rest should be here within a few weeks from the crime lab."

Crystal nodded her head as she watched Roman remove a small package from his jacket pocket. He slid the orange envelope over to her.

"This is it," Roman mumbled.

Crystal quickly opened the envelope and dumped the contents onto her desk. There were three items. Crystal grabbed the hotel swipe card and looked at it.

"That's the duplicate hotel key that was under the bed," Roman informed. "It had no prints on it and was probably wiped clean."

"Oh, okay," Crystal groaned. "And I guess this is her earring and fingernail file?"

"Yes."

Crystal twisted her face up. "And this is what Mark was bugging you for? These three items?"

"Three items?" Roman said. "What about the contact lens?"

"Contact lens?" Crystal surprisingly whispered

Roman frisked his body for another package. He reached in his other jacket pocket and removed another orange envelope.

"I'm sorry," Detective Roman said. "Here is the last envelope. We also found a contact lens in the hotel room. It wasn't the victim's contact lens. We're thinking it may have been in the room before they got there or maybe our guy left it."

Crystal felt a cold chill rush down her arms as she grabbed the last envelope from Roman. She opened it and saw a small evidence bag inside. Her heart started pounding when she saw the brown contact lens. Roman watched her closely and noticed her mood was changing as Crystal examined the contact lens. He repositioned himself in his chair.

"What do you think?" Roman said.

"I can't believe this son-of-a-bitch!" Crystal barked. "This son-of-a-bitch!"

"What Detective? What is it?" Roman quickly asked.

Crystal frantically picked up the phone and dialed the conference room. After a brief moment she heard someone pick up the other line.

"Hello…yes this is Detective Crystal. Please tell Detective Mark to come to his office immediately. It's an emergency. I think we found the real Breath Taker. Please tell him to hurry. It's an emergency! Tell him to come now!" Crystal quickly hung up the phone and stood up behind her desk. Roman watched her as she paced back and forth and began to talk to herself.

"This son-of-a-bitch!" Crystal repeated. "Why didn't I see it before? This son-of-a-bitch!"

"I don't understand Detective. Who is it?" Roman asked. "I thought they caught the Breath Taker already."

Crystal ignored Roman. She rushed back over to her desk and quickly opened the drawer. She pulled out her service weapon and reloaded it. As Crystal went to close her drawer she heard a loud crash from the front of her office. It was Mark rushing through the door.

"What the hell is going on DC?" Mark yelled as he ran through the door and entered the office.

In an unexpected move, Crystal immediately ran over to Mark and punched him square in the jaw. The loud commotion startled Roman. Mark fell against the wall from the impact of the punch and grabbed his face. Crystal quickly backed away from Mark and raised her gun at him. Everyone in the room was stunned by her reaction. Even Roman stood up and backed away from the desk.

"Put your hands up motherfucker!" Crystal yelled at Mark as he tried to gather himself.

"Whoa!" Mark stuttered as he slowly rose to his feet. "What the fuck did you do that for?"

"You are under arrest for the murder of Brenda Owens and Captain Shane Reilly," Crystal sternly said. She was staring right into Mark's eyes when she delivered the news.

"Are you insane?" Mark yelled. A nervous smirk came to

his face as he checked his lip for blood. "DC, I didn't murder anyone. You were there when Captain Reilly made his move. Put the gun down."

"I'm not going to tell you again!" Crystal yelled. She raised her weapon slightly higher to show him that she was dead serious about his arrest. "Put....your fucking...hands up. You're under arrest Mark! Detective Roman can you take Detective Mark into custody."

"This is ridiculous," Mark said. Now, he wasn't smiling anymore. He looked over to Roman, who was still stunned.

"I can't do that Crystal," Roman stated. "Where's the proof?"

Before Crystal could answer another female officer burst through the door to investigate the commotion. She quickly turned to Mark.

"What's going on here?" the female officer yelled.

"Please, take Detective Mark into custody!" Crystal yelled at the female officer.

"No!" Mark quickly replied. "As your Acting Police Captain, I'm ordering you to arrest Detective Crystal for assaulting a police officer."

"What?" the confused female officer said to both of them.

"Do it now!" Mark yelled at the female officer. "Arrest her!"

The female officer raised her gun and pointed it at Crystal. The room fell silent as the tension mounted. Crystal never acknowledged the other officer as she kept her attention on Mark.

"I know it was you Mark!" Crystal continued. She was becoming more emotional with every word. "You set him up! How could you do that?"

"I don't know what in the world you're talking about DC!" Mark yelled. "You're obviously delusional."

"And you're a murderer," Crystal countered.

"Prove it!" Mark angrily yelled.

Crystal quickly reached for her desk and grabbed the clear evidence bag. She raised it up and showed it to Mark.

"Contact lens!" Crystal snapped. "Brown contact lens!

Found the day before you went to get your new contact lenses Mark. What did she do…put up a struggle and hit you in the eye before you killed her?"

"This is ridiculous!" Mark barked. He frantically looked over to Detective Roman, who was now staring at him differently.

"Is it ridiculous?" Crystal said. "Who else could've put me and Captain Reilly at the same place at the same time? It was you."

Mark was becoming increasingly nervous. The spotlight was on him. The room fell silent again as he looked around.

"Is that all you got DC?" Mark whispered. "A contact lens? You're going to need more than that to make me stand down."

Crystal didn't say a word as her eyes twitched a little. She was also becoming nervous. She knew her allegations could land her in some serious hot water if she was wrong. And now that she put the heat on Mark, she knew he was going to hold this vendetta against her forever. She quickly looked around the room and stopped at Mark's computer. A light bulb went off in her head that made her expression change.

"You're right Mark," Crystal calmly spoke. "Detective Roman can you please sit down at my partner's desk and fire up his computer. I think I have all the proof I need."

Detective Roman was reluctant to follow the order, but he sat back down at the desk and turned on the computer. Mark nervously looked over to Crystal as he tried to figure out where she was going with her next move.

"You knew who the Breath Taker was this whole time didn't you Mark?" Crystal quickly questioned. "That's why we couldn't catch him. Because it was you! And when the Captain was getting close you decided to set him up."

Mark never said a word. His eyes grew wider and wider with every word from Crystal's mouth. The female officer next to him kept her weapon on Crystal as she continued to speak.

"But one thing you didn't count on was the brilliant mind of Captain Reilly," Crystal said.

"It's asking me for a password," Roman said, as he kept his hands on the keyboard.

"Give him the password?" Crystal said to Mark. "It's your

computer, give him the password."

"I'm not giving him shit!" Mark blurted out. His response seemed to heat up the room a few more degrees.

"Don't worry Mark; my *real* Captain already gave it to me," Crystal shot back. She took a deep breath. The drama in the room made her heart thump with anticipation. Mark's jaw tightened.

"Detective Roman," Crystal continued. "Try these three letters. E- S- P!"
Crystal put a tighter grip on her weapon as she heard the clicking of the keyboard. Roman carefully typed the three letters.

"It worked," Roman surprisingly said.

Crystal closed her eyes and let out a gasp of relief. She knew she had her man.

"Oh my God," Roman said. "He has everything on this computer. Reilly's cell phone records, internet passwords, the other victims' address…everything!"

Crystal turned back to Mark. His face was frozen with a demonic expression. Mark realized he'd been exposed. He turned to Crystal and stared at her. The female officer looked over to Crystal as she also was shocked at the news.

"How could you do it Mark?" Crystal calmly asked. "What possessed you to kill those women?"

Mark didn't say another word. He looked down for a brief second and decided to make a run for it. Crystal didn't know how to react as Mark grabbed the female officer next to him. He quickly knocked her to the ground and bolted out the door.

"Goddamit!" Crystal yelled as she tried to chase him. She was held up for a second as she tripped over the female officer struggling to catch her balance. Roman stood up and ran behind Crystal as both detectives chased after Mark. They watched as he scurried out the front door and into the parking lot.

"Shit!" Crystal yelled, as she continued running.

Roman was right behind her when they made it outside the precinct. Mark was no where to be found. Crystal looked around and spotted his car in the back of the parking lot. She raised her gun and rushed over to the car. More officers rushed out the building with their weapons drawn. Crystal became intensely nervous as she ran up to Mark's car. Mark was inside the driver seat, but he was reaching over to his glove box.

"Don't do nothing stupid, Mark!" Crystal yelled as she ran in front of the car.

She watched him grab a small bottle and twist the cap off. He quickly put the bottle to his lips. Crystal was confused. She rushed to his car door and tried to open it but it was locked. Mark continued to drink the contents from the bottle as Crystal banged on the window.

"Get out the car, Mark!" Crystal began to shout. "Don't make this harder than it has to be!"

Mark started gagging as he tossed the bottle to the side. Crystal watched him as he struggled for air.

"Oh my God!" Crystal screamed.

She took a step back from the car and pointed her gun at the back door. She fired a loud shot that shattered the back window. Roman rushed over just in time to see her reach through the shattered glass and pop the front lock. She opened the driver side door and pulled Mark out of the car. He was still violently gasping for air. His face was nearly blue as Mark was tragically losing the battle to stay alive. Roman rushed to the other side of the car and opened the door. He grabbed the bottle and noticed that Mark had just drunk a lethal dose of Hemlock oil. He shook his head at the irony.

"I think it's too late for him," Roman stated. "He literarily took his own medicine."

Crystal slowly shook her head in disbelief as Mark struggled for his life. She watched in horror as his neck swelled from the poison and his airways closed up on him. Mark tried to speak but he was unable to.

Another cold chill rushed through Crystal's body. She battled with a mix of emotions watching her partner. The emotional side of her was sad to see Mark suffer such a gruesome fate. To watch his body convulsing in pain and his lungs being shut off from the precious air by the poison. She felt remorseful. But in the very deep, dark and secretive corner of her heart, Crystal's cynical side smiled at the fact that she had finally caught the real Breath Taker. And the sight of him taking his final *breath* in her presence was that much sweeter.

HOUSE OF SIN
J. TREMBLE

ONE

How the fuck did I end up like this? I stared at the knife dug deep in my chest, while on the cold bathroom floor inside the House of Sin. This was not supposed to be my future. I had so many big plans. I should've been the next Johnny Cochran, winning major cases that would change the world. Never in my wildest dreams did I see myself becoming an exotic dancer having to shake my most prized possession, *my dick* for money.

It all began in my Howard University dorm room a couple of weeks ago. Staring at the tuition bill with my name, Jerome Stewart printed across the top, I realized the cost of my education was going up, but my scholarship was remaining the same. Being the first person in my family to go to college meant I had a lot of pressure to graduate. I grew up in the Simple City projects on public assistance with my mother to take care of me and seven other siblings. Other guys in my dorm just picked up the phone and called home for more money, but I didn't have that luxury.

My only option was to get a loan from Big Gee, the numbers guy that my old freshmen year room-mate used for his bets on the horses. I thought I could just pay my tuition and then repay the loan when my income tax refund arrived. I didn't know how these loans worked. How was I supposed to know that the interest would grow so fast? Before I knew it, I was into that loan shark for twelve grand. Big Gee gave me two weeks to come up with his money or he would send some guys over to break my legs.

I remembered spending hours sitting at my oak desk staring out my large windows trying to come up with a solution to my problems. My concentration was so focused, that the phone had stopped ringing before I noticed it. With two quick flicks of a permanent marker, another day was marked off my desk calendar. Leaning back in my chair, I continued to dwell on my situation, which was slowly sucking all the energy out of me.

The deadline for my payment was one day closer. As I opened the desk drawer to put the marker away, a small card caught my attention. The owner of the House of Sin had slipped the card into my shorts one evening at the gym after eyeing me like one of her favorite treats. She talked a real good game, but she didn't fit into my plans. Any other time, the card would've gone into the trash, but my options were dwindling down to none. After shaking my head a couple of times, I reached for the phone and dialed the number. She answered, listened to me as if she'd been expecting my call, then told me to come down for a quick look later that evening; 10 o'clock sharp. It was already past eight, so after hanging up, I went to get dressed. Something deep in my gut told me it was the wrong move to make, but I didn't have another choice. My back was against the wall.

When I looked at the address, the one good thing was that the club was right up the street from my school. I must've driven past it without even noticing, a thousand times. When I pulled up in front of the building an hour later, unnoticing it before was now quite obvious. The club didn't look at all impressive. It was a red brick building with paint chips peeling off the sides and a large rusty door, at the corner of Georgia and Sherman Avenue North-west. Even the Christmas lights around the perimeter of the building with several missing several bulbs looked ghetto.

A few women were in line when I parked my car in the gravel parking lot of the Murry's Store across the street. Majority of the women were on the heavy side, but I noticed a dime or two. They all stared me down focusing on the way my jeans cuffed my bulge. They way all their eyes followed me, I felt pretty uncomfortable about all the looks, since I was the only guy in line. The bouncer even gave me a crazy look when I asked about the cover charge.

"You do understand that this is a male strip club, right?" the bouncer asked.

"Yeah, I'm here to meet Mary Ann," I replied.

"Oh, then there's no cover for you, but there is a two drink minimum at the bar, even if you are here to see Mary Ann," he said, patting me down.

I felt like a little boy as the bouncer did his job. My six foot two inch frame was nothing next to him. After being a little humiliated, I slowly walked into the club through a black curtain. I glanced back to see all the women still checking out my ass before the door closed. There were cherry oak tables and chairs on both sides of a long wooden stage. Black leather sofas and bar stools lined the walls. Long brass poles touched the ceiling. I took a seat in a booth next to the bathroom and watched the women yell and holler as if it were New Year's Eve.

"I'm feeling freaky tonight. Let's get this party started!" a dark skin woman yelled from the crowd.

A chubby woman at the bar held up her singles. "Hell yeah, I've got money to spend, and I want to feel some big dicks rubbing up and down my body."

Moments later, the long black curtains on the stage opened slightly and out walked a petite woman with short straight black hair. She had on a tight leopard print dress that stopped right beneath her butt cheeks. Even though she had on three inch heels, she still had to raise the microphone to accommodate her five foot two frame.

"Welcome to the House of Sin!" she shouted into the mic.

The women began to scream and shake their hands filled with money high into the air. Suddenly, the DJ quickly blasted, *Duffle Bag Boy* by Playaz Circle through the many speakers. Women popped out their seats and danced in small groups along side the cherry oak wood stage with brass poles that outlined the perimeter.

"My name is Mary Ann, but you can call me Sensual."

"Hey Sensual!" the crowd of women shouted in unison.

"I've got just one question. Are you ladies ready for a good time?"

"Yeah!" the crowd shouted.

"If you're ready for a good time, let me hear you say, "hell yeah!" Sensual belted, walking back and fourth on the stage.

"Hell yeah!" everyone screamed.

Sensual waved at some of the regular guests and blew kisses to others. "Please get that money ready. The first dancer of the night will be Mr. Marlin Tucker better known as Tranquil!" Sensual shouted as she pulled the microphone stand off the stage.

"Oh, yes. I love Tranquil's dick. He can get some anytime, anywhere!" one of the ladies yelled.

The music quickly switched from the house shaking rap song to Keith Sweat's, *Make It Last Forever*. Seconds later, the black curtains opened and a gurney with a body covered in a white sheet stood in the middle of the stage. The crowd went into frenzy when Tranquil strolled out wearing ass-less hospital pants, no shirt, hospital booties over his feet and a surgeon's mask covering his mouth and nose.

Tranquil started by dancing around the stage seductively. The light reflecting off the baby oil on his muscular chest caused the women's scream's to pierce my ears, especially when he danced his way to the right side of the gurney. Tranquil lowered his body to check for a heart beat, then pulled an arm from under the sheet to feel for a pulse. When he didn't feel anything, he twirled away from the gurney and snatched off his pants.

The screams got even louder. The women rocked in their chairs as they watched the sweat bead up on his smooth bald head. The muscles in his dark chocolate legs bulged as his dick swung inside his white homemade dick sleeve.

"Look at the size of that dick!" a lady yelled out.

The regular club goers knew right away that she must've been new. All the dancers at the House of Sin had dicks. The smallest pipe on any of the guys would probably measure at ten inches.

Suddenly, Tranquil yanked off the sheet and exposed his female, plastic blow up doll lying on the gurney. He picked her up and danced around holding her in his strong muscular arms. He then pressed her against his chest and walked near the edge of the stage.

I watched as the women threw money onto the stage and shoved more into the strap around his thigh. Tranquil moved back away from the edge, paused in the middle of the stage, looked around the club then stuck his dick inside the manufactured vagina of the doll. When the plastic woman exploded seconds later and flew around the stage, the women yelled again as the curtains quickly closed.

"Now, that's how you get the party started," Sensual said, walking back onto the stage. "Remember ladies, the guys do their routines then the real fun starts when they come down there with you and work the crowd." Sensual gave a salivating woman in the front row a high five.

"The next pair of dancers coming to the stage shouldn't need any introduction. If you think you're seeing double, it's because you are. The Latin twins known during the day as Rico and Nico Brown. Give it up ladies for Scandalous and Insatiable."

When the women began clapping and screaming, Sensual walked off the stage and told Princess, one of the money collectors to finish the introductions. After making her way from backstage, she waltzed out front and up to my booth. She looked different from when we first met. Her light brown eyes sparkled in the club lights, and the wonder bra she wore made her double D's look like missiles. I even noticed that Sensual had a little hour glass to her shape as I sat drinking a Rum and Coke on ice. She slid in the booth next to me.

"So, Jerome, what do you think so far?" she asked with a wide smile.

"Is this club all yours?"

"Yep, it's all mine. My brother wants to get in on the action, but I keep him at a distance. Why'd you ask that question?"

I gave a short smirk, lifted my shoulders and put my glass back on the table. "It's really electric up in here. Are the women always this out of control?" I responded trying to change the subject.

"Women are no different than men. When the lights start lowering and they get a few drinks into their systems, anything is possible. I've been doing this for a long time. I know for a fact that my customers are going to love you. You'll make a killing here. However, I was just wondering what made you change your mind and call me. You didn't seem interested when I gave you my card," Sensual said.

I didn't want to tell her about my debt with Big Gee, so I said the first thing I could think of. "I need some rims for my car and my tuition has increased. The partial scholarship they gave me will only cover about three fourths of what's needed. The last fourth of the tuition and the cost for my books make it crucial, so I need to find something that pays well and pays fast. That's why the call to you wasn't a hard one to make."

A loud scream from the crowd caused both of us to raise our heads and glance over at the stage. A huge smile came over Sensual's face as she saw, David Lagner better known as Unpredictable shaking it on stage. She loved how her only white boy worked the predominantly black crowd. He gyrated his hips to the old-school tune, *Play That Funky Music White Boy* by Parliament.

Damn, where did the twins go that fast, I thought as I watched the white guy dance. "Shit, if the white boy can do this, I can too," I said, looking at Sensual.

"Don't sleep. The white boy is bad. I tell him all the time that his great grandfather must've fucked a slave girl because his eleven inch dick is no joke."

"I can't wait to get on that stage."

"So, are you saying that you're gonna take the job and join the House of Sin dream team?" Sensual questioned.

"Hell yeah. I want the job."

Sensual stood up. "Great, the first thing we have to do is

give you a name. What do you think about Incredible?"

My eyes squinted. "You already have an Insatiable and Unpredictable. I don't think you need another dancer with similar syllables."

"Well, do you have a name in mind?"

"What about Big Bone?"

"My brother told me you would be great for business. That's why I came to the gym to check you out. That's why I asked you down, but in order to get a name like that, I gotta check out what you're working with down there. Pull that Big Bone out."

"Who's your brother?" I asked curiously.

"Don't worry about that, just show me your dick," Sensual ordered.

I didn't hesitate. I reached down and unbuttoned the front of my pants then used one hand to pull down the front of my pants and underwear. Using my other hand, I pulled out and held my thick penis for Sensual to inspect.

"That's a nice size piece you have, but I don't think it's worthy of the name, Big Bone. Your dick looks real smooth like the skin of a snake or the fabric of a night gown. How about Cobra or Silk?"

"Neither works for me. My dick is no reptile. Besides, most women are afraid of snakes, and I don't want any woman to be fearful of my Johnson. That's not the picture I have of my dick. It's more like a never ending playground for women," I replied.

A large smile took over her face. "I've got the perfect name. You'll be called Stamina." Sensual sat back down and held up her drink that had automatically been brought over to her. "Let's make a toast to my newest dancer, Stamina."

I gave a half smile. The name had a good ring to it. I grabbed my drink, tipped it in her direction and took it to the head. When I finished shaking my head from the chill, I looked over to see the last dancer, Gyro on stage. The dancers face was very familiar to me. *That's the metro bus driver who works downtown on the H line,* I thought.

Gyro worked the stage to the song, *Low* by Flo-Rida. His long black and tinted gray dreadlocks swung all around his head.

Gyro had muscles on top of muscles. I couldn't remember him looking so fit sitting in the driver's seat.

"Do you wanna make a little money tonight?" Sensual asked.

A vision of me going back to the dorm and a couple of Big Gee's boys jumping from behind corners whipping my ass up and down the hallway popped into my head. I quickly answered, "Hell yeah."

"Come on then Stamina, let's go back stage and find you an outfit. You'll just work the floor tonight serving drinks as the guys work the stage. I'll work you into the schedule for this weekend," she said getting up.

I followed like a hen-pecked man as Sensual gave out high fives making her way to the back room. A few women smacked my ass as I walked through the crowd trying to keep up with my new boss. When I looked back and gave a flash with my pearly white teeth, several other women yelled for me to work it. I felt like a hooker down at the construction site on payday.

Once in the back, Sensual instantly instructed me to search through outfits hanging up on a metal rack. However, I didn't see anything that caught my eye. I stopped at a pair of leather chaps with the ass cut out, but decided that shit wasn't me. On another hanger was a red silk cape with gold trim around the collar. *Neither of these will go with the name, Stamina.*

Moments later, Sensual pulled out a pair of black silk boxers and a multi-colored bow tie. "Here you go."

I looked over to see the outfit in her hand, then slowly shook my head back and forth, thinking *what the fuck*?

"Don't even trip," she said. "Get used to this crazy shit. The women love it."

With extreme hesitation, I grabbed the boxers and the ridiculous tie, and quickly decided that some baby oil was needed to go along with the crazy ass attire.

Moments later, all the dancers walked in from the club's main room. They paused when they got to the clothes rack. All of them looked at me with a puzzled stare.

Sensual frowned. "What the hell you guys waiting on? This

is no time for introductions. Get y'all ass back out there and make that money. Those ladies are ready to get their groove on. Don't disappoint any of them. It's like I always say, a good dick will make a woman happy and a happy woman will give that good dick her entire pay check, especially if that dick makes her feel like she's the only one. Now, go out there and make them feel like they're the only special one!" she shouted to get their attention.

Not wanting to hear another one of Sensual's lectures, the dancers quickly snatched their outfits off the rack, changed, then made their way back out front. A few seconds later, the DJ cranked the music.

"You too. Hurry up and put your shit on," Sensual said, clapping her hands. "Time is money." She waited for me to change into my tiny boxers. Afterwards, I rubbed my chiseled body down with some peach body oil until my muscles shined. She eyed my body up and down. "Damn, you look good. Now, let's go."

I began serving drinks immediately after Sensual walked me out to the long Silver Dollar Mahogany bar and introduced me to the bartender. I was amazed at how aggressive the women were with their hands. I'd never been pinched, smacked or groped so many times in my entire life. I felt a little dirty at first, but then figured it would keep Big Gee from killing me. It wasn't until I noticed the other guys picking up women, burying their faces into their crotches, fingering pussies under skirts and slapping their dicks against the women's face before I began to loosen up.

I was taking a drink order over to the bartender when I noticed a beautiful woman sitting at the far end of the bar. When she looked up, our eyes immediately met. I gave her a small head nod and grin. The woman returned a smile, then glanced back toward the dancers.

I slowly walked over to her. "Can I get you another drink?"

"No, I'm fine," she replied.

"You sure are...very beautiful actually. My name is Jerome, but you can call me Stamina."

"It's very nice to meet you, Stamina. I like that name. Did Sensual give it to you?"

I paused for a second. "Yeah, she did, but like I was about

to say, if you want to see some real dancing you need to come back on Saturday. I'll be making my debut," I smiled.

The woman looked me up and down, and then laughed.

"What's so funny?" I asked.

"If you're going to work around all these ladies, you'll need to control your manhood a little better. How can you just let him reach out and touch me before you even know my name?"

I glanced down and noticed my dick was getting ready to rip through the silk boxers, almost touching her lower leg. *I'm a total asshole*, I thought.

"It must be you. I've been poked, pinched and smacked by so many women without it getting hard until now. I guess he knows a truly attractive woman when he sees one," I said, trying to save face.

Gyro was in the middle of a twirl when he noticed the two of us at the bar. When he saw my erection damn near rubbing up against the woman, he immediately stopped dancing and walked toward the bar. Sensual quickly stepped in front of him.

"I'll take care of Sunshine. You just finish the set, and we'll talk about this later. He's new, he doesn't know any better," Sensual stated.

Gyro smacked Sensual's hand off of him, and continued toward us. "Hey, drink boy, that's the wrong woman!" he shouted at me.

I turned to find Gyro standing behind me. My erection quickly disappeared when I realized how big he was up close. I couldn't help it, but a small laugh slipped from my mouth when I noticed that he was also very old.

"I was just checking on the lady's drink," I finally replied.

"The kid doesn't know any better. Tonight is his first night. How would he know that Sunshine is with you?" Sensual asked, walking up and getting between us.

"What's wrong baby? I hope you weren't threatened by the size of his dick," Sunshine added getting up to rub Gyro's chest.

Gyro looked me up and down. "Little dick ain't got nothing on me. If anybody should feel threatened it's him. If I catch him in your face again, I'll break my foot off in his young ass."

"I need to see you in my office," Sensual said to me.

I glanced over Sensual's shoulders and made eye contact with Sunshine in the mirror behind the bar. Gyro was about to go back to work, but when he caught the two of us staring at each other, he snapped.

"What the fuck?" he yelled nudging me in my back. "I saw that shit!"

Sensual quickly pulled me behind her and stepped in front of Gyro. "Saw what?"

"Your little pretty boy was making goo-goo eyes at my woman even after I warned him. I saw him in the mirror!" Gyro belted.

"Old man, you need to grow some fucking balls. If you're so afraid of someone fucking your girl, you need to leave her at home or step up your game," I responded with a smirk.

Gyro balled up his fist. It appeared as if he was about to swing on me, but I was ready to defend myself. Moments later, one of the bouncer's ran up and grabbed him. Gyro started to pull away, but Sunshine grabbed both sides of his face, which quickly calmed his old ass down. Sensual then snatched my arm and dragged me into her office. She pulled me so hard that I lost my balance a couple of times.

"Sit your ass down," she ordered once the office door slammed.

"What did I do? This is like high school. I talk to a pretty girl and then bum, some weak ass nigga gets insecure and wants to square up."

"This ain't about high school. It's about you respecting other people. You gave Sunshine another look even after Gyro made a scene. That's your insecurity, not his," Sensual commented.

"Look, I'm sorry. What do you want me to do? I'll go back out there and apologize to old boy and his girl. Will that be enough? All I want to do is make some money to pay my bills," I replied.

"I'll handle Gyro and Sunshine. You just go home and get yourself together. You'll start this Saturday and your shit better be on point. All eyes will be on you."

I nodded my head. "Trust me, you won't be disappointed."

"Good."

"Now, can I go back out there?"

"Your young ass must be hard of hearing. No, I said go home," Sensual said, pointing to her office door.

After walking back into the dressing room, I took my time changing my clothes hoping that Sensual would change her mind and tell me to go back to the bar, but she didn't. When I walked out the dressing room and back onto the main floor, I locked eyes with Gyro as I slowly made my way across the club. He gave me a small shake of his head to let me know that this wasn't over. I simply gave him an "I don't give a fuck" smile in return and left.

TWO

I spent the remainder of the week in the gym making sure my body was tight and changing my routine, so I wouldn't run into Big Gee or his boys. Between the anticipation of my first night at the club and my phone ringing off the hook from Big Gee looking for his money, it was hard for me to concentrate in my Biology class. When I hit the number one to activate the messages on my voicemail, there was Big Gee yelling into the phone…as usual.

"You better have my fucking money or I swear to God, your mother won't even recognize your body when I'm done with your ass."

I had to make some money, and make it fast. The teacher was giving out a homework assignment, but instead of paying attention, I just stared at my watch. The long hand had barely touched the twelve and I was already making my way toward the door. I thought, *the hell with homework right now. The only thing I need to be taking home is some dough.*

By Saturday evening, my nerves were out of control as I parked my car and walked toward House of Sin. They turned to major butterflies when I entered the club. Looking at the stage, I began to visualize how my routine would go so I wouldn't be completely unprepared. Making a fool of myself wasn't an option. Walking in the back, I stopped outside of Sensual's office door that was slightly ajar, especially when I heard her and Tranquil yelling. After hearing the name, New Boy a couple of times, I knew they were talking about me. I instantly peeked through the crack.

"You have to be fucking with me?" Tranquil shouted.

"Look, I make the schedule around here," Sensual replied.

"It's my turn. I'm supposed to come out last. This is my Saturday. You can't give my night to the new boy."

Sensual laughed. "I do believe I'm the one who owns this place. I say who dances, when they dance, and how long they dance."

Tranquil took a deep breath. "When I started, you had me come out first every night for a month. Now, you're just gonna let that new nigga walk in here off the street and bump me. This shit is wrong!"

Sensual leaned back in her large leather chair and lit a cherry Black and Mild. Tranquil's little hissy-fit made her chuckle. "Whatever, Tranquil. I'm not changing my mind, so go ahead in the dressing room and bitch to the other guys like you always do."

As I watched Tranquil stand up, I quickly kept walking, so he wouldn't catch me eavesdropping. Besides, I wanted to make it into the dressing room before he did. Moments later, I slowly pushed the dressing room door open and stepped inside. The room had a real tense feeling as I walked in and the door closed behind me. I looked around wondering what all the guys were thinking as they stared at me like a museum exhibit. No one said a word.

Tranquil marched into the room shortly after with a huge frown on his face. He slammed the door, then threw a chair across the room into the far wall. "That fucking no good bitch!"

"What's wrong now, Tranquil?" Gyro asked.

"Fucking Sensual, she bumped me tonight from coming out last. I've waited a month to get my turn at prime time. I needed a big payday tonight."

"I was the bomb last Saturday. I guess she must want the white God to close the house again," the white boy, Unpredictable said with a laugh.

"Shut your white ass up. Who did she put in your place?" Gyro asked in a more serious tone.

"The new boy, I think she said his name is Jerome or something like that."

The room went completely silent. They all stared at Tranquil as if they were waiting on the punch line. Then all eyes fell on me, which caused Tranquil to look in my direction as well.

"You must be fucking Sensual's old ass," Tranquil said.

All the guys burst out laughing. Not wanting to be played for a fool, I was about to say something, but suddenly remembered my talk with Sensual. *Calm down, don't start no shit, you need to make some money*, I thought to myself. I ignored his invitation and obvious taunting. If I didn't need this job I would've smashed his punk ass, but I wasn't going to let anyone ruin this for me. Big Gee's boys and their threats put my priorities in order. So, I placed my duffle bag on the table and began to take out my stuff.

"Is that space over there free?" I asked.

One of the twin's Nico stood up. "You can use that spot over there," he said, pointing to an open counter.

"I guess there's a new sheriff in town, and I think his name is Stamina," the other twin added.

I looked around not knowing what was going on and again ignored their comments. Slowly, I walked over to the empty chair, sat down on the metal chair and reached down to untie the shoe strings on my Timberland boots. I pretended not to be concerned with what the guys were talking about, so I kept my head down.

"How are my men tonight?" Sensual asked stepping into the room. "Time for a dick inspection."

The guys moaned, but they quickly got up and formed a

line side by side; military style. Tranquil took his time, but eventually got in line too. I remained in my chair wondering what she meant by dick inspection. At that moment, they all reached inside their pants, pulled out their dicks and held them up like water hoses. I couldn't believe what they were doing.

"What you waiting for fresh meat? I always check out my men before we open the doors. It would be awful for business if any of my customers were to see an infected penis rubbing between their breast and thighs," she informed.

"The lady just likes to admire over sixty inches of good prime dick," Gyro said laughing.

"If the rookie is longer than ten inches, Sensual would control two yards worth of penis," Nico butted in.

Sensual smiled when Nico's words hit her ears. She glanced over at me still sitting in my chair. "Get your ass in line and take out that dick for inspection," she said in a harsh tone.

I slowly rose to my feet then walked over and stood next to Tranquil. When I opened my jeans and pulled out my dick, all the guys looked over expecting to see something amazing that would explain why Sensual put me in the prime spot.

"New boy ain't packing nothing special," Tranquil smirked. "You gave him my spot and all he has is that?"

Sensual didn't pay Tranquil's remark any attention. "Okay, it's time to oil your bodies and work those muscles. I feel tonight is going to be a big payday." Sensual smiled widely before walking out the door.

"This is some straight up bullshit!" Tranquil shouted.

Sensual stuck her head back into the room. "Oh yeah by the way, Tranquil, you'll be opening tonight." She looked him up and down then slammed the door.

Nico burst out into laughter. It didn't take long before the other guys joined in. I was the only one not laughing. Tranquil walked over to the chair he'd flung across the room and carried it back to its rightful place.

It seemed like he wanted to say, "Fuck it." He probably even thought about cursing Sensual out and leaving, but didn't. Hell, I'm sure that nigga had bills just like the rest of us. Tranquil sat down, rubbed his hands over his face then proceeded to get dressed since he was going out first.

As time passed, the screams from the women outside the dressing room started to get louder. I felt the butterflies zooming around inside my stomach as I heard Sensual opening up the club. I snickered a little when Tranquil got up to leave the dressing room in his ass-less cowboy chaps. The other guys shot me a cold stare.

"It ain't cool finding humor in another person's pain, Stamina, or whatever your damn name is. What goes around comes around. You need to remember that if you're gonna last here," Gyro said, standing up to put oil on his stomach.

Suddenly, the head bouncer, Rock came into the dressing room to tell us that the club was completely filled. Trying to get myself pumped, I sat in my chair working my dick. I wanted to be at full erection when it was my turn to step out on stage. The other dancers left the room one by one until I was all alone. Forty-five minutes later, the flashing red light over the door acknowledged my need to get on deck.

I walked out in my silk shorts, tied my dick to my right thigh and waited patiently behind the black curtain with my back facing the crowd. The butterflies had now turned into major knots deep inside my stomach. I closed my eyes, took a deep breath and tried to get control of my emotions.

"Alright ladies, you know what time it is," Sensual said. "It's time for the last dancer to hit the main stage and do his thing, and do I have a special treat for you tonight. For the first time here at the House of Sin, get your money ready for the club's newest heart throb…Staminaaaaaaa!" she roared.

The cheers instantly became deafening. The bass from the song, *Perfect Match* off the old School Daze sound track, shook the glasses on the tables near the stage. Then the black curtains slowly lifted into the ceiling. I turned to the crowd hiding my face with a black Mardi Gras mask connected to a stick.

The colorful lights shone off my glistening body as I moved around the stage to the music. I slowly made my way over to the pole down on the stage. When I threw the mask out into the crowd, it almost started a riot the way the women went wild. I climbed my way up the pole about half way, then stopped. Using my arms, I held myself up while gyrating my hips in a humping motion. Showing the ladies my moves, I continued the humping motion until I made my way back down to the stage. Ladies began to throw money on the stage instantly; ones, tens and twenties were everywhere.

"Work that pole again!" a woman shouted from the crowd.

"Come on ladies, let's see if we can pump him up to climbing the pole one more time," Sensual commented over the microphone.

The chant, "One more time, one more time," came from all the women in the room. I couldn't leave them hanging, so I twirled around the pole and began climbing up again. This time, I didn't stop at the halfway point. The women began to shout, "Go, go, go," until I reached the ceiling. Feeling like Superman, I grabbed a black beam then freed myself from the pole. Eyes widened in amazement as I hung over their heads.

When I swung my legs up to lock them on the beam, and hung upside down, the screams grew even louder. All the other dancers were now focused on me too. Releasing my legs, I let go of the beam with my left arm and began doing one arm pull ups to show the bulging muscles in my back. The women held their breath not knowing what I would do next.

I used my free hand to reach down and rip my silk boxers off and untie my dick from my thigh. After making my way back to the pole, I looked down and saw several women walking to the stage and using their stacks of money to make it rain. It reminded me of the ticker tape parade in New York City on Thanksgiving.

Knowing the party wasn't over; I had one last move to give the anxious crowd. I slowly lowered my body back down the pole with my legs spread wide so they could get a good look at my dick, and it worked. The entire club went berserk.

"Wow. Now, that's how you make your debut. That's how you put it down!" Sensual shouted repeatedly as I danced my way off stage. "Put your hands together again for our newest dancer, Stamina!"

The ladies continued to walk up and throw money onto the

stage while Tranquil looked on in anger. I'm sure he couldn't believe my payday. He watched as the collectors needed more and bigger plastic storage bags to collect all the money off the stage and floor.

I could hear Sensual saying, "Don't forget ladies, Stamina will be right back out to mingle with you after he changes. So, let's keep this shit going and find yourself one of the guys already on the floor and get your freak on."

My heart raced like a thoroughbred at the Kentucky Derby as I walked down the hallway. There were several women standing at the bathroom at the end of the corridor. I tried to slow my heart beat before I got close enough for them to notice my anxiety.

"Oh, my goodness, you were fantastic," a pretty, heavy set woman said.

I stared at her forty double D's and simply nodded my head then flashed my award winning smile. I tried to slide past her, but other women started to walk up and began to encircle me. They began rubbing my chest, grabbing my dick to make sure it was all me, and smacking my ass. I became very uncomfortable at how aggressive they were getting.

"Clear the hall," a deep, scratchy voice shouted from behind me.

The women turned to see Rock, coming down the hallway. They quickly jumped against the wall as if they were waiting in line for the bathroom.

"Oh, it's you jamming up my hallway. I know it's your first night so I'm going to say this only once. There's absolutely no working the ladies back here," Rock warned when he got closer to me.

"I was just trying to get to the dressing room," I countered.

"There's a short cut through the double doors in back of the stage. If you come this way, the women will never let you pass, and you'll miss all the real money out front."

"These women are like dudes. If you wouldn't have shown up, they probably would've raped my ass," I said.

Rock laughed. "These are just the drunk freaks who can't handle their liquor. They get real hyped, but their money is short.

You'll see what the top flight women sip on and where they hang out once you come back out on the floor," Rock replied.

"Good looking," I said before ducking into the dressing room.

I quickly freshened up and decided to wear a pair of silk Sponge Bob Square Pants boxers, white drop socks and my fresh brown double sole Timberland boots. It was a crazy outfit, but I knew those women could care less what I wore. I then put a white sleeve on my penis, allowing it to hang out the little slit in the front.

The noise level grew louder as I walked toward the floor of the club. Some of the dancers were causing all the commotion because of what they were doing. The twins were on the runway playing dick volleyball. It was the craziest shit I'd ever seen. Their hands were tied behind their backs and they used their dicks to hit a balloon over a little toy net.

Tranquil had several women throwing money at him as he made his dick two step with a towel. On the other side of the club, that white-boy Unpredictable had the ladies in a frenzy. He'd climbed up on a customer, positioned his dick between her breasts and simulated the act of fucking the shit out of them. Other women were smacking his ass until his butt cheeks were rosy red. It was a complete madhouse.

I didn't know where to go or what to do, but luckily Sensual was already heading my way. I stood there and made my chest jiggle as a couple of ladies walked past.

"There's my star," she boasted, before turning to me. "I had no idea you knew how to work the pole. All these bitches are horny as hell from watching you work the damn ceiling beam, too. That shit was crazy."

I smiled. "I just did what came natural. So, what do I do now?"

"It's time to make some real money. You can walk around and let women put money in your shorts or you can give them a one song lap dance for twenty dollars. For fifty dollars they can have you in the Naughty Rooms for about ten minutes."

"The Naughty Rooms, what happens there?" I asked stupidly.

"Anything goes back there. It all depends on what you're willing to do for the money," she laughed. "It's so cute how green you are. I guess you've just been paying for pussy all your life."

My eyes tightened. "You have me mistaken. I've never paid for pussy a day in my life."

"Sure you have. Whenever you paid for the movies, dinner, a show, breakfast, the hotel, a trip or anything else, you've put a down payment on the pussy. You just used objects instead of cold hard cash," Sensual said with more laughter than before.

"Damn. I never thought of it like that."

Sensual put her right hand on my shoulder. "Take it slow. Work the room until you get comfortable. Always remember that you have the right to say no if they want something you don't want to do. Still, at the end of the night, it's all about the money. The house gets ten percent of whatever you make."

Sensual started to pull me to another section of the club. "I almost forgot. I wanna introduce you to a group of women who already gave me fifty so they could be the very first to work you out."

What the hell did she mean work me out, I thought, but followed Sensual over to a booth that was shared by four very beautiful women. There were also four empty bottles of Moet and the waiter was just dropping off two more. Two of the women were Black, one was White and the other was Asian. If I had to guess their occupation, I would've said all of them were models.

"Stamina, I would like you to meet the First Ladies of the Washington Redskins. Ladies, this is Stamina. Take it easy on him. He's still a virgin in the House of Sin."

"Hell yeah, don't worry Sensual, we'll take good care of Stamina," one of the Black women said with a large smile. She looked at me and batted her eyes. "Hi, I'm Mya."

"Nice to meet you, Mya," I said, grabbing and kissing her hand.

As the DJ switched the song to Jamie Foxx's, *Blame It On The Alcohol*, the club exploded, including the four women who instantly jumped up. When they formed a circle around me, I quickly began working my body, rotating my hips and slowly swinging my dick up and down.

Minutes passed and the songs kept changing, but I didn't pay it any attention. My focus remained on the four women repeatedly putting ten and twenty dollar bills in the waistband of my boxers.

"Let's get the lap dances started Jessica," the Asian chick blurted out.

"Fuck that, I say we take fresh meat downstairs and see if he can work that amazing rod between his legs or if it's just for show," Mya chimed in.

Suddenly, the little phat ass Asian woman grabbed my wrist, and pulled me through the crowd of dancing women. My heart rate increased, and sweat appeared on my forehead as we got closer to the door with the sign, Naughty Rooms hanging over it. I was nervous as hell.

I caught Sensual's eyes watching me. Obviously, my facial expression had revealed how I felt at the moment. I was able to read her lips when she mouthed, "Shit, I better put one of the twins on standby." Little did she know, I wasn't about to let her down…or give up my money. I circled my head to crack the bones in my neck in order to loosen up and get myself together.

My erection got even harder as we walked down the steps and past several occupied rooms. It wasn't long before we entered the last room on the left, which looked like something out of a freak movie. It had a swing hanging from the ceiling in the middle of the room along with a full size inflated air mattress against the far wall and chains with hand-cuffs on the back of the door. I even noticed shelves with several pairs of silk sheets folded, new dildos, bullets, blindfolds, and a variety of lotions, creams and body paints.

The other three ladies were fast on our heels and they wasted no time taking off their clothes once we were all inside the room. It was almost as if they did this on a regular. I was still looking around when the little Asian woman's warm lips wrapped around my dick, which completely surprised me. I glanced down to see her head working like a bobble head with the power of a shop vac.

One of the ladies removed a pair of silk sheets from the shelf and began making up the air bed. I looked over to see another woman putting a large black dildo into a plastic harness. *I know she's not about to use that on anyone in here,* I thought to myself.

Suddenly, tiny pins and needles began to work their way up from my toes to my legs. The bobble head doll tried to pull my dick out her mouth when the first ounce of thick cum squirted, but I grabbed the back of her head to keep my dick fully in her mouth. She began coughing uncontrollably.

"Oh no. I know that bitch ain't over there choking from a dick suck. Wait until this bed is done. It's on," Jessica said jokingly.

"I hope he makes me choke next," the white girl, Crissy chimed in.

I released her head once my dick went empty. I chuckled as she continued to gag on the amount of cum that now was dripping from her skinny lips. My dick went limp for only a second, but the sight of Crissy bent over in a doggy style position, taking a ten inch rubber penis up the ass from Mya made my dick recuperate instantly.

Several minutes passed, and to my surprise, Sensual suddenly pushed the door open. It took me a moment to adjust my eyes, but the flickering from the strobe light in the hallway allowed me to make her and Nico out. Obviously, privacy wasn't a rule for Sensual. The way her eyes widened, it looked as if she couldn't believe what was going on. Crissy was now on the swing with her legs spread eagle as Jessica pounded her pussy with the black dildo. Mya was eating the pussy of the Asian woman on the air mattress, while I banged her from behind. We must've looked like a human jig-saw puzzle or jumbo blocks of Lego's.

Nico tried to enter the room, but Sensual wouldn't let him. She pulled him back, closed the door, and seconds later, I could hear their footsteps walking away from the door. The girls and I ended up fucking until the club closed.

Once security cleared the Naughty Rooms and the bathrooms, the bus boys started clearing the tables and cleaning the floors. As all the dancers started taking showers and getting dressed, Sensual strutted her tiny frame into the dressing room with a huge grin.

"How are my men doing? What a hell of a night," she said.

"Tonight was off the hook. It had the feel of the first of the month or payday weekend. They were coming off that money with such ease," the other twin, Rico said.

"Stamina must've hit the mother load. I'm not clocking his money, but his routine got it all going. That roof shit made the bitches horny as hell. Then he had the Fabulous Four down in one of the Naughty Rooms until closing," Nico added.

"That routine wasn't anything special. He got my fucking money for doing some gay ass gymnastic shit. New Boy should give me half for getting my prime time slot!" Tranquil shouted.

I looked over in his direction, but didn't say a word. The other dancers were waiting for a response from me. They laughed once they realized none was forthcoming. Moments later, Gyro emerged from the shower drying his body.

"What did I miss?" Gyro asked.

"Tranquil still crying like a little school girl cause Stamina got the prime spot. But now we can see what you think," Nico said.

Gyro frowned. "Think about what?"

"We were talking about Stamina's routine. That shit was the bomb right? The women were throwing that money like there was no tomorrow after he worked the fuck out of that pole," Nico continued.

Everyone's eyes were locked on Gyro waiting for his reply. I pretended not to be interested, but stared over at him through the corner of my eye. Tranquil folded his arms and looked directly at me.

"I've been doing this a very long time, and I can honestly say that I've never seen anything like that ever. Even though I hate to do it, I gotta agree with Nico. New Boy took the women over the top with his routine."

"That's what I said. Fuck, I wanted to throw some money on the stage when he worked the pole," Nico replied.

"You know what, fuck you Nico, fuck you Gyro and fuck

all the rest of you. I still say that tonight should've been my payday and I don't give a damn what anyone has to say," Tranquil said, pointing at everybody.

"Okay calm down. It's way too much testosterone popping off up in here. Let's just clear up the money thing and you guys can continue this stupid ass conversation out in the parking lot, the IHOP, or wherever you niggas go," Sensual finally said.

She called for the collectors to come in and pass out the plastic bags to each of the dancers for their routine on stage. On a good night, two or three bags were considered good, but they brought me five bags, which were completely full. Then, to top it off, Sensual walked over and gave me an envelope filled with more money.

"This is your money from the Fabulous Four. Each one kicked in four hundred a piece for their time in the Naughty Rooms. Count that with the other money from your routine."

After Sensual took her ten percent, most of the dancers ended up with around one to two thousand dollars for the night. I hit the House of Sin for forty-five hundred. This was the best night of my life. I got paid a rack of money for fucking four different beautiful women, exercising on a pole and exercising on a ceiling beam. This definitely wasn't a bad gig.

"One last thing, the best dancer of the night is Stamina," Sensual announced.

That was the straw that broke Tranquil's back. At that moment, he rushed me, tackling me to the floor, then began swinging like crazy. I buried my face into his side so he couldn't get a clear punch to my face. After dodging a few more of his swings, I gave him a swift knee to his groin and rolled him over onto his back. As I got ready to deliver a punch of my own to his face, Gyro snatched me off of him.

The twins grabbed Tranquil when he jumped to his feet, pinning him against the far wall. When the door flew open, Rock and another bouncer burst into the dressing room like two pit bulls. Sensual just stood there watching us with a smirk on her face.

"Everything okay in here Ms. Mary?" Rock asked.

"You know how it gets when jealousy gets the best of some

guys egos. Tranquil is feeling a little hurt that Stamina is the big dog of the night. I was about to give him the five hundred dollar bonus for being voted the best dancer when Tranquil lost it," Sensual replied.

"Get your hands off me. I'm cool. For real fellas y'all can let me go!" Tranquil shouted.

Once the twins slowly released him, Tranquil walked over to his space and grabbed his duffle bag. Even though Gyro stayed in front of me, I still put my hands up just to make sure Tranquil wouldn't try and sucker punch me on his way out. Sensual continued to laugh. She seemed so unenthused.

"Oh yeah, one more thing. The Fabulous Four rented out the House of Sin for a bachelorette party for one of their friends this Thursday night. We're gonna have an old fashion Lock-In," Sensual paused to see the guy's expressions. "It's mandatory that everyone be in attendance. We're gonna have all of you and five women locked in here from midnight to eight in the morning. This should be a good payday for all of you. These women are coming with deep pockets and we're gonna try to empty them before they leave."

You could hear the walls being pounded on and kicked as Tranquil walked down the hall. He continued to holler and curse with each step.

"Hey, forget about him and come collect your money," Sensual said to me.

I walked over to her and took the extra five hundred then wrapped it around the rest of the stack of money. *Another couple nights like this and my debt to Big Gee will be paid in full,* I thought. When Sensual left, the guys started talking about going to IHOP, so I decided to hang out. Hell, I was even surprised that they'd invited me in the first place.

I followed the guys to the IHOP on New Hampshire Avenue. All the other clubs had just let out, so the parking lot and restaurant was packed. We pulled in and found a couple of spots in the far back next to the trash cans. I thought it was going to take forever to get a table, but to my surprise the guys had that already worked out.

The twins walked up to the hostess and gave her a kiss on both cheeks at the same time. One even reached over and smacked her ass. She giggled then told them to follow her. They motioned for the rest of us to come on. Surprisingly, there was an empty booth on the other side of the restaurant with a reserved sign on it.

"You nigga's got a reserved spot in fucking IHOP," I said sitting down.

"We have reserved spots all over town. You'll learn that the women who come to see us come from all walks of life. They just want to take care of us any way they can," Gyro replied.

I still couldn't believe that he was even talking to me after the Sunshine incident.

After we ordered, the ladies in the restaurant kept stopping by our table feeling and touching on the other guys. They all kept asking me for my name and telling me how they couldn't wait to see me dance. Looking around the restaurant, I saw this little cutie from back in the day sitting in the corner with a couple of her friends. I ended up leaving the guys to go finish my western omelet with her.

I nodded my head when the other guys found some action and left minutes later. By the time I finished my food, Big Gee and three of his boys had rolled inside.

My eyes instantly widened. "Oh, shit."

I ducked down hoping they didn't see me, but of course they did. Standing up, I tried to make a dash out the back, but the door was locked. When Big Gee sent his boys after me, they snatched my ass up and dragged me outside to the alley.

Big Gee went to his trunk and came back with two pair of long tube socks and several bars of soap. They handcuffed me to the tall metal gate around the dumpster. I watched as they slid the soap into the socks and tied knots at the end.

"Remember no face shots. Those bitches at the club won't want him if he's all bruised up and swollen," Big Gee commanded.

How the fuck did he know that I was working at the club, I pondered.

However, the thought quickly disappeared from my mind when the first loaded sock hit my open rib cage. Each one of Big Gee's goons took turns swinging their loaded socks into my torso and legs. It felt as if they were filled with bricks. When I tried to call out for help, they only swung even harder. Besides, only the alley rats would probably hear my cries. I doubted if anyone was going to interfere.

"Boy, did you think that I wouldn't find out?" Big Gee asked when his boys took a pause. "Check that nigga's pockets."

When they went inside, it didn't take long for them to find the stack of money I'd just earned. One of them threw it over to Big Gee. At that moment, somehow I found the strength to look up and watch Big Gee count it out like a bank teller.

"Let that fool go." As his boys did as they were told, I instantly fell to the ground. Big Gee walked over to mc and stepped on my hand. "This is for me having to look for you. Your bill is now fifteen grand. Don't make me hunt your ass down for the rest of my shit."

THREE

When Thursday quickly came, I wondered where the week had gone. My body still ached from my little run in with Big Gee. It was hard for me to take notes in any of my classes with the many fantasies about what would happen at the Lock-In competing with the nightmares of what Big Gee was going to do to me if I didn't get his money. After going back and forth with the same thoughts all day, I got to the club around eight o'clock that night.

Most of the guys were already there getting ready. I locked eyes with Tranquil as he went to his area. All the guys watched carefully to see if anything was going to pop off again. However, Tranquil didn't say anything. I shook my head once I realized that he was still mad. He was so fucking emotional; just like the bitch he was. After several more minutes of uncomfortable silence, Gyro finally turned the radio up.

"I've got stay hard cream, blue pills, Viagra, Cialis and some of that good Chinese herb to keep your big dicks going from start to finish. What you want?" Sensual asked, walking around stopping at all our areas.

Most of the other guys went for the Viagra or Cialis, but I wasn't down for putting chemicals into my body. When Sensual got to me, she could see the reluctance in my eyes. She held out the tube of Stay Hard cream and laughed.

All of a sudden, there was a knock on the door. Sensual looked at her watch and realized that time had been flying. After we were finally ready, she hurried all of us out front to greet the women once Rock opened the main door. The Fabulous Four entered the club looking even more beautiful than I remembered from a few nights back. It shocked me when I realized that their friend and guest of honor was LaTonya Sims. She was the girlfriend of the star football player at Howard University who was expected to go in the first round of the upcoming draft. As I studied LaTonya, everyone went around introducing themselves. I pretended not to know LaTonya's name as I kissed the back of her hand. Now, I even knew that, Ming was the Asian's chick's name. Not that any of the introductions mattered because I could tell everyone was ready to get down to business.

Rock went behind the bar and began pouring shots of Patron into several glasses. All of the dancers along with the ladies held up their glasses, and then tossed them back continuously until Sensual finished up the monetary business with Mya.

"It's two minutes to twelve. Rock is about to lock the door and watch it from his car to make sure nobody disturbs you. I'll be in my office. Once the key turns, the House of Sin and all that's inside belong to you Fabulous Four," Sensual said, turning on the house system. "I'll turn the music off at eight in the morning and hit the lights to let you know time is up. Now, it's no need to waste anymore time with small talk. Enjoy yourselves ladies...and gents."

I tossed back a few more shots as Rock closed the door and I heard the key turn. Sensual had also disappeared as the lights went down to party mode. The ladies did exactly as Sensual instructed and quickly grabbed a partner then separated throughout the club.

I gave a sigh of relief that Jessica had grabbed my arm, pulling me toward the stage. LaTonya waited until all the women selected a partner and ended up with Tranquil. After realizing that she was nervous, he took the lead and escorted her downstairs to the Naughty Rooms. The fuck fest had begun.

The screams and moans from the ladies were heard coming from all parts of the club. I had Jessica calling out, "Big Daddy" as I long stroked her. I had her bent over the end of the stage like a criminal on a police car.

Gyro had Ming sitting on his dick, walking her around the club like she was an attachment on a Halloween costume. The twins had Mya and Crissy in the V.I.P. lounge banging their backs out and switching like a doubles tennis match. The only ones that I didn't see were LaTonya and Tranquil.

I lifted Jessica's leg and stuck my face into her dripping pussy. She'd just finished with her second then third orgasm, but surprisingly didn't fall over in exhaustion. She pushed me off of her and yelled out, "Switch!"

At that moment, Mya and Jessica pulled Gyro onto the stage, and forced him down on his back. Mya sat on his face as Jessica straddled him. I watched as they rode him like seasoned cowgirls. My dick jumped when they began kissing one another's breast and biting on each others nipples staying in rhythm with their gallop.

Before I knew it, the twins had switched partners. Nico had Crissy near the bar and Rico took Ming over to one of the sofas, pounding her in the ass within seconds. I was left alone for a second, so I decided to sneak up on Crissy who was getting fucked doggy style over a bar stool. I smacked her face with my dick a few times just to get her attention. Like a trained sex slave, she reached up and started sucking my shaft with amazing force. I looked into the bar mirror and couldn't help but laugh. Our bodies looked like they were in a tug a war game and Crissy was the rope.

After I burst a full load of my thick juicy cum into her

mouth, I decided to go check on Tranquil and LaTonya. Crissy held on to my penis for a moment until I was able to free her grip. At that moment, I slowly made my way toward the Naughty Rooms. I could hear moans as I started down the steps. Once I got to the correct room, I wasted no time; just simply pushed the door open. LaTonya was riding Tranquil backwards; bent over with her face stuck between his legs. Tranquil spanked her plump ass with a mid-size black leather belt shouting, "You better not stop!"

My dick wanted to drag my body over and dive into her mouth as she rose slightly and slid her tongue across her full seductive lips. Suddenly, LaTonya opened her eyes to see me in the door way. Her body froze as if she'd seen a ghost.

"What the hell did you stop for? You better work this dick!" Tranquil yelled, while whipping her with the belt even harder.

The two of us continued to stare at one another. When Tranquil realized that I was standing at the door, he immediately pushed LaTonya off of him. Tranquil didn't know what to make of me watching them so intently.

"You gonna come in here and help me work her or just watch?" he asked.

Not expecting that kind of response from him, I stood with a confused expression on his face, but didn't respond. Instead, I watched LaTonya very closely. Her nipples were thick, just the way I preferred. I started at her tight hour glass body that was sweaty from fucking and took in the sweet smell of her Clive Christian's No.1 perfume. All that made me want to join them, but I didn't.

I had so many thoughts running through my head as I turned away. *She should be at home watching porn instead of here getting fuck by a complete stranger if she's that horny. I wish I had ole boy's number. I'd call him up and tell him to come on down and check out his future wife.*

I stepped back and slowly closed the door shaking my head in the process. I needed to clear my thoughts, so I rushed into the ladies bathroom to splash some water on my face. *Why am I tripping? This ain't my girl, but for some reason, I'm feeling her,* I thought while splashing more water. Just then, the bathroom door squeaked and the light went out at the same time. I turned in an attempt to see through the darkness, but saw nothing. I could only feel a slight breeze letting me know the door had been opened and there was someone in the bathroom with me.

That's when I felt a sharp pain hit my chest. The excruciating feel immediately sent me onto the floor. The sounds of feet scrambling then running out the bathroom were all I heard. I gathered up enough strength to get back to my feet while grabbing on the edge of the sink. Inch by inch, I stumbled over to the door, slid my hand all over the wall, and finally clicked the light switch. I looked down to find a long knife with a black handle sticking out of my chest. When I saw blood running down my body like a leaking faucet, I panicked.

"Help!" I shouted, loosing what little strength I had.

I called for help again but my pleas went unanswered. I pulled on the door, hoping to get it open, but my body lost all hope. I fell backwards onto the cold marble floor once again. I could hear voices, but couldn't find the strength to call out. I felt the end coming, but couldn't figure out why someone would do this to me.

"Where's Stamina? I want to feel that dick inside me again. I bet he's downstairs with LaTonya fucking like Jack rabbits," I heard Ming say.

Her voice was so close. Instead of continuing down the hall closer to me, I could hear her still talking, headed toward the Naughty Rooms.

"Have y'all seen Stamina?" she asked someone.

I assumed she was talking to Tranquil and LaToya, but didn't know for sure. I wanted to yell out, but couldn't. I had no control over my own voice. It seemed everything was fading, including my vision and my ability to hang on.

Moments later, I heard other people coming down the steps. Somebody was talking about needing to use the bathroom. *Finally, somebody was going to find me*, I thought.

I hoped.

I prayed.

I was hanging on for dear life. Suddenly, I heard the footsteps getting closer and finally the door opened. The high-pitched screams seemed to shake the foundation on the building. Seconds later, I could hear several different footsteps running downstairs. I'm sure it was an attempt to see what was going on.

"In here, in here!" I heard Ming scream.

When everyone ran inside, Crissy immediately sprung into action. She was on her knees checking me for a pulse with one hand and holding my arm slightly with the other.

"Somebody call 911!" Mya shouted.

"None of us have cell phones. They're not permitted in the club," Jessica responded.

"I still feel a pulse," Crissy replied.

"I'm going to get Sensual!" Gyro yelled. "Don't touch anything. Baby girl, you keep talking to him," he instructed to Crissy. "Let him know that he's going to be alright. Make sure you keep pressure around the knife to slow up the bleeding!" he continued to shout before taking off.

I laid on the floor feeling lightheaded, and listening to the frantic mood surrounding me. I wasn't sure whether I would make it much longer, so I started reflecting on my life and all the wrong that I'd done. Before long, Gyro returned with Sensual.

"What the fuck is going on?" Sensual asked when she walked into the bathroom. She seemed to be calmer than the rest. That is until she finally saw me; hanging on for dear life. "What the fuck happened. I need to know right now!" she belted.

I found the strength to raise my head. They all began to look at one another. No one said a word.

"I mean somebody knows something. We're all locked in here, so that means the ruthless motherfucka who stabbed him is still in here." Sensual started pointing around the room. "Y'all ain't gonna be the death of my fucking club. I'm gonna find out who stabbed him before the doors are unlocked!"

"We need to call the police," Crissy said through her tears.

"We ain't calling shit. What the fuck are we gonna tell

them? You want your husbands to find out on the evening news that y'all were at the strip club getting fucked…using their money?" Sensual questioned.

"Then what do you want us to do?" Jessica asked. "Stamina needs help. Aren't we going to call an ambulance?"

Sensual pulled out her cell phone. "I've got my own doctors," she told everyone with confidence. She started dialing, then moments later spoke sharply into the phone. "Gee, I need your help. I've got caught in a fucked up situation."

My heart stopped about the same time that I heard Sensual take a deep breath and switch her cell on speaker phone.

"I don't want to say anything over the phone, Gee, but trust me…I need for you to get here with some of your crew and deal with some folks."

Just before I blacked out I could hear Big Gee say, "I'm on my way!"

TO BE CONTINUED...

Flexin & Sexin : Sexy Street Tales Volume 2

JOY RIDE
NICHELLE WALKER

PROLOGUE
MONEY, POWER, DRUGS
WELCOME TO MIAMI

Growing up in The Port of Miami I saw a lot and experience a lot. When people hear Miami they hear luxury and good times. Tourists flood this city looking for parties and drugs. My daddy, Jason capitalized off of Miami's nightlife. On my twelve birthday I realized my father was a pimp and all the women he claimed where my aunties were his workers. My daddy ran an underground dollhouse called Secret Society. I saw ho's come and go and men pay to play. Prostitution was illegal in Miami but my daddy told me if you had the right people in your pockets you can do whatever you wanted.

I was an only child and my father raised me alone. My

mother chose drugs over me so I never knew her; my childhood was strange. I saw way more than any little girl should have witnessed growing up. Even though my dad raised me in a whorehouse he truly wanted the best for me. He forced me to attend private school and then college. I was raised to be classy and not a ghetto whore like the women who worked for him. He never let me hang around them because he said they were poison and he'd die before he had a whore for a daughter. My dad was very serious about the way he wanted me to behave and carry myself. I believed it had to do with my mother being like she was because he always made me promise him I would never sell my body for money. I had every intention on becoming an accountant but once my daddy passed away my plans changed.

I didn't see the need to close down my daddy's dollhouse that he had made millions off of. I knew if I took over his company I could get paid and continue to life the good life. I took my degree and my daddies dream and turned it into a *Joy Ride*

ALL WOMEN ARE HO`S

There's a difference between being a whore or a ho. It's actually very simple; whores lack common sense and most of the time they have very low self esteem. A lot of these busted whores missed the basic fundamentals to tricking. I couldn't stand whores, but they made me a lot of money, so I kept at least five of them on deck. Whores are usually loud and run their fucking mouths too much. They carry themselves like trash, act like trash; hell some of their pussy's even smell like trash.

I learned a lesson about tricking from one of my daddy's bottom bitches Miss Gia. We had words once and when I called her a whore she cut me up. "Little bitch I'm not a whore, I'm a trick." I laughed because she sounded foolish to me, but she laughed as well and told me she was gonna kick me some game.

"Baby girl I ain't a whore, whores get pimped; tricks get

rich," she continued. "All women are ho's by nature, but tricks are the only ones about their paper. A trick is fifty bitches deep. She sucks a nigga's dick until she puts him to sleep; wakes him up with something good to eat. A good trick mind fucks a man until he can't think, makes him feel like he can't breathe when she leaves."

Miss Gia took a seat, lit up her cigarette and rolled her eyes at me. "While you're sticking your noise up at me, you're a ho, too." She laughed as she continued her disrespectful tone. "You're just like me. You might as well embrace it or it will control you and turn you into a whore."

I stood there in shock. I couldn't believe she had called me a ho. "I'm not a fucking whore!" I screamed at her. "I will never be like you!"

"Good," she laughed again. "A real woman never tries to be like the next bitch; she always tries to be better." Miss Gia took in a deep breath, put out her cigarette and spoke the realist words I ever heard.

"Sweetie we all are ho's, the difference is knowing when to turn your ho off. You have to embrace your womanhood by nature. We like sex and by nature we like to please. You have to own your inner whore so she won't control you," she said, "Keep your mouth shut, act like a lady, stay classy and embrace your inner whore. If you don't, she will control you. Never tell anyone about what you do behind closed doors. Your business is your business, and always own your pussy."

I didn't understand a word she said until the first time I had sex. The things I did and enjoyed, I would've never imagined myself doing. Once I embraced my inner ho, I vowed to always control her. I promised myself I would never be a whore. I owned my pussy!

TRICKING AIN'T EASY

Ring, Ring, Ring
What the fuck? I thought as I rolled over out of my sleep. I

hated getting my sleep broken; it was the worst. I checked the clock and got pissed. It was seven in the morning. I never slept late, but anyone who knew me knew not to call before nine. "Who the fuck is this?" I screamed as I answered.

"I got busted."

"What?" I asked trying to recognize the voice on the other end of the phone. "Busted? Who's this?"

"Yeah, it's Apple. Joy I need you."

Apple was a pain in my ass; this ho was definitely taking me to an early grave. Apple thought she was so slick. I knew she'd been up to no good. "And?"

"I need you to come and bail me out."

"Bitch please. Did you get busted selling pussy on my watch?"

"Come on I got caught with some blow. I'm sorry I need you to help me."

One thing I couldn't stand was people taking my kindness for weakness. Apple knew she was gonna get right back into trouble again. I'd bailed her ass out at least five times this month. "Apple I'll get you out this last time, but you're doing two jobs without pay. I'm not here to baby sit you or be your damn mommy. "Where are you?"

"South Beach."

"South Beach? Bitch you a mighty long way from home aren't you?"

"Come on Joy."

Apple stayed in the hood, and couldn't even afford a cheese burger in South Beach. Her pimp boyfriend took all of her money. I wasn't a fool. I'd heard she was messing with Troy on the low. "Let me tell you this Apple, I'm no fool, if I find out you seeing Troy behind my back you're fired."

"Joy, if I was seeing Troy I wouldn't be hustling pussy. I swear on my momma grave I haven't seen that nigga. You know Dee ain't having that shit."

"Fine I'll be there within the hour!" I yelled as I slammed my phone down.

I slid from beneath my oversized canopy bed and slipped

into my Channel slippers. It was defiantly time for me to hold another meeting with these ho's. My workday started at ten, sometimes nine. I didn't jump out of my sleep unless I was checking my paper. Her ass better be glad she was sitting on a golden pussy or she would be short. I swear Apple and Dee were the worst drug dealers in Miami.

I turned on my heated floors, jumped into the shower and sat under the hot water for a minute before getting out. Once I dried off, I brushed my teeth, washed my face and covered myself in my Ed Hardy lotion. "Oh Lord, it's too early," I complained to myself.

I took off my silk scarf and let my long hair fall down. I'd just gotten my hair freshly layered, so it fell right into place. My chocolate skin glistened from that new skin polish I'd been using. I pulled out my Armani Exchange dress, slipped into my flat golden wrap sandals, sprayed on my Ed Hardy perfume, and put on some light make up.

Everybody called me Co Co because of my silky smooth skin. I was way darker than my dad considering he was a light bright. My dad told me I took after my mother. He said I was dark like her, shaped like her, and even walked like her. I heard she was looking for me, but I wasn't checking for her ass. I appreciated the good looks and banging body she gave me, but I wasn't checking to be her friend, especially since I'd accomplished a lot without her ass. I graduated college at twenty-one and finished my masters degree two years later. I was only twenty-five, making paper and I owned my own business. I was a successful independent PYT, and I chose to be single because I rather make love to my money.

I jumped into my Range Rover and headed over to the police station. *Apple has to be the stupidest bitch I know,* I thought turning the corner. I didn't see why she kept running drugs for her nothing ass boyfriend. He never bailed her out when she got locked up, which pissed me off. That's why I work for myself and I'm by myself. I didn't need a man in my life causing me problems and making it hard for me to focus. I was living my own American dream. I was young, rich, and a paper chaser. Who could ask for more?

Once I got to the police station, I headed to the front desk. I didn't know how much her bail was, but the last time she got into something like this it hit me for two stacks.

"Hi I'm here to bail out Apple Johnson."

"Okay Miss. You can take a seat and fill out these forms."

"How much is her bail?" I asked the clerk.

She looked down a list longer than my hair. "It's going to be five grand for her to walk."

"Five Grand!" I yelled.

Apple was for sure twerking that pussy tonight. This bitch was outta her mind wasting money like this. With hesitation, I slapped my American Express Black card down on the counter, handed her the forms back and took a seat.

This was Apple's third arrest for the same shit. I couldn't understand how she got bail. Maybe she ratted on her boyfriend? Regardless, it didn't matter; I was tired of coming to get her out. *These people probably know me by my first name. I don't need this shit in my life,* I thought. I hated the police and I hated wasting money. I certainly didn't need any extra heat or these people wondering where all my money was coming from. *This is it, I'm done,* I told myself. Apple made me a lot of money daily, but it wasn't worth the heat she kept bringing me.

THE SET UP

The police took forever to release Apple's and my patience was growing shorter by the minute. The station was filthy and the stinky drunk-ass man I was sitting next to had breath that smelled like ass. I took out my Ed Hardy perfume and sprayed it in the air to kill some of his sour odor.

"Baby girl I'm I bothering you?" he asked.

I wanted to say, "Yes, you smell like a shitty diaper," but my daddy raised me better than that. "No, I'm just waiting for my friend."

"Hmm if she looks as good as you then I know what she got picked up for?"

"Excuse me!" I snapped at him.

"You know, I seen you women running loose in this city. I can't afford you."

I was insulted. *No this bummy nigga didn't come at me like that.* "I think you need to mind your own business."

"I'm sorry if I offended you, but how much does it cost?"

I was furious. "Nigga you couldn't afford it if you wanted to. You need to be easy before I slap the stank off of your ass."

The nerve of this dusty nigga. I was beyond ready to go. I was giving Apple another fifteen minutes before I bounced. I didn't have to sit and be disrespected by a bum. I scanned the room looking for an empty seat, but the station was jammed packed.

"Why you got so many phones?" he asked, looking at both of my cell phones in my hand.

Since I didn't want to hold a conversation with him, I spoke with anger. "I'm a business woman!" I turned my head. "What the fuck is wrong with people these days?" I mumbled under my breath. It was just a personal and business phone nothing exciting. My clients didn't have my personal number because there was no need for them to have it.

My patience was running short. I started to play Uno on my Blackberry in an attempt to calm down my nerves. I was on my last pull when my phone rang breaking my game. "Yeah, this is Joy," I answered expressing that I was pissed.

"Hey, baby this Troy, what's going on?"

"Troy it's been a while." I hadn't seen Troy in a minute; I heard he was having hard times.

"Man, I've just been trying to get my money right. I wanted to come through and bring my partner."

"Okay, but you know I need all his information before hand, and he needs to be screened."

"Good, I'll tell him to stop through. His name is Major Thompson, he's an investment banker. His money right, don't worry about him. He cool peoples, Joy. I wouldn't send him if I didn't know him like that."

"Alright, tell him to come by on Wednesday and I'll see you on your regular day."

"Yeah Ma, stay up."

I didn't mind taking on a new person. Shit, that was just more money to be made. Troy was cool peoples and he had spent a lot of money with me. Apple loved Troy so she would be happy to hear that he was coming back. Seconds later, I looked at my watch and got up, I was leaving. "Fuck Apple," I said.

"Joy!" she screamed as I grabbed my purse.

"Bout time. I was about to leave your ass!" I yelled.

"Sorry Joy. Thanks so much for helping me."

Bitch please, you gonna repay me."

Apple looked tired. Her eyes had rings around them, and her skin looked pale. Apple was gorgeous when she didn't let her boyfriend run her down into the mud. Some women just didn't know what's no good for them. I pride myself on being an independent woman who didn't need a man to run her life.

I gave girls like Apple a chance to make some real money, but the truth is; you could never change who a person was. I couldn't understand why women couldn't see that the wrong nigga can take you from the top to the bottom quicker than you can blink your eyes.

My father never wanted me to get into this game because it didn't leave me many options. I didn't consider myself a ho like the other girls. I was a business woman. I only slept with a handful of my clients, and it was a way to have sex without any feelings. I didn't disclose myself or my identity. I was undercover when I was with those men, so unlike the others girls, I still had all my options.

"What happened to you now? You need to get your life together, Apple," I scolded.

"Man, Dee asked me to hold his shit and left me in the car. The police pulled up behind us and next thing you know, I'm getting busted."

"When will you learn that Dee don't give a shit about you?"

"He does, he loves me."

"Please," I laughed as I rolled my eyes, "aint no man wifing up a ho."

"He does love me. He tells me everyday. You're just mad

because you don't have a man!"

"Apple have you looked at yourself lately? You're falling off. Your skin's fucked up, and you look like a dead woman walking. You're a call girl. He's gonna tell you what you want to hear so he can continue to pimp you outta your money. You're right, I don't have a man, but guess what…I don't need one! I got money. Everything else doesn't matter."

"You don't have anybody to love you," Apple replied.

"So, you think a man loves you when he slaps you around, or tells you to hold his work? If he loved you he wouldn't cause you any harm."

Apple looked at me and shrugged her shoulders in denial like most blind bitches. "He does love me."

"Girl get a clue that nigga is using you. And you're causing a lot of heat for me by keep getting locked up. I don't need any extra drama in my life so stop it already."

Apple was a confused bitch, and I wasn't gonna let her or any of those raggedy bitches run my company down. I didn't need any extra heat, especially from the police. Joy Ride was listed as a legitimate Spa, however what goes on behind my closed doors is past illegal. My club was very exclusive, only the premier and elite had a membership. You could only be referred in; I made it that way to weed out the undercover police and investigators.

Apple looked at me, "I know he loves me Joy you just don't like him."

"So, how did you get out of jail?" I asked changing the conversation.

"What do you mean?"

"I'm no criminal, but I know when you get locked up for the same thing three times you're toast."

"All those other times got dropped. What you trying to say?"

"I ain't saying nothing. Talking to you is like talking to the wall. I just want to make this clear, the next time you need help don't call me."

Apple rolled her puffy eyes at me. "I won't."

"Good!" I snapped back. Keeping a flock of ho's is a damn

headache. "And you're doing the Mayor tonight."

"Man hell no. He too freaky."

The Mayor was one of my problem clients. I should know, I did him once. He even paid extra for his kinky behavior, but it was too much. "You don't have a choice, and you better take care of him Bonnie, just thank your Clyde," I instructed.

"The last time he bit my clit. I can't stand him," Apple whined.

"Me neither that's why I'm sending you."

Apple better twerk that pussy for the Mayor because I needed him on my side. He helped make the Joy Ride possible and I couldn't fuck that up. Outside of him being a sick, twisted white man he was cool peoples with a lot of power.

X MARKS THE SPOT

Joy Ride was very successful and stayed in high demand. I serviced several upscale special clientele ranging from A list actors to the sleazy Mayor. I sealed all my client records, and put them under code names for protection. When you ran a business like mine, less was better. I gave all the girls code names and fired anybody who had an outside relationship with any of my clients. Managing ho's was harder than putting out a forest fire. Once you got one bitch under control, another one was spreading their legs like wildfire. Just keeping the girls in order kept me on the clock twenty-four seven, but I couldn't complain. My money was right and life was good for me. I had everything I needed and wanted.

I kept my personal clientele list down to only three. Running the office was hard work because of the salon and spa. I had to make sure I kept all my ducks in a row. I saw my clients every other day and they always came back even when they said they wouldn't.

I soaked my body in my Jadore bubble bath. Mr. X loved the way it smelled on my skin. I never got involved with any of my clients outside our scheduled one hour session. My Code name was Crave, and I covered my identity with a mask that I kept on the entire evening. All my clients wanted to be with me; I even had to dismiss a few because they stalked me. I had two rules I lived by; *money over nigga's* and *no feelings* in my job. I knew sometimes a good piece of dick could make you go against what you promised yourself. Luckily, I'd never had any dick that knocked me off my square.

Mr. X was waiting for me. I smelled his scent in the hallway. I like having sex with him because he was well endowed. His football skills made him a beast in the bed. The way he touched and teased me was unbelievable. I stepped into the room with my red six inch Gucci heels and long Co Co brown legs oiled up. My red lace boy shorts only covered some of my fat oily ass. I knew X liked my shaped because I was well proportioned. My thick nipples stuck out like gum drops and my real 36 D breast sat up high without a bra. My stomach was cut like Mel B and my thighs were thick like Alicia Keys. My body was serious and X loved every inch of me. When I was younger it was hard for me to embrace my dark skin and full Angelina Jolie lips. Once I figured out what full lips could do to a man, I thanked God and my momma for giving them to me.

X looked at me and smiled harder than I had ever seen him smile before. *I knew he would be back*; *they always come back*, I thought. "Long time no see. I thought you weren't coming back?" I asked as I grabbed him by the jaw and licked my tongue around his lips. X liked to be ruffed up, which was his main problem with his wife. She didn't know how to slap him around.

"I need you," he said as his manhood came alive.

"I thought I told you to work on your marriage with your

wife?"

X looked up at me and licked his lips. "I tried, but I can't shake you."

I laughed at him. Men were so predictable. That's one of the main reasons I didn't have one. "You can't shake Crave," I said as I grabbed his dick and squeezed it until he jumped.

X grabbed me, ripped my lace bra, and pushed me against the wall. After getting on his knees, he licked my pussy lips softly. "You smell so good," he moaned as he licked me in all my favorite spots. "I bought my wife that same perfume, but it didn't smell good on her," he advised.

I loved X. He was a man that knew a woman's body. He knew how gentle to be, but at the same time he knew how to get ruff just the right way. X took his long fingers and rubbed my clit back and forth while his other hand cuffed my right breast. I tossed my head back and braced myself self to receive some good head.

"I need you," he whispered in my ear while bringing me to my peak. "I want you Crave."

X begged and pleaded with me, but I'd heard this all before. I'd been doing this shit long enough to know nigga's didn't mean what they say. Men always talked crazy shit when they're knee deep into some mean pussy. I didn't get myself caught up in the moment. I mind blocked all my emotions when I was Crave. I was just here to do my job, and falling in love was not part of it.

"What do you want me to do to you Poppi?" I asked after I caught my breath.

"I wanna look at you," he said as he stepped back and admired my five foot eight inch curvy frame. My chocolate skin was shimmering from the lotion I put on. My Ja'dore followed me everywhere I moved. "I wish I could see you," he begged.

"You know that's out of the question so why ask?"

"I love you girl," he moaned as he stroked his well endowed member.

I walked over and kneeled down in front of him. "You love this, not me," I advised him as I licked down the shaft of his third leg. I knew just how he liked it, and I always aimed to please. I let my salvia stream down his shaft like a river before I wrapped my lips around him. I took him down with one stroke and licked him like a lollipop.

"Oh, I can't leave you alone," he grunted. "She can't fuck me like you!" he screamed.

I kept my rhythm steady going at him like a beat to a drum. X tried to pull away, but I wasn't having it.

"Fuck!" he yelled as he gripped the desk tightly. X tried to break loose of my head hunter grip, but I had him on lock. I never let go and I always finish what I started. I knew his peek was coming near. X's body started shaking and wiggling. "Please stop," he begged once again. But I wanted him to release all that stress he was holding in my mouth. When X's peak reached, he snatched me by my hair forcing me off him.

"Damn nigga!" I screamed at him. My hair was real, not some fake beauty supply shit, so I felt every tug. I finished him off with my hands and let him explode all over me.

"Oh my God girl, I'm surprised you're not married."

"How do you know I'm not?" I asked him curious to know his answer.

"Because."

I looked at X and he closed his mouth before he put his foot in it. Just five minutes ago he told me he loved me. Being a ho was a hard job. Men loved to fuck ho's, but they never wanted to wife them.

"Well ho's need love to, right? I mean you can't seem to keep your dick out of me," I snapped back at him.

"I'm sorry," X said as he grabbed my hands and put my fingers into his mouth. He sucked my fingers one by one making my body shiver. As I felt my heart racing, all I could do was close my eyes tight. X picked me up, placed me on the bed, pulled my ass down and slid into me. "Umm," he moaned. "This shit so good I swear."

Our bodies moved in union to the sounds of Eric Cire's, *Sensual* while X's words roamed my head. I started to question; did I want more out of life? His manhood tapping the bottom of my ocean made me want him to be mine. I tried to shake the feeling I was having, but couldn't. X's words sliced through me like a knife. Part of me did want a life where I was a wife or maybe a mother. Part of me did want to be wanted for more than just sex.

As our bodies touched, I felt a passion that I never felt with him before. I felt desired. I gripped his back as his strong arms held me in the air. I didn't know why my emotions chose to run wild. I'd been in this place many times before.

"Shit," I moaned into his ear as he bounced my body up and down like a basket ball.

My body connected with him. "Take all of me," he whispered softly in my ear. I felt my body shaking and knees getting weaker by the minute. I knew I was cuming harder than before.

"Oh, daddy it's coming down!" I screamed.

"Yeah, I want to feel it all over me," he said as he picked up his pace. The feeling was coming so strong, I couldn't contain myself. I arched my back in as far as I could. My juices flowed hard like a flash flood all over his dick. X fell to his knees and licked my sweet juices like a thirsty dog. "You taste so good baby."

After forty-five minutes of going at it, we both fell back on the bed to catch our breath. "Damn girl you a beast."

I just looked at him. Usually I would have a lot to say, but this time I was speechless. I just couldn't understand why my emotions were all over the place. I knew he was married and didn't give a damn about me. I was vulnerable and I didn't like feeling that way. I quickly sat up.

"What's the matter?" he asked.

"Our time is almost up," I said trying to flee the room and the feelings that I was having.

"I'll pay extra. I want to talk to you like we always do."

"Da—I mean X," I stuttered trying to catch myself from calling him by his first name. Nobody was supposed to know any of the clients name, but the owner. "I think we should call it a night."

"I need you," he said as he hugged me tighter.

I took in a deep breath. "Okay," I said as I laid back down next to him. I felt awkward and strange next to him. I'd never felt this way before about anything. I was always sure of myself and knew what I wanted. "What's on your mind?" I made sure that I didn't look into his eyes.

"You, I really want to be with you."

"Please." I laughed, "You're married and have a beautiful wife and kids. I'm not worth messing that up for." *Plus didn't yo dusty ass say I wouldn't find a husband because of my job?*

"But I'm not happy with her and the sex is so bad."

"You can train her; talk her into doing different things."

"She doesn't want to. She's just a plain Jane."

After I listened to him complain about his wife, I couldn't help but question myself. *I'm I wanting more out of life?* I knew I'd be the perfect wife. I knew exactly what men wanted. "I think you can work things out with your wife. Don't lose what you built over some pussy no matter how good it is."

X just looked at me and at that moment I knew that I did want more. I wanted a relationship and somebody I could share my life with. X didn't love me. He loved Crave, and that was the bottom line. Falling in love with my clients wouldn't do me any good. I couldn't cross that line and if any of them found out who I was, I'd be ruined.

X`D OUT THE GAME

Because I couldn't stop thinking about X and the way he made me feel, I had to reassign him a new girl. I couldn't risk losing everything I'd built because my emotions and good dick blocked my vision. *That what's best* I told myself.

"Excuse me," a soft voice whispered to me breaking my thoughts.

I looked up, snapped out of my daze and caught my composure. "Yes?" I asked her trying to see the reasoning for her coming into my office without knocking.

"I need to get a date with Crave."

I looked at her strangely. My clients only came by referral. I wasn't surprised that a woman stood in front of me. I was more surprised that she asked for Crave by name. I only serviced a few people and I knew neither of them gave out my name. I ran a tight ship with two male escorts and six females. "I'm sorry who and what are you looking for?"

"I want a session with Crave."

I looked at her noticing she looked familiar to me, like I'd seen her somewhere before. "What type of session? A massage or a hair style? I can find somebody who can hook you up, but there's nobody here by that name."

Her mocha skin and short spike hair looked like a women I'd seen before. Her slender frame and pretty white teeth couldn't be mistaken. As she flashed her seven carat Harry Weston diamond wedding ring, it came back to me where I'd seen her. I just fucked her husband the other day.

"That's bullshit. I want to see her tonight, so you better get her ass on the phone and tell her she has a meeting."

I laughed at her trying to act like she was from South Central. "Look Ma'am I don't know what you want with this person, but you need to leave."

"Look bitch, your ho is fucking my damn husband, so don't try to play stupid! I found plenty of credit card receipts dated back to last year. Now, unless you want me to expose your ass, you better tell her to be ready by nine."

I laughed even harder at her goofy ass because she didn't have anything on me. I ran a tight ship and all the girls signed agreements. "Expose me how?"

She laughed at me this time. "The funny thing is, my best friend's husband was cheating on her. I think the girl's name was Smokey, and Smokey told us she works here."

"Well, she's a damn lier," I retorted even though she was right. I fired Smokey three months ago when I found out she was fucking a client off the clock.

"Really," the woman said as she played a tape of Smokey giving a confession. Joy Ride was full of secret door ways and passages. Smokey told them every little detail right down to where I could be found.

My heart started racing and my hands became sweaty. I

made sure I kept my cool because I didn't want her to think she'd gotten the best of me. "So, let's talk."

"There's nothing to talk about. Tell Crave I'll be back at nine. And if she's not, my brother works for the IRS and I think I'll show him my credit card receipts so they can make sure you're filing the correct amounts."

"Will do?" I replied. I knew these bitches were going to be part of my downfall.

X's wife waltzed out the door with half of my livelihood in her hand. *How could this happen?* I asked myself repeatedly. I didn't know what this lady could possibly want with me. I was stuck between a rock and a hard place. I couldn't call the police and tell them a lady had just threatened my illegal business. I had no choice but to get myself prepared for anything.

YOU, ME & SHE

I took two shots of Hennessey to ease my mind. I was nervous as hell. I packed my .22 in my purse just in case I had to put a cap in a bitch's ass. I haven't had a fight since sixth grade and wasn't looking forward to fighting a woman over a man I didn't want. Things like this came with the business; women always blamed the other woman for their spouse cheating. Women never wanted to look in the mirror at the real reason their man was straying. However, there were only two options; either he was a dog or he wasn't getting something he needed at home.

I sat at the edge of the bed and knocked back another shot. I would be lying if I said my stomach wasn't turning knots. When I heard footsteps coming closer to the room I was in, I adjusted my mask, stood up and waited my fate. Seconds later, the door opened and X's wife peered in, but she wasn't alone. A tall gentleman was with her. He was blind folded and was definitely in for a surprise.

"You ready baby," she said as she kissed him on his neck.

"Yeah, I'm passed ready," he replied.

When she removed his mask, his eyes immediately popped open. I was so nervous I almost peed on my damn self. I tried to get myself ready for whatever she had coming to us. X didn't say a word. He just stared at her like a lost puppy. The entire room was lost for words.

"What the cat got your tongue now?" she said breaking the silence among us.

"What's going on?" X asked his wife.

"That's what I want to know," I added, "I don't have time for your marital problems."

"Bitch you gonna have time for whatever I have time for."

X's wife reached into her purse and I got posted up for some action. She took out all his credit card receipts and threw them at him.

"I can explain," he said.

"There's nothing to explain. Since you like fucking her, go ahead and do it right now."

I didn't know what type of game she was trying to play. She knew she didn't want him in my bed. "Come on I don't have time for these games," I responded.

"I'm not playing games. My husband is in your bed for some reason and I want to know why? So unless the both of you want to get on my bad side, I suggest we get down to business."

X looked at me then back at her. "Baby let me explain," he said as a last attempt to stop this madness, but his wife wasn't having it. She took a seat in the chair and motioned her hand for us to get closer.

"Take off your mask," she ordered. "I want to see what you look like."

I shook my head. "Absolutely not. If you wanna do this, I'm keeping it on."

"Fine," his wife said.

I took in a deep breath, *what in the hell did I just get myself into?* I asked myself repeatedly.

I walked over to him and grabbed him by his collar. I made full eye contact with him while I licked my lips. When I took my tongue and ran it across his lips, X's body began to tremble. He'd never been this nervous before. I moved in closer and whispered, "Listen this is the only chance you have to show her what you like. Give it to me like you would like to give it to her."

Like a trained soldier, X took me by the hand, swung me around and pinned me to the wall. He ripped my panties off forcefully and picked me up and planted his face between my legs licking my wetness. I opened my eyes and looked at his wife I wanted to make sure she wasn't trying to kill a bitch on the low. She sat there and stared at me while her husband licked me like an animal.

"Hmm," I moaned as his tongue went deeper into my bosom. "Oh fuccck!" I said as X received all of my juices into his mouth.

Once he finished, X let me down and I went in. I licked his lips, pulled his shirt off, pushed him down on the coffee table and crawled behind him. I licked his back and planted soft kisses in the middle of his arch. I made my way over to his shoulder blade kissing it softly. I tried to show his wife everything X liked so she could take him home and save some money. X's wife wanted some… I could tell. I took my fingers and motion for her to come over and join in.

At first she hesitated, but after another look at her husband's rock hard dick she obeyed me. She kneeled down beside me and I smiled at her. "Tell your wife how sexy she is," I commanded.

When he looked at her, I saw the love he had for her. "You're beautiful," he said.

"That's not what I told you to do. I said tell her how sexy she is."

She looked up at me like a virgin having sex for the first time. X took his hand and rubbed his wife's face, "You're the sexiest women alive," he said.

"Kiss him," I ordered. His wife hesitated again. The look of embarrassment came over her face like she was ashamed to get loose with her husband.

"Kiss him," I ordered more forcefully this time.

She rose up, closed her eyes, kissed him and pulled away.

"No!" I yelled, "I said kiss your husband damn it." I pulled her up, pushcd her toward him. "Now, put your tongue down his throat!" She looked at me confused and unsure about doing what I ordered her to do. However, when I bucked my eyes at her, she finally reached in and kissed him on the lips softly.

X grabbed the back of her neck and forced his tongue down her throat. At first she tried to pull away, but I pushed her back into him. After five minutes of struggling she wrapped her arms around him, closed her eyes and let herself go.

"That's it, take it, let yourself go," I coached reinsuring her that it was okay to get loose with her husband.

X started undressing his wife, ripping her cloths off like a dog in heat. She seemed to loosen up as she started to unbuckle his pants.

"Kiss his neck," I whispered in her ear, "he likes his neck kissed." She did as I said and slid her tongue down from his lips to his neck. She kissed and sucked his hot spots. I couldn't believe after being together for more than ten years they never touched or kissed like this. She then took her tongue and flicked his ear lobe softly. "Yeah, give him more," I moaned. I saw her inner freak coming out and she was well over due for a visit.

X picked his wife up and placed her on the table. He removed her shoes and pulled down her pants and underwear, then started to lick and kiss her toes. She covered her eyes, but I made her remove her hands.

"Enjoy it!" I demanded, "This is what he likes; you want to please him right?" She shook her head yes. "Well, let him have his way with you," I told her. "Let him please you. Let him take control of your body."

X was a beast in the bed; he knew all the spots to kiss, touch and caress. He always had me wetter than a faucet. X licked her inner thighs sucking them in the right places so softly. The arch she had in her back told me she was enjoying the treatment. X made his way to her large pussy lips, slowly sucking them one by one. He placed his index finger in her, slowly pushing it in and out of her sugar walls. At that moment, she tired to run, but I made her sit still and take that monkey spanking.

"Take it," I scolded.

"Oh my God!" she screamed out as tears rolled down her cheeks.

Once she released her juices, X pulled her down some and slid his thick muscle inside her. Their bodies intertwined with each other and after a while I no longer existed. I grabbed my robe and looked at them. At that point, I felt good. I felt like I'd saved a marriage from falling apart. I left them to finish what they should've been doing from the start…making passionate love.

SOMETHING MAJOR

I got a call from X telling me that he and his wife worked out their differences. He advised me that she promised she would let the past be the past and I didn't have to worry about her causing me anymore trouble. He also told me that he was glad things happened the way it did. X claimed he never wanted to hurt his family or mess up his house, he just wanted more. Some women thought rich men cheat automatically because they had money and options. Shit little did they knew, broke nigga's in the hood had the same options these days.

I've always been convinced most men cheat because they were missing something. When money comes into the picture, women tend to get laxed. X's wife felt she was entitled because she was there before the money. *More money more problems,* Biggie said it the best. However despite all the drama, I was glad I could help bring them back together.

"Ms. Mendez your 11 o'clock is here," my assistant Devon advised me.

"Send him in," I told her.

I fixed my golden toned lipstick and ran my fingers through my freshly blow dried hair. With X leaving Joy Ride, I was free to take on two more people. I was unsure if I would take on any new clients personally. I really wanted to focus on building a bigger brand. I spoke to some of my Japanese clients about opening up a night club. I knew the night scene in Miami craved me. I could capitalize big time off the party scene here. I also wanted to build a ranch in Las Vegas were it's legal to sell Kush.

When my door swung open, a tall dark chocolate well built gentleman entered my office. His skin was perfect. I'd never seen a man's skin glow like his. His Issey Miyake cologne shook my hand before he did. I hadn't seen a brother this serious since I ran into Morris Chestnut on the strip. His broad shoulders poked out like a basketball player, and his wife beater revealed every muscle and cut he owned.

"How you doing Ms Mendez?" he said sounding like Barry White's twin brother.

Damn, I thought to myself, he was too good to be true. He was either married or gay. I knew he had to be one or the other. A man with his looks and seductive voice could pull a woman without any help.

"You must be Major?" I asked reaching out for a hand shake.

He smiled. "Yes."

Damn right, your something Major. "So, why do you need services?" I always asked my client personal questions for security purposes. A business like mine could get very dangerous. You need to be careful who you trust and let into your life.

"Well, I travel a lot so my partner was telling me if I was just looking for fun this is the place to be."

"So, you can't have fun in Miami?"

"Yeah but, I'm trying to have clean fun, you know just do me and not worry."

I tested everyone for STD and AIDS twice a month. I advised the girls to use condoms, however them ho's didn't listen well. I ran a business that was not only confidential, but safe and entertaining.

"Okay," I advised Major handing him paperwork to fill out and forms to sign. "Are you married?" I asked while blushing like a little school girl. He looked at me and smiled. "I'm sorry if I'm getting too personal. I have to ask for safety purposes. I don't personally care."

"No, I'm not married. Are you?"

"Nope, I'm single."

"Wow, I'm surprised. You're so beautiful, very breathtaking."

"Thank you. You're making me blush," I said as I looked away. "Is there any type of girl you prefer?"

"The best. I prefer the best."

"Well, I have just the girl for you. Her name is Crave. She's the best girl here at Joy Ride. There's only one rule; she wears a full mask and will not take it off. If that's cool with you then I'll set a date." I wasn't passing him off. I wanted to see if he tasted as good as he looked.

"Well, Ms Mendez."

"Call me Joy."

"Well, if I call you Joy you have to let me buy you lunch."

I hesitated at first, going out to lunch with a client was very dangerous and against company policy. Major wasn't worth me losing my business. *Hell it's just lunch and it's my rules, so I can break them if I want,* I told myself. "I guess I can do lunch." Fuck it, it was time for me to live a little and start exploring my options. Going out with Major wasn't a big deal; I was ready to find me a man. There was no harm in letting this man take me out and treat me good. He was just paying for the ass twice without knowing. Major looked too good to pass by and soon I would see if he's packing something major below.

MAJOR TALENT

Lunch with Major went great. We talked to each other for hours that day. I really felt a connection with him and since then we'd been seeing each other almost every day. When Janet Jackson sung, *"funny how time fly's when you're having fun"* she was kicking the truth. Three months had passed and I was convinced Major was everything I wanted in a man. I called myself taking things slow with him because I wanted to make sure he was the one. I hadn't even had sex with him because I wanted to make sure he was packing. I liked what he stood for as a man, I just didn't do the little dicks. Major had been spending so much time with me that he hadn't stopped in to see Crave.

He was great, career oriented, no kids, money in the bank and fine. He was an investment banker and knew the stock market very well. He talked me into getting some stock. He liked that I was very career focused and pushed my idea for opening up the club. Sometimes I felt like he was too good to be true. He understood that I didn't want to have sex right away and said he wasn't looking to rush me. When he finally made a date with Crave, I was excited. I was anxious to see what he was working with. We had a few make out sessions, but I would stop before it went too far. I made up a lie and told him I was out of town on business so he could really give Crave the business without worrying about bumping into me.

By the time Major and I hooked up, he'd told me all that he liked sexually. I was going to use that to my advantage. His favorite color was blue, so I lit some candles that gave off a blue effect. I found some blue rose petals, threw them over the bed and trailed them to the bubble bath I ran for him. I made sure I smelled good. Major loved the way my Be Delicious smelled when I mixed it with my Juicy Couture. My Blue French Laced Cami dress hugged every curve I owned. My five inch deep blue YSL peep toe heels looked fierce on my never ending legs. My entire body shimmered in gold like my Mac gloss. I put on a mixed CD I'd made full of R Kelly, Joe and The Isley Brothers best hits.

I wanted Major to feel connected with Crave. Although I kept her hidden, she was still a part of me. I planned on putting something major on Major. I didn't plan on showing him who I was at all. I just wanted to learn him and figure out what he liked so when I did him as Joy he would be hooked on me.

When I heard his footsteps at the door I put on my blue

mask and let him in. After I opened the door I stepped back so he could enjoy every inch of my firm stacked body.

"Damn, Crave, how did you know I fucks with blue?" Major asked as he came in and closed the door.

"A guess," I replied, pushing his back to the door. I took off his shirt and threw it down. Major's body was right and his hands were huge. And he wasn't shy to touch me. He took his hands and grabbed my ass and pulled me close to him.

"Damn Shorty you so fucking soft," he said to me talking in slang.

The more Major spoke and acted so tugged out I felt like he was two totally different people. He was talking a little too hoodish for an investment banker. He did tell me he grew up in the projects, but this man that was standing in front of me was totally different. I guess this was his freaky side and the way he carried himself when I wasn't around.

Major acted like a lion hunting his prey right before he captured them. He stroked his longs fingers across the crotch of my lace panties making me shiver. He took his long thick index finger and pulled my panties to the side and slid into my wetness.

"Shit," I moaned while he fingered me hard switching from one finger to two. Major reached in and kissed me softly while he pushed his fingers into me deeper and faster. "Oh, daddy I'm about to cum baby."

My peak was approach faster than a police car. I started rocking my hips so I could explode like a volcano. Once my juices streamed down his fingers, he took his hand and rubbed it across my lips. Major was a freak, he was working on an A+ and he hadn't even hit the pussy yet. I took Major's fingers and licked them one by one. Once I licked all my sweetness off, I unbuckled his pants. His dick was poking out of his jeans, and I wanted to wrap my lips around it.

"Wait," he said as he took off his shoes, removed a gun and pulled off his pants.

I was shocked he was carrying a gun on him. What type of danger would an investment banker be in? "Are you a bad boy?" I asked him.

"Hell yeah, a real bad boy and I need a spanking."

"That's why you keep a gun? I mean I hope you ain't a crazy killer."

"No," he said as he grabbed me, pushed me on the table and spread my legs apart. "I need it to protect myself from crazy motherfuckers. My job is dangerous."

Dangerous, I thought. Major placed his head between my legs, pulled my pussy lips apart and licked his long tongue up and down my pearl. I wanted to ask him more questions, but my mind got cloudy once he started to eat my pussy like it was his last meal. I couldn't do anything but take the tongue spanking he was putting on me.

I wiggled my ass around trying to find a position so I could catch my breath. Major tongue game needed to be outlawed. My body went through withdrawals. I wanted to run like a little girl, but he had me gripped too tightly. There was no running. My body started shaking; I just wanted to take a ten minute break.

"Please give me a minute," I begged, but he didn't stop.

The more I tried to break away, the more he ate and pushed his index finger onto my spot. I finally reached the point of no return. I grabbed Major's ears, closed my eyes tightly and let myself go.

I never came that hard in my entire life. My body was motionless. I wanted to call this session a night and get my gangster back up. Major had gotten the best of me. I didn't even want to look at him in face; I was embarrassed. I sat on the edge of the table looking away from him trying to figure my next move. He wasn't supposed to get the best of me; I was never out of control when I had sex.

"What are you thinking?" he asked me.

"Nothing."

"You cool?"

I finally built up enough nerve to look at him. I didn't know why I became nervous. "Yeah," I said shyly.

At that point, Major wasted no time grabbing me again. He snatched me off the table, picked me up and tossed me onto the bed. My heart was racing; I couldn't take the lead from him. This man was something major!

Major grabbed a condom and rolled it down his dick; once I noticed his ungodly size I got scared. He was packing and the look on his face told me he was looking to do some damage to me.

"Get yo ass over here and take this dick," he commanded pulling me by my legs forcing them open. My body cringed as his slid into me. "You got some good pussy," he moaned into my ear. Major's dick was long and thick, every time he pushed himself into me my stomach turned. I knew I had to sit still and take that dick like a grown woman, but he was killing me. My body was shaking as my hot spot got abused by Major's long dick. "Oh, girl I want to feel it raw," he pleaded.

"Okay," I moaned without thinking how dangerous it was to let him put his bare dick inside of me. Major ripped off his condom, turned me over, and slid his bare dick inside of my sugar walls. "Oh, shit, give me more!" I screamed wanting him to move a little faster. He felt so good inside of my wetness, bare.

With every stroke, I felt all of him and I liked it. After an hour of switching positions I pleaded with him to release himself. Major pulled out of me, grabbed me by the hair and stuck his dick into my face. I knew what he wanted, most men are visual. I opened my mouth, stuck out my tongue, grabbed Major's dick and stroked it until all of his juices shot all over me. I caught most of it before I wrapped my mouth around him and sucked the rest.

Major looked satisfied and I was in total shock that he was so good. I had never experienced a connection with a man like that. I wanted him. I knew he was the one that I could be with forever.

MAJOR`S LEAGUE
THREE MONTHS LATER

Being with Major under two different identities was very draining. At times I became jealous at the way he looked and touched me when I was Crave. When I was Joy he seemed very reserved, like he was another person. I felt he was himself when he was with Crave. When he was with Joy he talked very proper and wore suits, but with Crave he talked in slang and acted very hood. His whole body was tatted up and he always carried a gun. I caught him in several lies, but I was forced to hold my tongue. He told me he didn't drink and attended church, but he reeked of alcohol when he came to see Crave.

I felt he was being phony as if he was trying to impress me. I knew he was feeling me; he talked about how much he liked me while I laid with him. The good thing about seeing him undercover was that he told me all of his business freely. He was open about every thing with Crave and our sex life was phenomenal. I hadn't made love to him as Joy and honestly he wasn't trying to sleep with me either. He touched and teased me, but remained very respectable. He spent the night often and never tried to pull my panties off.

I was scared to cross the line with him and give him some on my own. I didn't know how to come across sexually as Joy. I'd always had sex under my alter ego and didn't know how to just be plain. I also didn't want to ruin my chances with him. He didn't seem to care that Crave was a call girl. He was really digging her. I wasn't blind to the fact he had feelings for the both of us, but I knew once I started sleeping with him he would love me only.

Some days I wanted to come clean and tell him I was Crave. I just couldn't ruin everything I worked so hard for; but I felt myself losing him and I hated it. He called me and told me to set him up an appointment with Crave which was unusual. He only saw her on the weekends and it was just Tuesday. I wasn't complaining, I was down for his dick any day of the week. I loved having sex with him; he was the best I ever had.

MAJOR CONSEQUENCES

Major was over an hour late for our appointment and I was pissed off and ready to go. I'd never been stood up in my entire life. I packed up my pleasure bag and took off my six inch YSL pumps. I had just turned off my radio when I heard a knock at the door. I took my sweet time answering it, since I'd already waited for him for hours. When I finally got the door open Major was standing there looking sad.

"I'm about to go!" I yelled, rolling my bag out the door.

"Please, can you come back in? I need to tell you something, it's important," he advised.

I looked at him. I started to leave him there, but I was in love with this man so I stayed. I dropped my bag down and sat on the bed. Major came over, grabbed me and rubbed his hand across my clitoris. I needed his touch. My body had been craving him since that morning.

"Give it to me," I moaned into his ear as his hands caressed my breast.

Major pulled off my dress and ripped my panties off. My heart started to race, but I didn't want him inside of me yet. I wanted to give him some oral pleasure. I got down on my knees and unbuckled his pants and let them drop to the ground. I pulled his boxers down, took my tongue and circled the head of his dick slowly.

Major ran his fingers through my hair and pushed his long dick down my throat. I received all of him like a champ without gagging. I wrapped my throat muscles around him tightly and sucked him until I felt all his babies swimming around my mouth. Major commanded me to swallow them while he licked my lips.

"Turn around and bend over," he ordered. I bent over, grabbed my ankles and waited for him to push himself inside of me. Major entered me slowly teasing me, "You want that don't you," he mocked.

"Yes, please give him to me," I begged.

Major wrapped my hair around his hands and forcefully shoved his entire love muscle inside me. I shifted positions trying to find an easier way to receive his thrust, but I couldn't. I was in pain, but it felt so good I wanted more from him. I started bouncing my ass back on him arching my back, going up and down on him rapidly. Our bodies connected for more than an hour before our sexual peaks reached. My legs started shaking so bad I couldn't move. I arched my back up high as Major pushed himself into me so deep I stopped breathing. After our juices flowed, we both fell back on the bed and caught our breath.

"Shit, boy I needed that," I said to him.

"Me too. I'm sorry I was late, but I got caught up into some shit."

"It's cool; it was worth it. So, what's so important you had to see me today?" I was curious to see what was going on with him. Major looked at me like something was wrong. I knew whatever he was going to say it wasn't going to be good. "What's up?" I asked him once again.

"I really like you," he said as he rubbed his fingers through my hair. "Would you consider coming away with me? Maybe move to a different town?"

"What about Joy?" I couldn't believe he was sitting here trying to play me when he just told me to meet him at ten.

"Man forget Joy. I need to know if I took you away from this would you roll."

What the fuck is this nigga talking about? "What's going on Major?"

"Listen, there's some shit about to go down and I'm in love with you, so I want to get you out of here."

I couldn't believe my ears. He's in love with Crave. *What about me?* I was so upset, I couldn't think straight. "What's going down?" I wanted to know what the fuck his lying ass was talking about.

"I need you to trust me."

"Trust you?"

"Yes," he said as he got up, took out his wallet, and showed me a police badge. "I'm a police officer. In twenty minutes there's gonna be a raid. I don't have feelings for Joy. I was sent undercover to shut down this whore ring. Everybody's going down and getting charged and can face serious jail time."

Major reached in to take my mask off, but I snatched away.

"Listen Crave you have to trust me. I don't want you to go to jail. I care for you and want to be with you seriously. I don't care about your past. I want to be your future. Please let me save you. I could lose my job getting you out of here. Everything I've built is at risk; my job, and my money, but you're worth it. I tried so hard to find out who you are. Your name is not on any paperwork. I need for you to tell me who you are so I can get you out of here, there's no time to waste."

I couldn't believe it; Major had played me from the beginning. I should've known better than to get open. All the signs were there. I just ruined my whole life over a piece of dick that didn't want me. *Major claims he loves Crave so much I wonder will he still want to save her when he finds out she is me.* I still had unanswered questions. Why did I deserve to loose everything that I'd built?

"Okay Major, I will take my mask off, but I have one question. How did you guys find out about Joy?" I needed to know how just a week ago I had everything and now everything was crumbling. For three years Joy Ride was untouchable; I had money, power and respect and now it was over because I fell for the wrong man.

"Well, one of her girls Apple was busted with her boyfriend, NBA player Troy Gibson. They got caught with a lot of drugs and were seeking major jail time. They made a deal with the DA to turn over this place. We've been trying to shut this place down for the longest. The only way we could do it was from the inside."

"Troy, plays ball?"

"Yeah, he got dropped from his team some months ago, and him and his girl have been running drugs out of this place."

It all made sense to me. I couldn't see how I was blindsided, all those men requesting Apple multiple times a day. That ho got me, all along I thought she had a golden pussy, but it was a crack pipe. I knew Apple would be part of my downfall. She played me like a games of darts. She was sneaking around with Troy behind my back and selling drugs out my business. I should've followed my first instinct and fired her ass, but I had to be greedy. Everything my daddy worked hard for, all that I sacrificed was all in vein now.

"Well Major, I really hope you meant what you said. Why

would you risk it all for me?"

"Because you're the one my daddy told me about. Once I found the woman I couldn't live without, she's the one."

"The one?" I laughed "So, you will still love me no matter what I look like when I pull this mask off?"

"It doesn't matter. I care for you. You're the one," he reassured me.

I turned around so he couldn't see me just yet. I took off my mask, ran my fingers through my long hair, and laughed. "Well Major, I really hope you enjoyed your *Joy Ride* because it's over for one of us." I advised him as I turned around and let him see the woman he was in love with. Major flashed on the lights to catch a good glimpse of me and hung his head down. He didn't speak. His face said it all and everything else *faded to black.*

THANK YOU FOR TAKING THIS JOY RIDE.
THE END

MEET THE AUTHORS

ERICK S. GRAY

The author of the urban sexomedy BOOTYCALL *69 has been known for his well thought out plots and ability to keep readers interested with every turn of the page. This entrepreneur is also the owner/founder of Triple G publishing and is making moves in other markets as well. Born and raised in the south side of Jamaica, Queens, this gifted author has brought himself out on a high note with his first endeavor. He continues bringing you good stories as he shows in his collaboration with Mark Anthony, and Anthony Whyte, STREETS OF NEW YORK VOLUME 1 , Ghetto Heaven, Money, Power, Respect. Nasty Girls and It's Like Candy.

Erick S. Gray is showing that young African-American males don't all fall into the same categories of drug dealer/thief/statistic. His future is filled with promises of more intriguing and diverse stories for the masses to digest.

Books By Erick S. Gray

It's Like Candy
Ghetto Heaven
Money Power Respect
Booty Call *69
Nasty Girls
Crave All Lose All
Love and A Gangster
Heartbreaker

ASHLEY & JAQUAVIS

These two New York Times best-selling authors hit the scene at the ripe age of seventeen when Carl Weber discovered them. During their freshmen year in college, they both received publishing deals and have not looked back since. With a smash hit novel "The Cartel," they have solidified themselves as two of the best in their genre, together or apart. With a roster of fourteen novels published and a hefty ghostwriting resume they have made a successful career for themselves. Their highly anticipated next series "Murderville," will be backed by Cash Money Records/ Atria.

Books By Ashley & JaQuavis

Dirty Money
Diary of a Street Diva
Supreme Clientele
Girls from The Hood 4
The Trophy Wife
The Cartel
The Prada Plan (By Ashley Antoinette)
The Dopeman's Wife (By JaQuavis Coleman)
The Cartel 2
Kiss Kiss Bang Bang
Coming Soon: The Cartel 3 (Coming July 2010)

www.ashleyjaquavis.com

TREASURE E. BLUE

Many have called Treasure E. Blue the reincarnated Donald Goines. This prolific author without doubt is one of the most shocking and controversial writers that we have seen in decades.Blue's background is almost as compelling as his mouth-dropping debut novel entitled Harlem Girl Lost. Using the streets as a means of survival, he soon found himself involved with some of Harlem's most notorious elements. Retiring form the game at the tender age of sixteen, Blue managed to become one of the youngest people to receive his G.E.D. in New York State. Joining the military at seventeen, he developed a voracious appetite for books going on to read well over 2000 novels. After serving his country honorably, he joined the New York City Fire Department and worked as a Supervising Fire Inspector in the Bronx. Blue is a father of four and won praise for his screen writing skills. He is also an active member of the American Studies Association. Blue has an uncanny way of not only telling a story, he makes you feel it emotionally as well.

Books by Treasure E. Blue

Harlem Girl Lost
A Street Girl Named Desire
Keyshia And Clyde

Web : www.myspace.com/treasureblue
Email: treasureeeblue@yahoo.com

DASHAWN TAYLOR

Dashawn Taylor is an innovative and contemporary novelist. A New Jersey native and graduate of Rutgers University, Dashawn's art of storylines has been compared to today's top sellers with an urban edgy style. His writing captivates both young and mature audiences. Dashawn's work has been featured on BET, NBC, FOX, Essence Magazine, Don Diva Magazine, Real-Hiphop.com along with a number of online magazines and blogs. In 2009, Dashawn was nominated Best Male Author of the Year.

Books By Dashawn Taylor:
From Poverty To Power Moves
Kissed By The Devil I
Kissed By The Devil II
The Final Kiss (Coming Spring 2011)

www.dashawntaylor.com
www.nextlevelpublishing.com

J. TREMBLE

J. Tremble was born and raised in Washington D.C., and is a product of the district public school system. He graduated from Missouri Valley College with a B.A. in Psychology then went on to receive his Masters in Elementary Education from Howard University. He was given the nickname, "King of Erotica" after his first novel, Secrets of a Housewife made the Essence Bestsellers List several times. J. Tremble currently resides in the Maryland area with his wife and children where he works as a school teacher, boy's & girl's club coach and tutor for at-risk boys with the D.C. Juvenile probation office. He's also a member of Phi Beta Sigma fraternity, Rho Delta chapter. J. Tremble is currently working on a variety of future projects including the follow-up: House of Sin – The Novel.

Books By J. Tremble

Secrets of a Housewife
More Secrets More Lies
Naughty Little Angel
My Man Her Son

www.twitter.com/jmakesutremble
Facebook- Search- Jay Tremble
jaytremble1914@yahoo.com

NICHELLE WALKER

Author Nichelle Walker hails from the fabulous city of Chicago, Illinois. Nichelle found her love for writing early in life. During her high school years she penned several successful screenplays, short stories and her first novel. While matriculating through college to attain a degree in Accounting, Nichelle put her love for writing on the back burner only to find herself constantly wanting to write and tell her story. While on a three week break from school and unhappy with losing touch with her creative passion, she wrote her highly anticipated novel, Doing His Time. Not wanting to wait on a publisher to decide her fate, Nichelle founded her own publishing company NWHoodTales Publishing. Nichelle Walker is excited to introduce her company and her novel to the world and show why her company's motto is "We Keep Them Pages Turning." Nichelle is also the founder of **nwmasssmedia.com** and **nwhoodtales.com.**

Books By Nichelle Walker

Doing His Time
Money Over Men
Heartbreaker
Secrets & Lies (Coming May 2010)

http://twitter.com/Nichelle_Walker
www.facebook.com/NichelleWalker.
NWMassMedia

COMING SOON

A NOVEL BY
MISS KP

One of the Best Street Series of All-Time

By New York Times
Bestselling Authors
Ashley & JaQuavis

www.ashleyjaquavis.com

DISCARD

ORDER F

MAIL T~~O~~:
P~~O Box~~ 23
Brandywine, MD 20613
301-362-6508

FAX TO:
301-856-4116

Ship to:

Date: Ph

Email:

Make all

Qty.	ISBN			Price
	0-9741394-5-9			$ 15.00
	0-9741394-2-4			$ 15.00
	0-9741394-7-5			$ 15.00
	0-9741394-3-2			$ 15.00
	0-9724003-5-4			$ 15.00
	0-9741394-4-0			$ 15.00
	0-9741394-6-7			$ 15.00
	1-934230-99-5			$ 15.00
	1-934230-98-7			$ 15.00
	1-934230-95-2			$ 15.00
	1-934230-94-4			$ 15.00
	1-934230-93-6			$ 15.00
	1-934230-96-0			$ 15.00
	1-934230-92-8			$ 15.00
	1-934230-89-8			$ 15.00
	1-934230-91-X			$ 15.00
	1-934230-87-1-			$ 15.00
	1-934230-86-3			$ 15.00
	1-934230-88-X			$ 15.00
	1-934230847			$ 15.00
	1-934230855			$ 15.00
	1-934230820			$ 15.00
	1-934230839			$ 15.00
	1-934230782			$ 15.00
	1-934230669			$ 15.00
	1-934230804	From Hood to Hollywood by		$ 15.00
	1-934230707	Sweet Swagger by Mike Warren	Jun-09	$ 15.00
	1-934230677	Carbon Copy by Azarel	Jul-09	$ 15.00
	1-934230723	Millionaire Mistress 3 by Tiphani	Nov-09	$ 15.00
	1-934230715	A Woman Scorned by Ericka Williams	Nov-09	$ 15.00

Total for Books $

Shipping Charges (add $4.25 for 1-4 books*) $

Total Enclosed (add lines) $

* Prison Orders- Please allow up to three (3) weeks for delivery.

For credit card orders and orders over 30 books, please contact us at orders@lifechaningbooks.net

*Shipping and Handling of 5-10 books is $6.25, please contact us if your order is more than 10 books.